BLUE HALO S

CALLUM

NYSSA KATHRYN

CALLUM

Copyright © 2023 Nyssa Kathryn Sitarenos

An NW Partners Book
Ebook Cover by L.J. Anderson at Mayhem Cover Creations
Paperback Cover by Deranged Doctor Design
Developmentally and Copy Edited by Kelli Collins
Line Edited by Jessica Snyder
Proofread by Amanda Cuff and Jen Katemi

❀ Created with Vellum

One wedding, one fake relationship, and a threat no one saw coming.

Attending a wedding is dead last on Fiona Lock's list of priorities. She has two options: stay home and let the family gossip mill speculate on why she isn't there; or attend the wedding and pretend she's just fine. The decision is obvious. Not only does she choose option B...she may have mentioned a boyfriend she doesn't have. With the nuptials imminent, the race is on to find her "perfect man" who doesn't exist.

When he's not running the security business he owns with his friends, ex-Marine Callum Thomas spends his down time indulging in his favorite hobby—reading. Of course, it's not just the books luring him to the library every other day. It's also the sexy, sassy librarian, Fiona, who can't resist putting Callum in his place at every turn. When he discovers she's in need of a fake boyfriend, he's determined to claim the role...and then slowly, cautiously win over the prickly woman he can't get out of his head.

His plans are quickly disrupted when Fiona starts receiving threats, drastically speeding up his timeline. Callum knows any distance between him and Fiona is no longer an option. Letting her out of his sights could mean danger creeping in...and potentially losing Fiona before she's even his to claim.

ACKNOWLEDGMENTS

Thank you to my book team; Kelli, Jessica, Amanda and Jen. You guys are rockstars, and no story would reach its full potential.

To my ARC team, thank you for being the first readers and my greatest fans.

To every person who picks up and reads this book, thank you. You make sure the next gets written.

And to the two most important people in my life, Will and Sophia, thank you for your support and love. You are my world.

CHAPTER 1

Amanda: I'm doing the stationery for the wedding and need the name of your date.

Fiona's fingers tightened around her cell, each word in the text from her sister glaring at her. She'd known it was coming. Hell, she'd actually been expecting it earlier, seeing as the wedding was less than a month away. Yet, here she was, feeling completely unprepared for it.

Oh, man. A date. She'd told her sister she had a real, living, breathing date for her wedding. And now, not only did her sister expect her to bring said date, her entire *family* did too.

It was official, she was screwed. Completely and utterly screwed.

She massaged her temple as the beginnings of a headache pricked the backs of her eyes. The lie had just kind of slipped out at the last family dinner, somewhere between talk of flower arrangements and you're-going-to-die-alone looks.

And now she was paying the price.

She started typing out a response but quickly deleted the words. Then she started typing again. Same thing. Argh. This was dumb. She had to just tell her sister there was no date.

Her phone vibrated while she was midway through text attempt number three.

Amanda: If there's no boyfriend, it would be best to just admit the truth.

Her jaw clicked and her spine straightened.

Excuse me? It was one thing for her to be a lonely liar, but another for her sister to call her out on it with no proof.

Maybe moving an hour and a half away from the woman wasn't enough. Maybe she should have tried for another time zone. Or better yet, another galaxy.

"Fiona Lock!"

She jumped at the use of her full name and spun to find her library manager, not only in the same aisle as her but marching toward her with a beet-red face. Great. Just what her morning needed.

"How many times have I told you *not* to use your phone at work?"

Uh, zero? Not that she'd be admitting that to a man who could win an award for biggest ass of a boss. Actually, no. He wasn't always an ass. Sometimes he was ridiculously nice to the point she almost felt like he was coming on to her. But as soon as she didn't reciprocate that...hello, asshole again.

"Sorry, Rick."

His cheeks reddened further, something she hadn't thought possible a moment earlier, and he shoved his glasses up his nose. He was a tall, thin man and kind of reminded her of Kevin Bacon...only a much less likable version. Not that she'd met Kevin Bacon. She just assumed he wasn't a grumpy middle-aged man who gave people whiplash with his mood changes.

Rick huffed. "That will come out of your break time. You have ten minutes left."

Yep, definitely in the running for that ass award.

She plastered a phony smile to her mouth while holding in the slew of curses she wanted to throw his way. "Sure."

She moved out of the aisle, almost surprised when he didn't call after her with some other problem. Maybe her knee-length skirt was somehow inappropriate for work. Or she'd filed a book incorrectly. He'd been fine with her when she was hired eight months ago, almost always teetering more on the flirtatious side. But over the last few weeks, he'd done a complete flip on her. What she'd done to piss the man off, she had no idea.

She stepped into the shared staff room to find Jenny, the only librarian close to her age, dropping her bag into a locker. The woman had only started working here a month ago, but God, she'd saved Fiona from a lonely existence. She was on the shy side but always friendly.

When Jenny's gaze hit hers, the woman's smile slipped. "Hey. You okay?"

Not only did the woman have the cutest bangs and bob Fiona had ever seen, she also had big red-rimmed glasses and a cute mole on her cheek. There was a small scar beside her right eye, but it didn't detract from how pretty she was. She fit "librarian" to a T.

"Yep, just Rick being Rick again."

Jenny gave a sympathetic smile. "I know you think you're the only one he picks on, but trust me, you're not. Today he told me I was late when I got in at nine oh one. Nine oh one! That's basically early. The man has a serious stick up his ass."

Yeah, Jenny wasn't wrong. "Let's not say it too loud. He's probably bugged the place and is wearing a hidden earpiece to listen to these kinds of exchanges."

"Let him hear us. I'd like him to try and find more librarians. Everyone else is on retirement row." She squeezed Fiona's arm before walking out of the staff room.

Fiona grabbed her apple and was about to sit down when her phone rang. She almost expected it to be Amanda, wanting to ride her ass about this date stuff. Nope. Her cousin's name popped up on the screen. Thank God.

Fiona moved back into the library, then out the front door, where she sat on the bench beneath a pine tree.

"She called you, didn't she?" Fiona said before Stacey could get a word in.

There was a beat of silence, and Fiona could just imagine her cousin cringing. "Yeah, text then call."

Of course. Because it wasn't harassment with just one mode of contact. "Did she also tell you she thinks I'm lying about the whole having-a-boyfriend thing?"

"Kind of. But it's not lying, remember? It's fudging the truth."

"Stace, it'd only become fudging the truth if I'd miraculously found a boyfriend between then and now...which I haven't." Hence, straight-up lie.

"Amanda was pretty firm that she needed a response within the week."

Oh, man.

"I know," Stacey said, as though she could hear Fiona's thoughts. "It's soon. But don't you have a guy friend who could just, you know, come over to Twin Falls and pretend?"

Fiona laughed out loud, a big, yeah-the-hell-right kind of laugh. "Even if I'd made a male friend in this town in the last eight months—which I haven't—our friendship would not be at the let's-play-house stage."

That was like a good ten-year friendship thing, right?

"Let's just call it what it is," Fiona continued before Stacey offered any other ideas. "I'm screwed and all out of options. I'm going to have to admit to my god-awful sister that I'm dateless and will be watching alone as she marries the man who broke my heart."

The words had barely left her lips when she turned her head and spotted Callum stepping up to the door of the library. A deep breath filled her lungs, and her heart beat to a new, faster rhythm in her chest. Not because he was a million feet tall with biceps so

4

thick they looked like tree trunks. But because his beautiful light brown eyes were looking directly at her.

Stacey's voice turned to a buzz of background noise. The brush of wind on her face lost its coolness, and the world faded away to just her and him. Then he winked, one side of his mouth lifting, before he disappeared inside the brick walls of the library.

Her chest deflated and she exhaled so long and so loudly, it was a wonder she had a speck of oxygen left in her.

Christ, why did he have to be so pretty?

Callum was one of eight men who ran Blue Halo Security here in Cradle Mountain. They were all former military. All huge, and beautiful, and dangerous—in more ways than one.

How much of her conversation had he heard? The man had good hearing...*really* good. He and his team had been part of a non-government-sanctioned project that involved experimental drugs. Those drugs had made the men faster and stronger than they should be, and able to hear things they shouldn't. Had he heard her pathetic admission about needing a boyfriend? Oh God, where was that hole in the sand for her to bury her head?

"Earth to Fiona! Are you still there?"

Crap. She forced her attention back to the call. "I'm sorry, I..." *Saw a man I absolutely do not like and got distracted while I was simultaneously thinking about how pretty and off-limits he is?* "Nothing. I'm going to text Amanda that I'm coming alone."

Yep, the words sounded as painful out loud as they did in her head. What would typing and sending them in a text feel like? Razor blades to her fingertips? Electrical bursts up her arms?

It sounded like she was being dramatic. She was not. Amanda and her fiancé were the worst humans on the planet. Okay, maybe not the planet, but the worst in her world after what she'd found them doing while Fiona was still with him...

"Don't you dare!" Stacey basically shouted. "You have the week, just give it until then. I'm going to spend my evening researching real-life wedding dates for hire."

The corners of Fiona's mouth twitched. How many times had she and Stacey watched *The Wedding Date* growing up? So many she'd lost count. She'd never thought she might actually need a date for hire. "Okay. You do that. But I'm only hiring him if he looks like Dermot Mulroney."

One-sided smiles and dark eyes...yes, please.

When thoughts of the actor spidered through her mind, another set of eyes bombarded her. Light brown eyes.

Dammit, Fiona. Get it together! You are not at a point in your life where you can afford to date another attractive, sexy-as-sin man.

"Deal," Stacey said easily, like there was a good chance she might actually find this made-up man, when really there was none. Zilch.

"All right, I have to go before Rick comes out here."

"Okay, I'll call you once I find something."

She laughed. "I'll be eagerly awaiting that call."

Once she hung up, she took a massive bite of her apple, knowing she'd only get a couple in before needing to get back inside.

Her heart gave a little skip at the fact Callum was in there. The man came to the library often, usually after borrowing one of her favorite books, the ones on which she put the little tags of recommendation. The books were never returned as they'd been borrowed, though. He always seemed to damage them in some way. Often with a fold of a page or a stain on the cover.

She told herself that was the reason she couldn't crush on him, but in reality, she wasn't that shallow. What she *was*, was scared shitless of getting her heart broken again.

With a resigned sigh, she stood and moved into the library, throwing the apple into the trash after a second bite. Immediately, and completely without her permission, her gaze searched the stacks for Callum. The library was small, designed with some self-borrowing machines at the front and a manned circulation desk behind them. There were aisles of books beyond, extending to the back wall.

Third row…that's where Mr. Million Feet of Muscle stood. His head was down, and he was reading the back of a book. One she'd popped her recommendation tag onto that morning.

Her brain tried to short-circuit at the way his biceps flexed as he turned the book over. God, why did the man have to be built like God's gift to women?

Because that's how they get you, the burned voice in her head whispered.

With a shake of her head, she looked away before he could spot her staring. *Do not focus on him, Fiona.*

Quickly, she found a trolley of books that needed to be shelved and chose the aisle furthest from Callum to start in. The third book from her cart needed to go on the top shelf. Because the library wasn't big enough for a lot of aisles, the rows of books went up quite high instead. Only the librarians used the ladders to get books from the high shelves, though. They were mostly study aids. Books people knew they needed, so they didn't have to read a blurb.

She grabbed a ladder and placed it beneath the shelf, then climbed to the top. She'd just slotted the book in when her phone vibrated from her pocket. She cursed. God, was that her sister again? What was it this time? Was Amanda messaging to tell her she knew she was going to die alone? Because that wasn't news to Fiona.

She shouldn't check it. She knew she shouldn't. Yet her stupid hand still slid into her pocket and pulled it out. She was smart enough to cast a quick, covert look around her. No Rick. Good.

Unknown number: You better keep your hands off what's mine, bitch.

What the hell? She re-read the text three times, convinced that she must be misreading, but nope, the words were still there and unchanged every time.

Who would send her—

"Fiona! What did I just say?"

Rick's angry voice boomed through the aisle, so loud and menacing that she flinched—and the one hand still on the ladder tugged it forward. It rocked, and she tried to right it, but her efforts only made the rocking more violent, until both she and the ladder were falling back.

CHAPTER 2

The corners of Callum's lips tugged into a smile as his gaze ran over Fiona's intricate handwriting on the small recommendation tag.

This razor-sharp crime thriller will leave you awestruck as the author takes you on a journey of windy turns.

Truth be told, he didn't even need to read Fiona's words. Her name on the tag was enough. Her recommendations had never led him astray before.

He glanced at the door, recalling the words he'd heard on his way inside. Words about needing a date for a family wedding. About already having told her family she had a date when she didn't.

He hadn't been trying to listen, but it had been damn impossible not to. He'd heard everything. Right now, he could hear the breath slipping in and out of the woman by the corner window. The ticking of the second hand on the older man's watch one row over. Even the beating of the woman's heart at the end of the aisle.

And he knew the exact moment Fiona stepped back into the room, but that wasn't because of any altered DNA. It was his acute awareness of her. She drew him in like a moth to a flame. It wasn't just that he found the way she put him in his place sexy as hell. It was the way her chestnut eyes glowed when she looked at him. That she tried to put on a tough exterior, but he saw the vulnerability below the surface.

When he looked across the library at her, she wasn't facing him. In fact, she was staring at a cart of books like it was the most interesting thing in the room and marching toward it like she was on a damn mission.

He bit back the chuckle that threatened to break free. He'd been coming to this library for months. It felt good to get back into reading. The security company he ran with his team took up a good chunk of his time, but he'd needed something else. Something just for him.

He spent a couple minutes picking up and putting back other titles, Fiona's recommended book firmly in his grasp. Then he walked down the back wall, checking each aisle. He told himself he wasn't looking for her, but that was a damn lie. He searched for her every time he was here. Hell, it was why he got through the books so quickly and only borrowed one at a time—so he had an excuse to come back.

It wasn't until he reached the last aisle that he saw her. His lips twitched. Had she chosen this one because it was the farthest from him? That was something she'd do.

She was on a ladder, wearing a cream-colored top that pulled tight against her ample chest and a yellow skirt that flowed down to her knees.

Damn, she was cute. The kind of cute he wanted to tug closer to peel back the layers of. The kind of cute he could become lost in.

He started toward her, wondering what kind of witty retort she'd give him today. He was halfway to her when she gave the other side of the aisle a quick glance before cursing and pulling her phone from her pocket. The corners of his lips kicked up at the sound of that curse word on her sweet lips.

Oh yeah, she was cute, but she had a mouth on her. A mouth with lips so full his gaze was always drawn to them.

The smile slipped from his mouth when the color left her face. Whatever she was reading, it wasn't friendly.

From the other end of the aisle, Callum spotted a male librarian step into view. His gaze zeroed in on her, an angry scowl pulling across his features. Then he shouted.

The one hand that anchored her to the ladder jolted, tugging the entire thing off the wall and off balance. She tried to right herself, but the ladder only rocked more. Then she was falling.

Callum was moving before he could stop himself, reaching her just in time to catch her body before she hit the ground.

Eyes that had been scrunched shut flew open, colliding with his. For a moment, they were both silent, her heart beating so hard in her chest it was like a hammer.

Then she spoke. Quiet words in a tone so soft, so gentle, that they slid over his skin like silk. "Thank you."

He was used to her witty retorts, even her eye rolls. But this softer side? Yeah, he liked this too. Plus, she felt good in his arms. So good, he struggled to set her down.

The asshole's voice cut down the aisle again, accompanied by the stomps of his feet against the carpet. "See, this is what happens when you mess with your phone at work."

A muscle ticked in Callum's jaw. When Fiona pressed a hand to his chest, he reluctantly set her down, then turned to the jerk who had clearly forgotten how to speak to women.

"Fiona—"

"You owe her an apology," Callum cut through, inching in front of her.

The man's eyes widened. "Excuse me? Who are you?"

"It doesn't matter who I am. I saw what happened, and you owe her an apology."

The man spluttered. "I'm the manager of this library, and I warned Fiona not to be on her phone at work not ten—"

"You also yelled at her while she was in a precarious position, which caused her to fall. If I hadn't caught her, she could have broken her neck." That statement was too fucking true.

The man's cheeks reddened.

A shuffle sounded behind him, then Fiona appeared at his side. "You're right, Rick. I was on my phone when you told me not to be. I'm sorry."

The man huffed, his gaze flicking to Callum uncertainly, then returning to Fiona and hardening. "Well...good. Sorry I yelled."

The insincerity in the apology almost had Callum laughing. Rick shot one more unhappy glance his way before turning and walking away.

Asshole.

The color hadn't quite returned to Fiona's face. Not only that, but a lock of hair had fallen from her bun, onto her cheek, and Callum's usual restraint waned when his fingers twitched to reach out and slot the piece of hair behind her ear. He just stopped himself.

"You okay?" he asked quietly.

Her mouth opened and closed before she got any words out. "Yes."

He bent and lifted the phone she'd dropped from the floor. He was tempted to look at the screen, see if whatever had the color leaching from her face was still there. "You went a bit white up there. Everything okay?"

There was a flicker of something on her face. Uncertainty. Maybe even a touch of fear. Then she blinked, and a cool, calm expression took its place. She slipped her phone from his fingers and stepped back.

"Everything's fine. And while I appreciate you catching me, and saving me a broken neck, I don't need you fighting my battles."

He lifted a brow. "Letting *Rick* know he was a dick was more for me than you."

Rick the dick…had a good ring to it.

Surprise flickered over her features.

He lifted a shoulder. "I don't like pricks who put women in danger."

Her eyes flared, and her chest rose on an inhale. Then she stepped back again, out of reach.

Running away?

"Okay, well…thank you." She grabbed the trolley of books, her knuckles whitening, and took off down the aisle—fast.

Yep, definitely running.

Naturally, he followed, being sure to grab the novel he'd dropped first. "I grabbed your newest book recommendation."

He caught the slight brow lift.

"Planning on damaging him?"

She always referred to books as him and her. Like they were her babies. "No. But I never plan on it. They just become unwilling victims of my carnage."

The corners of her lips twitched. "I would appreciate you taking care of him. He's newer than a lot of the other books you've injured."

"If I bring him back in perfect condition, will I regain your book trust?"

She stopped, slotting a book onto a shelf. "Probably not. Once burned, forever damaged."

He was pretty sure she was going for humor, but he didn't smile, because there was something in her voice, something deeper, that indicated she spoke from experience. Had someone burned her? A guy? And now she had trouble trusting?

She pushed the cart a bit farther before stopping again. He paused beside her and lowered his voice. "I heard you need a date for a wedding."

Her spine straightened and she spun. "You listened to my conversation?" Her words were an aggressive whisper.

"Not intentionally."

Red tinged her cheeks, and she looked both ways before returning to him. "It's complicated. It's my sister's wedding, and she's..." Her voice was still low, but this time there was something else there.

Callum tilted his head. "Marrying your ex?"

Pain flashed through her eyes. Was he the guy who'd hurt her? "Yes. She's marrying my ex."

"I'll do it." Go to a wedding and pretend to date this gorgeous, feisty woman? Hell yes, he'd do that.

Her brows slashed together. "Do what?"

"Be your boyfriend for the wedding. It would be fun."

Spending time with this beautiful woman who, for some reason, had tangled herself into his every goddamn thought wouldn't just be *fun*. It would be a hell of a lot more than that.

"No." She shook her head vehemently, as if to underscore exactly how much of a *no* it was. "Absolutely not. I've already decided I'm going to tell her I'm attending alone."

Even though the words came out of her mouth, they were accompanied by a cringe. It was small, but he saw it. He saw everything with this woman, even the complicated layers she tried to keep hidden. And right now, she was trying to hide that it was important she didn't attend this wedding alone.

"Well, the offer's there if you change your mind."

Her eyes widened. Maybe she'd been expecting him to push or to laugh and say he was joking. He didn't do either.

"Do you have a pen?"

Her brows rose further. "A pen?"

One side of his mouth lifted. "Yeah, Fi. A pen."

She swallowed, grabbing a pen from the trolley. He slid it from her fingers, then took her hand and turned it over. Damn, her skin was soft. And better yet, she didn't pull away as he wrote his phone number on her palm.

"I've given you my number before," he said softly, "but in case you threw it out"—which was something he suspected—"here it is again."

He was almost certain she didn't breathe the entire time he touched her. He finished writing the digits, but like his thumb had a mind of its own, he gently caressed her wrist. He lowered his voice further. "You still doing okay after the bar incident?"

His chest burned at the memory of that night. A bit over a month ago, a gun had been held to her head at a bar. Every muscle in his body had seized, and all he'd wanted to do was protect her.

That was the night he'd decided to pursue her. Figure out what this damn attraction meant.

That pale skin turned whiter. "I didn't get hurt."

"Doesn't mean you're okay."

Not only had a pistol been aimed at her temple but the man holding her had been shot in the head—while Fiona was still in his arms. Callum's heart had stopped when that shot fired. How easy would it have been for the civilian to hit Fiona instead of his target? Too damn easy.

"I am."

Callum could usually detect a lie, thanks to his enhanced abilities. Little things gave people away. The dilating of the pupil. A hitch in their breath and alteration in the heartbeat...but for once, he couldn't tell. Because *she* didn't know if she was okay?

One more swipe of her wrist, then he lowered her hand and stepped away. "Text if you change your mind on the date thing, honey."

Then he winked before heading to the desk.

CHAPTER 3

"*A*re you sure you want to do this?"

Fiona swallowed as she crossed the parking lot with Jenny. It was dark, but that wasn't the reason she was afraid she might trip. It was the nerves. The ones skittering through her belly, causing her knees to feel weak and her ankles to wobble. Because this was the bar where, a little over a month ago, she'd been grabbed in the bathroom and dragged out by a criminal with a gun.

She swallowed. "I'm okay."

It was a half lie. She *had* been feeling okay. Right up until the building came into view and nightmarish memories started to taunt her. But that was exactly why she needed to do this. Why she'd asked Jenny to come get a drink with her. She hated feeling weak or like she couldn't do something. Yet, every time she passed this bar, that was exactly how she felt. The fear, the nausea...the helplessness. Yeah, there was definitely a bit of help-lessness. It sucked. Hell, she'd even started taking longer routes to get places just so she didn't have to pass this bar.

Nope. All of that needed to stop, and it needed to stop now.

"Okay," Jenny said carefully, watching Fiona closely from

behind her large frames and bangs. "But if you're not okay, we can go at any time. Really. Just say the word."

Jenny had only moved to Cradle Mountain after that terrifying night. Fiona had told her bits and pieces, playing it down like the entire event hadn't left her traumatized. But the night had been plastered all over the news and social media. Some people in the bar had even taken videos during her traumatic ordeal.

People were sick.

She swallowed as they stepped inside the bar, then paused.

Interesting. No pounding heart. No shortened breath or trembling limbs. She just felt...normal. In fact, the hum of people talking was almost soothing. The clinking of glasses against tables. The beat of the music.

A small smile curved her lips. See, this is why she'd needed to come here tonight, to show herself it was a safe place again.

She linked her arm through Jenny's, a new lightness in her chest. "Come on, let's get a drink."

She weaved through the crowd, only coming to a stop when they reached the bar. Jenny tugged at her skirt, and Fiona felt a flash of guilt for bringing her here. She hadn't been against it, just hesitant. Fiona had a feeling she didn't get out much.

A man with a lip ring stepped in front of them from the other side of the bar. He had a sleeve of tattoos down his right arm and piercing blue eyes.

"What can I get you, ladies?" His gaze paused on Jenny, one side of his mouth lifting.

Her friend blushed, and it made Fiona grin. She raised her voice so the man could hear her. "Whiskey sour, please." It was her go-to.

Jenny wet her lips and took a moment to respond. "I'll have the same."

The second the bartender moved away, Fiona nudged Jenny's shoulder. "He's cute."

"Yeah, he is."

"You should talk to him."

Her friend's brows rose almost to her hairline. "No, I couldn't."

"Why not? He was looking at you like he's interested."

She lifted a shoulder, glancing at him, then back. "Because I don't do that."

Fiona frowned. "Talk to cute guys?"

"Yeah."

The bartender returned and mixed the drinks in front of them before handing them over. Fiona went to pay, but the guy shook his head, eyes only for Jenny. "It's on the house."

Fiona's grin widened, but too quickly, Jenny mumbled a barely audible, "Thanks," and turned.

Fiona followed, lowering her head to Jenny's ear. "Just my opinion, but I think you should make talking to cute guys a thing. He's *hot!*"

And she didn't blame the guy. Her friend was cute. Tonight she'd put some waves into her bob and shadow on her eyelids, making her blue eyes look huge behind her frames. Plus, she wore a short skirt that showed off a hell of a lot of skin, paired with a tight black top that was low cut and made her breasts look amazing.

"Maybe after I have some liquid courage," Jenny said, stopping at a tall bar table. "And what about you? Are you going to talk to any cute guys tonight?"

She scoffed. "I don't think so."

"That wouldn't be because you're thinking about a certain tall, dangerous ex-Marine who saved your life, would it?"

Fiona gaped at her friend. She hadn't even told Jenny about that, though the news had spread like wildfire amongst the older librarians. "Absolutely not. Because I know nothing will ever happen there. I mean, you've seen the man. He's six and a half feet of drop-dead gorgeous. My ex wasn't half as good looking as him, and you know how that ended? In heartbreak. The next man I date will be short and chubby with a little bit of balding on top of his head."

Jenny made a face. "Really? He has to be chubby *and* bald?"

"Yep. He'll treat me like a queen."

"Hmm. Okay. So, Callum doesn't tempt you because you're waiting for short, chubby and bald."

"Yep."

"And if you saw him here tonight, you wouldn't be affected?"

"Absolutely not." She could coexist with the man and not turn into a puddle on the floor in his presence. She sipped her whiskey sour, almost wanting to give herself a pat on the back at her confidence in the matter.

"Great, because he's sitting over there in a booth, looking directly at you."

What? She whipped around so fast, the whiskey spilled onto her hand. When her gaze collided with Callum's heated light brown eyes, she almost spat out her drink. He wore a white shirt that pulled far too tightly across his chest, and his powerful fingers circled his glass, the veins in his hands standing out.

Oh, hell no. This was not how her night was supposed to go. Although, was it surprising he was here? He'd been here that fateful night she'd been taken hostage too. In fact, he'd driven her home that night. Was he always here? Was this his usual hangout?

God, she needed to find a new bar, because everything she'd just said to Jenny was a lie.

One big. Fat. Lie.

One side of his mouth lifted. The smile was almost mocking, like he knew exactly what effect he had on her, and he enjoyed it.

Argh. She tugged her gaze away to find Jenny with a knowing smiling and a raised brow.

"Don't say a word," Fiona warned.

"Okay." She sipped her drink, and her nose scrunched in distaste.

"Not a fan of whiskey sours?"

"No, I'm a beer girl through and through, but that guy had me in a fluster and I just ordered what you did."

Fiona laughed, even though she probably shouldn't have. "I'm sorry I'm not a beer girl. Although, I pegged you as more of a chardonnay-in-the-bath-with-a-book girl."

"I guess looks can be deceiving." She took another sip, yet again scrunching her nose. "Do all cocktails taste like this?"

Fiona chuckled again. "No. I'll get you a sweet one next."

They spent the next hour talking and laughing. In that time, Fiona did everything she could to *not* look over her shoulder at Callum. Every so often, the urge got the better of her and she peeked over her shoulder. And each and every time, the man's gaze went straight to her, like he could feel her eyes on him. *Dammit.*

On the third gaze collision, she looked away and threw back the last of her whiskey sour before stepping away from the bar table. "I'm going to pop over to the bathroom. On the way back, I'll grab us some more drinks. Beer or sweet cocktail?"

"No, actually, this is growing on me. I'll have another."

"Are you sure?" Jenny's nose scrunches said otherwise.

Jenny took another sip—and yep, another nose twitch. "No, you're right. I need a beer."

She thought so. "Sure."

She weaved through the crowd to the bathroom, brushing against heated bodies. God, it was busy tonight. It had been busy the last couple times she'd come too...before the incident. Not that she was surprised. It was a Friday evening, and this was probably the most popular place in town.

She stepped into the bathroom—and immediately stopped at the tightness in her chest. It wasn't expected, because she'd been doing so well. Maybe she *should* have seen it coming, seeing as it was the bathroom where the guy had grabbed her.

Her gaze rose to the window on the back wall, near the ceiling. It was closed, hopefully locked. That night it had been open. The breeze had brushed over her skin...a breeze she nearly swore she could feel in this moment.

She almost stepped back out...almost.

No. She was safe. Any feelings of panic or fear were in her head and *not* based on the reality of her moment.

Straightening her spine, she moved into a stall. When she stepped out, she turned on the tap, letting cool water rush over her skin.

A large, cold hand slipped over her mouth, rough and calloused, then she was pulled back against a hard stomach.

Fiona closed her eyes, her breaths coming too quickly. *No.* She was not back there. No one had a hand over her mouth. Nobody stood behind her.

She turned the tap off and grabbed some paper towels.

The muzzle of a gun pressed to her temple. Her stomach dropped. Her world stopped.

She stumbled back.

Stop it, Fiona.

"Hey, are you okay?"

A hand touched her shoulder, and she spun around so fast the towel slipped from her fingers. A young woman with bleached-blond hair stood beside her, hand on her shoulder.

She gave a quick, jerky nod. "Yes. I'm fine."

Quickly, she grabbed the paper towel, threw it into the trash, and walked out of the bathroom. She brushed someone's shoulder, and they gasped when their drink spilled.

Blood roared between her ears, but she still heard the gasps of the people around her. The rush of footsteps as people shuffled back, to get away. Because they saw what she felt. The muzzle of the pistol to her head.

She stopped, pressing a hand to her chest, trying to force air in and out of her body. But it wasn't just her lungs that felt tight, it was her throat too. The air itself was too thick to breathe.

The music had stopped. Everyone stared. Then a girl was talking to the man holding the gun to her head. The woman's words were too quiet to hear over the roar of blood between her ears.

She tried to pull herself back to the present. People hadn't stopped. The music still played. And there was no man behind her with a gun.

Two more steps.

The pressure of the gun to her head began to lessen. Was he letting her go? Would he release her? Her knees began to tremble with relief.

Then the sound of a gunshot cracked through the rush of blood between her ears. For a single heartbeat, she wondered if the bullet had hit her. If the shock and fear were numbing her from the pain of it cutting into her flesh. Then the body behind her disappeared, thudded to the floor.

The man who'd held her had been shot...not her.

Her gaze lowered to her shoulder to see wet, crimson blood. It coated her. Bathed her. Choked her.

CHAPTER 4

*C*allum watched Fiona's back as she headed to the bathroom. He'd been damn well unable to take his eyes off the woman all night. She wore a short red dress that clung to her curves and made her creamy skin look so smooth that he yearned to run his hands over it. She'd paired the dress with red heels, drawing attention to her toned calves and thighs.

It was fucking torture.

The second she disappeared, he dragged his gaze back to his team. Tyler, Liam and Jason sat around him. Together, they made up half the guys who ran Blue Halo. Logan, Blake, Flynn and Aidan had decided to stay home with their women, and for Blake, that included his five-year-old daughter, Mila.

"How's Emerson doing after everything that went down?" Jason asked Tyler.

Tyler's partner had recently been through hell when both she and her brother were targeted by a deranged psychopath.

He lifted a shoulder. "I think she's doing okay. Her brother's doing well in the care facility where he's receiving therapy, so I think that's helping her. She's still coming to terms with everything that happened with her ex, but she's handling it well."

Callum nodded, lifting his beer to his lips. "I'm glad she's safe and you're both happy."

His friend was different since meeting Emerson. There was a new lightness about him. He smiled more often, and longer, and left the office earlier.

"I *am* happy," Tyler said quietly, his lips curving into a smile. "Love will do that to a man."

Liam shook his head. "What is it with this town? It's like a damn love trap."

Jason bumped his shoulder. "The beautiful, strong women help."

Oh yeah. The women his teammates had found were strong. They'd had to be, with everything that had been thrown at them. Each had gone through their own nightmare in one form or another.

His gaze shot to the bathroom. Fiona was strong also. He still didn't know her as well as he wanted, but he planned to change that.

He was still looking that way when the bathroom door opened and Fiona came out—only she didn't look like she had when she'd stepped in there. Her skin was too pale and her eyes too wide.

What the hell?

She bumped into someone, then stopped and touched her chest.

Shit. Something was wrong.

He rose from the booth, ignoring the calls from the guys. As he walked toward her, he saw her attempt to step forward again, but she didn't get far before the last scrap of color leached from her face and she looked like she was going to crumble.

Fuck.

He moved faster, sliding past groups of people and bar tables until he reached her. He grabbed her upper arms, hating the violent tremble in her limbs. "Fiona?"

24

Her eyes were on her shoulder, her chest heaving so quickly each breath was a whip of air. "Blood..."

His throat closed. There was blood? Where?

He scanned her face. Her shoulders. But he couldn't see a damn drop. Was someone bleeding in the bathroom?

"His blood," she gasped. "It's all over me! Someone...someone shot him."

Realization hit him like a punch to the gut. She wasn't talking about here and now. She was talking about that night. She was having a flashback...a panic attack.

Quickly, he slipped an arm around her waist and tugged her close to his side. Her skin was too damn cold and her breathing still uneven. He maneuvered them through the crowd, sliding past people who were laughing and drinking, constantly watching both Fiona and the exit.

The second the cool outside air brushed his skin, he felt her breathing begin to slow. Heard her pulse return to an almost normal rate.

But he didn't move away from her. Instead, he eased in front of her and touched his palm to her cheek, trying to bring some warmth back to her body. "Talk to me, Fi. Are you okay?"

Slowly, her gaze slipped up his stomach, his chest, then finally, her chestnut eyes met his. When she spoke, her voice was low with an audible tremble. "I thought I was okay. It wasn't until I stepped into the bathroom that..."

That she realized she wasn't. It wasn't a surprise. The bathroom was where the asshole had grabbed her. Fuck, Callum wished he could protect her from the memories. He wanted to turn back time and keep Levi from taking her to begin with.

"I'm sorry." He felt responsible because it had been his team's job to catch the guy who'd grabbed her. They hadn't. At least, not in time.

Her lips parted. There was so much fear and torment in her expression that he couldn't stop himself. He pulled her against his chest and held her. For a split second, she was rigid. So still in his arms, he wondered if she'd push away. Then she eased into him, her shaky breaths brushing his chest. When her arms wrapped around his waist, she held him tightly, like he was the only thing keeping her grounded. Keeping her here, in this reality, and not in the past.

Minutes ticked by, calming the storms within each of them. It wasn't until a woman's voice sounded that he pulled back.

"Fiona." The woman stopped a foot away, one hand pressed over her heart and looking at them, unsure.

Fiona pushed back, and it took a hell of a lot of strength to release her.

"I'm sorry," the woman said quietly. "I couldn't find you. I asked the bartender if he saw you go anywhere, and he said some guy led you out of here. I was worried."

"I'm okay."

The woman nodded, then finally looked up at him, and her eyes widened. "I'm sorry. Am I interrupting?"

"No." Fiona stepped away from him, like she was cementing that there was nothing going on. "I just had a moment. I'm fine now, but I think my night's done."

He opened his mouth to say he'd take her home, because damn, he wanted to stay close. To make sure she was as okay as she insisted she was.

"Are you okay driving me home, Jen?" Fiona asked.

Her friend nodded. "Of course."

Fiona glanced up at him, the normal sassiness nowhere to be seen. "Thank you, Callum. You saved me again."

Then he had no choice but to watch her walk away.

CHAPTER 5

"So, when you say this place does good coffee, how good are we talking?"

Fiona's lips stretched as she looked at Jenny. "Really good. Like, dream-about-it-every-night-until-you-have-it-again level of good."

"Okay, now you're just teasing me."

"Nope. I only discovered the coffee shop a couple months ago. I can't believe I've been living in Cradle Mountain for almost a year and didn't find it till now."

In the week since the bar incident, Fiona hadn't had any more panic attacks, but then, she'd barely gone out—just to work and home and this coffee shop. Oh, and she'd read her way through half a dozen books because, well, that was what you did when you were trying to escape your world and enter a new one.

Jenny grinned. "You know my expectations are sky-high now, right?"

"You're lucky you found me."

Jenny nudged her shoulder. "I really am."

In all seriousness, Fiona was the one grateful to have Jenny. Her cousin Stacey had visited Cradle Mountain a handful of times—she'd actually been with her during that awful night at the bar—but having a cousin visit every so often wasn't the same as having a friend right here, every day. The other librarians were older and had their own little cliques. Plus, Fiona spent her spare time reading and taking walks, both of which were useless when it came to meeting new people.

When they reached The Grind, Fiona pushed inside and Jenny followed. Immediately, she grinned. It wasn't just the coffee she loved here. The interior was...well, the only word she could think of to describe it was quirky. The tables and booths were different colors, making the place look fun and happy. The walls were just as colorful, and the room was always full.

Fiona and Jenny went straight for a booth by the window.

"Oh my Lord," Jenny groaned as she sat. "The smell of coffee beans is magnificent."

"Ha. Wait until you try the stuff. You're going to be kissing my feet for bringing you here."

"I'm always up for some feet kissing," a woman said as she stepped up to their table. Fiona looked into the most exotic eyes she'd ever seen, one green and the other a beautiful brown. The woman also had pink stripes in the sides of her blond hair.

"I like anyone who brings more people to my coffee shop," the woman added.

"Your coffee shop?" Fiona asked. She'd seen the woman here before but didn't know she owned the place. She looked too young. Maybe mid-to-late twenties?

"Yep. This baby's all mine. My partner sometimes complains that I love this place more than him, but that's only true when he's bad."

Fiona laughed. "I hope that's not often."

She lifted a shoulder. "He has his moments. My name's Courtney. What can I get you ladies today?"

"I'm Fiona, and I'll have a latte, please," she answered.

Jenny nodded. "Jenny. I'll have a latte too."

When Courtney left, Fiona cocked her head to the side. "Now, are you *really* a latte girl?"

Jenny laughed. "I'm really a latte girl. I did not get tongue-tied in front of Courtney. Plus, what's the alternative? Black coffee? Yuck. If it's not a latte, it's a double-shot latte with two sugars."

"You're speaking my language."

Fiona's phone vibrated from her pocket, and her smile dimmed. It had been doing that a lot lately. She'd received three more messages in the last week from that unknown number, saying pretty much the same thing as the first. Now, every time her phone vibrated with a message, she was almost scared to look at it.

With a quick breath, she tugged her phone from her jeans pocket. Not the unknown number. Her sister. Which was almost as bad.

Amanda: Will you stop ignoring me! Are you bringing a guy or not? I need to know by tonight.

Fiona cringed. Yeah, she still hadn't replied to her sister.

"Okay, who's put that look on your face and why?"

Fiona looked up from her phone, not exactly sure what her friend was seeing. Anxiety? Resignation? The depressing acceptance that she'd have to admit the truth to her terrible sister?

"It's my sister," she finally said. "She's awful—and she's marrying my ex. Her wedding's in a few weeks, and I may have told a little white lie that I'm dating someone and will be bringing him to the wedding."

Jenny cringed. "Oh God. I'm sorry. She's really marrying your ex?"

"Yep. The one I told you about, who's equally awful. She actually started dating him while he and I were still together."

Jenny's eyes widened and she leaned forward. "No!"

"Yes again."

"Well, I can see why you lied."

Fiona sighed. "The worst part? I wasn't even surprised when

she did it. Don't get me wrong, I was mad as hell. But I swear, since the day I was born, she's hated me." And Fiona had never known why. Sometimes she thought it was jealousy, since Fiona and her parents got along so well. But their parents loved both of them.

"Why are you going then?"

That was a good question. Most wouldn't. "A couple of reasons. The first is my parents don't know about the cheating. They think I just fell out of love with him, then my sister started dating him. I adore my parents and the truth would kill them."

Her gaze flickered to the window, but she wasn't really seeing. "And more than that, I just...I don't want them to know how much they hurt me."

Because they *had* hurt her. More severely than anyone else ever had. And they'd damaged her trust.

"Okay. Yes, I totally understand." Sympathy shone in her friend's eyes, but then a second later it shifted into a mischievous look. "Well, I mean, you could ask—"

"No." She already knew who Jenny was going to say, and it was a big fat no.

So why do you keep thinking about asking him?

Even thinking it made her mentally cringe. She *had* been thinking about asking him. She'd been doing a lot of thinking about Callum in the last week. The way he'd caught her off the ladder. The way he'd saved her in the bar. The man was becoming her personal bodyguard.

No. Asking him was crazy. They weren't even friends.

Jenny lifted a shoulder. "I'm just saying. He clearly likes you, and he's saved you a million times now."

The words had just left Jenny's mouth when the door opened and three large men walked inside, all well over six feet, with wide shoulders and thick arms. And the last man in the door was none other than Callum.

Goddammit. Why did the world keep summoning him everywhere she went?

Immediately, Callum's gaze whipped to hers. The corners of his mouth ticked up in just a hint of a smile. Then he mouthed, "Hey."

And even though she told herself not to react, freaking screamed it in her head, her damn body betrayed her, her heart kicking into a gallop and her mouth drying.

Without realizing she was doing it, she thumbed her right wrist, where he'd grazed her skin as he'd written his number.

"Oh. My. God," Jenny whispered as she watched the men walking inside. "You can't say that isn't the universe telling you to ask him."

No. It was the universe tormenting her. She swallowed, swearing she could still feel him watching her. "It's not."

Jenny sighed. "Okay, but I think you're missing an opportunity."

She didn't tell her friend that the man had already offered to be her date, because then Jenny would push harder. For a fleeting moment, she imagined walking into her sister's wedding with his arm around her. With his heat touching her side.

No. No, no, no. He would be far too easy to fall for, and he wasn't in her plans. Her plans were short, chubby and bald. The opposite of Callum.

Thankfully, Courtney returned to their table with steaming lattes, which smelled so amazing she almost groaned out loud.

"Oh my gosh, Courtney. I think *I* might be kissing *your* feet for this." Fiona lifted the coffee to her lips, and yep, it tasted as amazing as the last time she'd come here.

"Kiss away." Courtney smiled. "Don't forget about the joke on the mug."

She pulled her mug down and read the side.

Once in a while someone amazing comes along...and here I am.

She chuckled as Jenny read hers out loud.

"You know what that sounds like? Not my problem."

They both laughed, and Fiona looked back up at Courtney. "These are awesome."

She lifted her shoulder. "They've become my little addiction. Call out if you need anything else."

Courtney left the table, but she didn't head behind the counter. Instead, she walked up to one of the Blue Halo men. Fiona's heart melted as she watched the couple lean into each other and kiss. Adorable.

"Oh my gosh, look at you."

She swung her gaze back to Jenny. "What?"

"You've got that ready-to-fall-in-love look on your face. Just ask him out already."

"I do not. And definitely not with Callum. Remember, I need—"

"Short, chubby and bald. Yeah, yeah."

She laughed. Jenny clearly didn't believe her.

"I hate this guy who hurt you. I want to kick him in the teeth, and I don't even know him."

Fiona scoffed. "Trust me, you're not the only one."

She wished *she'd* kicked him in the teeth the moment she'd found him in bed with her sister, but the shock had taken hold of her body and all she'd been able to do was stare at them, mouth open like a gaping fish, before turning and walking out.

"But," Fiona said, refusing to feel down about a past she had no control over, "it brought me here, so it can't have been all bad."

"And if you hadn't come here, we would never have found each other."

"What a tragedy that would have been."

"Exactly." Jenny took one more sip of her coffee before rising. "I'm just going to the bathroom real quick."

She had just left the table when Amanda texted again.

Amanda: You have until tonight, or I'm going to assume you don't have a date.

Fiona closed her eyes, then with a resigned sigh, opened them and started typing a response. She was halfway through her epic, fictional breakup story when the phone rang. Oh, man...it was her mother.

Fiona groaned. First Stacey, and now her sister had set their mom on her.

"Hi, Mom."

"Hi, baby. It's so nice to hear your voice. I miss you."

Her chest tightened. "I miss you too, Mom."

And she really did. She'd moved to get away from Amanda and Freddie, but the distance between her and her parents had been unfortunate collateral damage.

"I was just talking to your sister," her mother started. Fiona massaged her brow. "And she asked me to call about your plus-one."

"I was just responding to her when you called."

"Oh, good." Relief was heavy in her mother's voice. "She suggested he wasn't real, but I told her you would never lie about that. I know things are...complicated, with her marrying Freddie."

Complicated? They were more than that. But her parents didn't know she'd found them in bed together. When her sister and Freddie had come out as dating a few weeks later, her parents had been utterly shocked and more than a little stressed. She loved her mother and father, plus her dad had some health issues...so she'd lied again. Told them she was fine with it and happy for them.

Then they'd gotten engaged...

"I'm sorry this will be difficult for you. I tried speaking to her about it being too soon after you and Freddie split, but..." But her sister was a selfish bitch? "I don't think she understood the issue."

Of course she didn't. Amanda only ever thought about Amanda. "I'm okay, Mom."

Another lie that slipped off her tongue.

"But I'm just so glad you've got a partner to help you through it. All your father and I have ever wanted is for you and Amanda to be happy. This rift between you two these last several months, and having you move away…it's all been so hard."

She pinched her brow. The rift had been there for a lot longer than a few months.

"Hopefully," her mother continued, "with you having moved on, and Amanda getting married, we can leave the past in the past and be a family again."

There was so much hope in her mother's voice.

"So, will you tell me his name?"

Instinctively, she looked up to find the three Blue Halo men headed toward the door. Callum paused before stepping out, his gaze once again locking with hers. Then he winked at her, throwing her belly into a tattered mess.

"Callum."

The second the name left her lips, she cringed and scrunched her eyes.

"Callum. Well, I'll let Amanda know. And please tell him how excited we all are to meet him."

"I will. I love you, Mom."

"Love you too, baby."

The second the call ended, Fiona dropped her head into her hands. What had she done?

CHAPTER 6

"*I*'m not even gonna ask what has that look on your face. I already know...the librarian."

Callum's grin widened at Liam's words as they stepped onto the street. Hell yes, it was. "Her name's Fiona. And yeah, I smile when I see her. Sue me."

Jason scoffed. "You don't just smile, you light up like a damn kid at Christmas."

Callum couldn't even argue with his friend. He lifted a shoulder as they crossed the road. "I like her."

Blue Halo was only a block away from The Grind, which was only one of the reasons they visited so frequently. The other, of course, was Courtney. She and Jason were basically stuck at the damn hip.

"Oh, man," Liam groaned. "I'm gonna be the only single guy left. Who the hell's gonna be my wingman?"

"You think you need a wingman with those boyish good looks?" Callum asked.

"I like to think of myself as more of a rugged ladies' man kind of handsome."

Jason scoffed. "You can think of yourself however you damn well like. Hell, let's go with a baby giraffe."

Callum choked back a laugh as Liam gave his friend a shove in the shoulder.

"Seriously though, Callum," Jason said. "You gonna ask her out?"

"I offered to be her plus-one at a family wedding. That's a date." A date on a whole different level. "The ball's in her court now."

One side of Liam's mouth lifted. "Wonder if she'd say yes if I offered."

"Don't even fucking think about it." The words came out as a dangerous growl. He knew his friend was messing with him, but just the idea of her with anyone else was like a damn baseball bat to his gut.

"I'm kidding," Liam said, shaking his head. "It's clear to anyone who's seen you guys that you're into each other. Wonder why she's so dead set on pushing you away?"

Callum had been wondering that as well. "I'm a patient man."

He also didn't scare easily. When he wanted something, he damn well chased it until he had it.

They stepped inside the Blue Halo building and climbed the stairs to their office. Cassie, Aidan's partner, smiled at them from behind the desk. "Hey, boys. You bring me a coffee?"

Callum slid the second to-go cup across the desk.

Her smile widened. "This is why I work here."

Aidan scoffed from the doorway. "Excuse me?"

She swiveled in her chair, lifting a shoulder. "You're the second reason."

Aidan growled, and when he moved in on Cassie, Callum took that as his cue to get the hell out of there. He reached the hall just as Aidan's lips swooped onto Cassie's. He liked that his friend was happy, but he didn't need a front-row seat.

Callum settled behind his desk. He loved his job. The security business had become his life, and he was damn grateful to get to see and work with his team every day. They'd been thrown together by Project Arma against their will but amongst the wreckage had found family. Which was important to him, seeing as he only had his father, who lived in Seattle, and they weren't close.

He logged onto his computer and checked his schedule. A couple of cases to look into and some background checks to do. He'd always had a knack for technology and hacking, so when the team needed a tech guy, he'd been keen to take on the role.

He spent the next couple hours responding to job inquiries, setting up meetings with clients, and completing a background check for a job. It had just hit one o'clock, and he was about to get up and go to the workout room when his phone vibrated from the desk. Immediately, his lips stretched into a smile at the sight of the text.

Fiona: Were you being serious about the wedding thing?

He leaned back in his seat.

Callum: No.

Then he quickly typed to add…

Callum: But only about the part where I said I thought it would be fun. I don't think that. I think it would be damn amazing.

The two of them together for a prolonged period of time? Hell yeah, it would be amazing.

Callum: No.

Fiona's heart dropped, and the tingly feeling that had been tumbling around her belly since she'd decided to text him died.

She tossed her phone facedown onto the coffee table in her living room and scrubbed her hands over her face. What had she been thinking? Had she really asked Callum, a man who was basically a stranger, to be her pretend boyfriend at a family wedding?

Crazy. She was crazy. *Of course* he hadn't been serious. Someone should just kill her and get it over with because she couldn't show her face around him again.

With a long, pained exhale, she reached for her phone. It vibrated before she could touch it, and she snatched her hand back.

Had Callum just sent another text? Why? To tell her she was as crazy as she felt? To offer to dig the hole for her body because he knew she couldn't live with the embarrassment?

Slowly, like the phone was a bomb that might detonate, she wrapped her fingers around it and lifted so she could see the screen.

Callum: But only about the part where I said I thought it would be fun. I don't think that. I think it would be damn amazing.

Holy Jesus, Mary and Joseph. She was reading the text wrong, right? She'd tangled his words into what she wanted to read rather than what was actually in front of her?

Fiona: You're saying you'll go with me?

His response was instant.

Callum: Yeah, Fi. I'd love to be your date for your sister's wedding.

Her heart pitter-pattered so hard in her chest it was like it was trying to break free.

Fiona: The wedding's in Twin Falls. That's an hour and a half drive and we'd need to stay in a hotel...in a room I already booked...with one bed...

She wasn't sure if her words were supposed to discourage him or just make him aware. Either way, they'd be together for three days and two nights. And sleeping in the same bed? She broke out in hives at the mere thought!

Callum: You just sweetened the deal, honey.

What magical planet of perfect men was this guy from?

Fiona: My sister's awful. And I have these really nosy aunts and uncles who'll ask you about the intimate details of every life decision you've ever made. And the groom and I have a complicated past...

Complicated? What a damn understatement.

She waited for his response. When it didn't come as quickly as previous texts, she almost wondered if he was coming to his senses and reconsidering.

Then the phone rang. *Oh, God...*

Her hand hovered over the key before she finally answered. "You've changed your mind. That's okay. I shouldn't have asked. I'm sorry. It was crazy. I was just being desperate. But I shouldn't have tried to bring you into my mess—"

"Fi—"

"Just forget I mentioned it. Maybe we can still coexist, and I won't have to bury my head in the—"

"Fiona! I'm glad you asked. And like I said in the text, I'm happy to help."

She frowned. "You are?"

"Yeah. I only called because I figured no matter what I wrote, you'd respond with something else to deter me."

She stood and walked to her kitchen, needing to move. "You want more? The food will be terrible. We have to go a day before the wedding for a rehearsal dinner, where you'll be pounded with questions from my family, and you'll have to wear a suit."

"I've eaten terrible food in the military—can't be as bad as that. An extra night away actually doesn't sound too bad, I'm great with family, and I look damn good in a suit."

Uh, yeah, of course he did. He was cut like a bodybuilder. "I just..." She pinched her nose. "I'm not sure why you'd do this for me."

Hell, she wasn't sure why he did *anything* that he did for her. A week ago he'd saved her from a panic attack in the bar. Before that, he'd caught her when she almost broke her back falling off a ladder.

"Maybe," he said quietly, "I'm not the bad guy you pegged me as."

She nibbled her bottom lip as she looked out her kitchen window. "I don't think you're a bad guy. Just that you're a...guy."

A really good-looking one. A guy who had all the right words and knew how to make a woman want him.

There was a short pause. It was just long enough to have her squirming.

"Don't have a great history with guys?" Callum finally asked.

Just bad history with one guy. A guy she'd dated for just about her entire adult life, who'd hurt her in the worst possible way.

"Nope." She fiddled with the edge of the counter. "But that's not important. What's important is, I only want you to do this if you really want to."

"When's the wedding?"

"The weekend after next. I've got a room booked for two nights at the same hotel as the reception."

"I can't wait."

She opened her mouth to ask if he was serious but stopped at a sound from her bedroom.

She straightened, her gaze moving to the hall. For a moment, she was still, waiting for another sound. When it never came, she pushed off the kitchen counter and walked down the hallway. Her house wasn't huge, one story with three small bedrooms and two bathrooms. She opened her bedroom door, and a breeze brushed her skin.

One of the French doors was ajar.

The fine hairs on her arms stood on end. Had she done that?

Slowly, she moved into the room, scanning the space, every corner and crevice. Then her gaze shifted to the connected bathroom. With even slower steps, she went inside. Her makeup, moisturizer and perfume were out, but that wasn't unusual. She was often in such a rush she left things as they were.

"Fiona?"

Her attention dragged back to the call, and she shook her head. "I'm sorry. I got distracted for a second."

"Is everything okay?"

"Yes. I mean, of course it is." She swallowed to wet her suddenly dry throat, shaking off the unease. "I'll, um, send you the details."

"Sounds good." He took a breath. "You *sure* you're okay?" A deep, raspy concern filled his voice.

"Yes. Definitely. Thank you again, Callum. Talk soon."

Once she'd hung up, her gaze moved to her French doors. She must have left them open. The only other explanation would be that someone was in here, but...

Her neck prickled.

No. That couldn't be the case, because, well, it freaked her out too much.

Quickly, she crossed the room and stuck her head out to see the empty yard. See, no one was there. She tugged the door closed, and the lock made a loud click as she firmly turned it.

CHAPTER 7

*W*hat the hell was she doing? Had she lost her damn mind? Well, she had to have, because normal people didn't show up to the house of a man they barely knew, bag packed, ready to drive to a family wedding. It just didn't happen.

Christ, she needed her head examined.

She glanced up at his home from inside her car, across the street. How long had she been sitting here? Five minutes? Ten? She needed to go in. But that would make this insane situation real.

She'd been waiting for Callum to call and tell her he'd changed his mind. That he wasn't really going through with this. She'd never looked at her phone so much in her life. But nope, that call never came. Oh, he'd texted…to ask how she was doing. How work had been. What color suit he should wear.

More damn ticks to his name when she thought he'd already reached maximum capacity for perfectness.

Okay. Just do it, Fiona. Go inside.

With a quick, sharp breath, she climbed out of the car. She couldn't stop the fast glance in either direction. She'd been doing that a lot lately. Glances over her shoulder. Checking and double-checking the locks on her home. She wasn't usually a paranoid person...but strange things had been happening.

More sounds in her home. The feeling like someone was watching her.

The other day, she'd opened her drawer of T-shirts to find things looked like they'd been shifted around. Which was crazy, right? Apart from that day her French door was left ajar, her home was completely locked up.

She crossed the road, keys so firmly in her grasp they pressed painfully into her skin.

Her clothes looking messed with wasn't the only odd occurrence. This morning, she'd searched and searched for her favorite red sweatshirt but couldn't find it.

She was going crazy. Losing her goddamn mind. She must have taken the sweatshirt to work or just left it somewhere. Either that or it was under her bed or something, because things didn't just up and disappear by themselves.

And then there were the text messages...

Yeah, she'd received more, each more vile and threatening than the last. Calling her a slut and a whore, and warning her to stay away from what wasn't hers. She just needed to block the number and be done with it. Her name was never mentioned, so for all she knew, the texts were being sent to the wrong number.

With a quick shake of her head, she stopped in front of Callum's door. She couldn't think about any of that this weekend. She had a wedding to get through and a relationship to fake. That was going to take every ounce of her energy.

She lifted her hand to knock, but before her knuckles hit wood, the door opened—and her mouth went dry.

Holy hotness.

Callum stood in front of her, shirtless, sweat dripping from his body. Not only that, but his large muscles glistened, veins prominent under his olive skin like he'd just finished fighting lions in some arena.

"Hey," he said, his deep, raspy voice causing her belly to do a little heated jingle. "I was wondering if you were ever going to knock."

She opened and closed her mouth three times, trying to recall a couple words of the English language. It took five seconds. Five. Freaking. Seconds. "What are you doing?"

One side of his mouth lifted, showing a perfect dimple. "Opening the door."

So he was a funny man too. "Yes, but why are you shirtless and looking like...well...all big and sweaty?"

Okay. Not the most elegant wording, and he was always big. But shirtless and sweaty? Was the man trying to kill her?

"I was working out. I stopped a few minutes ago when I heard you pull up out front."

Oh, man. So he knew about her delay tactics. He didn't know she'd been tempted to keep on driving and forget this crazy little deal. Or maybe he'd figured that out. Wouldn't take much to connect the dots. Had he seen her jam her keys back into the ignition, fully prepared to run?

She cleared her throat. "You don't look very ready to go."

Understatement of the century.

"I'm all packed, just need a shower. I won't take long. Come in." He moved back, giving her room to enter. His biceps rippled with the motion, and she had to physically restrain herself from gawking at him like a desperate teenager.

What had she signed up for?

Carefully, she stepped past him, making sure to avoid any accidental touches. Even the smallest graze would probably turn her into a floundering mess. Or maybe she already was?

Not touching him was harder than it should have been. Not so much because there wasn't enough space, but because her hands twitched to reach him. Feel his heat, slide her fingers against his wet chest.

Get a grip, woman, she scolded herself.

Her gaze caught on the expansive staircase beyond the foyer. Then the large open living and dining area to the right, which led to a huge, modern kitchen. So the man wasn't just tall, funny and sexy, but he also had money.

Good one, God. You're really going out of your way to torment me now.

"You live here by yourself?" she asked.

"I do." The soft thud of the door closing echoed behind her. "I know. It's a lot of house."

"Well, you're a lot of man." The words fell from her lips before she could suck them in, and they fell like little explosions, detonating around her. She winced. "Oh God, I'm sorry."

He laughed. "Don't apologize, Fi. I like you uncensored." He leaned his head toward her, and this time when he spoke, his warm breath brushed her cheek. "And you're right, I *am* a lot of man."

A shudder raced down her spine. When he brushed past her, he touched her hip, causing her skin to just about break out in hives.

He crossed to his coffee machine on the kitchen counter, and she could only watch as a shirtless, glistening Callum made coffee in his glorious kitchen. It kind of felt like a dream. One of those types you didn't want to wake up from, because a god of a man was waiting on you in a mansion.

Only, it shouldn't feel like a dream. She'd promised herself she *would not* fall for Callum. They were friends…kind of. And they could never be more because she said so.

"What are you thinking so hard about over there?"

She jolted. "Just that I should offer to help with that coffee."

He gave her a knowing smile, which lit humor in his beautiful eyes. He knew she was lying.

When he handed her one of the mugs, their fingers grazed, and she had to hold in the gasp that tried to zip into her chest.

"Thank you," she said, her voice quieter than it should have been.

"You're welcome. Make yourself at home. I'm just going to jump into the shower, then I'll be ready to go."

Sweet baby Jesus, now she had to listen to running water while knowing he was naked in the shower. Great. "Okay."

He moved out of the room, looking all power and strength as he went.

How would that power feel in—

Stop it, Fiona.

He'd just hit the staircase when he swung a look over his shoulder. The side of his mouth kicked up, like he knew exactly what she was thinking about. Then he kept moving.

Where was that hole she could bury her head in?

She exhaled loudly and took a sip of her coffee, humming in appreciation. What the actual heck? His coffee tasted good too?

One bad thing. That's all I'm asking from you, universe. Something she could latch onto and use to remind herself she didn't want to date Callum.

She spent the next fifteen minutes moving around his living room, covertly checking it out. Everything was neat and tidy. There were no old coffee mugs on the coffee table. No dirty dishes in the sink. It was as far from the bachelor pad she'd expected as possible.

It had masculine touches—the brown leather couch that was devoid of throw pillows, the PlayStation beside the TV—but it was still so neat.

She'd just stepped into the open office to the left side of the foyer and was eyeing the masculine art on the walls when the doorbell rang.

Her gaze shot to the entrance, her brows pulling together. She remained still, not wanting to answer a door to a house that wasn't hers. But then a knock came. A firm one. Maybe it was the mailman with a delivery?

Quickly, she set her empty mug onto the desk and moved to the door. Her eyes widened when she pulled it open.

Not a mailman. A woman who looked to be in her mid-thirties, wearing the tightest jeans Fiona had ever seen, and *Christ*, were the woman's legs nice. She wore a top so cropped that her belly button ring was on full display, as was her cleavage at the top. Then there was her hair...gorgeous long brown hair, contrasted by piercing blue eyes.

Beautiful. She was beautiful. And hot.

The woman's brows slashed together. "What are you doing here?"

Well, there was a mark against her. That wasn't exactly a friendly hello. "I'm Fiona Lo—"

"I know who you are. I've seen you at the library. What are you doing *here*?"

The woman knew her? Fiona had never seen this lady in her life, and she was pretty sure she'd remember. And what the heck was with the attitude?

The woman's gaze moved behind Fiona, zeroing in on Callum's suitcase. Her eyes narrowed, her back straightening. "Is that yours? Are you staying here?"

Who the hell *was* this woman? "That's none of your business."

At. All.

Another narrowing of her eyes. *Yeah, narrow them all you want, woman. I said what I said.*

Before she could respond, footsteps sounded on the stairs behind her. Then Callum's heat permeated her back. "Hey, Kasey. Everything okay?"

The woman clearly wasn't okay, but she scrambled for a smile. "Callum! I thought I'd just drop by and see if you wanted to grab something to eat?"

And there it was. The thing she'd asked the universe for. The reminder that this man was not safe to fall for because he had women like *this* vying for him. And honestly, who would be able to say no to a woman who looked like this Kasey?

As if he heard her thoughts, a warm hand touched her back, and she had to fight to keep the touch from heating her cheeks. From seeping below the surface of her shirt and skin and finding every part of her that yearned for more.

"Sorry, Kasey. I'm going away for a few days. I'll see you when I get back."

Her eyes pinched, but to her credit, her smile didn't falter. "Okay. Well, you know where to find me when you get back... just next door."

Ding, ding, ding. There was the second thing. Callum not only had a sexy, beautiful woman vying for his attention...she lived right next door!

Kasey gave them one more tight smile before turning and walking away, her perfect ass swaying as she went.

Callum closed the door. "Ready to go?"

"Yep." One tight word. She couldn't even muster a smile.

She shouldn't be angry. Callum had done nothing wrong, and if anything had happened between him and Kasey, or was going to happen in the future, that was none of her business. She was nothing to him. Barely a friend. He was just doing her a favor. A massive, will-probably-never-be-able-to-repay-him favor.

Callum watched her for a beat longer, the intensity in his eyes boring into her, before giving a little nod and squeezing her arm. "Great. Let's hit the road."

CHAPTER 8

*C*allum shot a glance Fiona's way. She'd driven for the first hour, and they'd switched over about twenty minutes ago. He'd offered to drive the entire distance, but she'd insisted. Not that he was surprised. Independence seemed important to this woman.

Since leaving his place, she'd been overly polite. He'd tried for a couple of jokes, but either he wasn't as funny as he thought, or her mind was elsewhere. He was going with the latter. He wasn't annoyed by her demeanor. More intrigued. What caused this woman to get her guard up so easily?

He knew Kasey's visit had affected her, but her attitude wasn't in proportion to that brief interaction. Whoever had hurt her had made her trust fragile.

"I think we should play twenty questions," Callum said, breaking the ten-minute silence that had passed since his last attempt at conversation.

Her gaze turned from the window to him. "Twenty questions?"

"Yeah. Get to know each other a bit better. Also, get details of our relationship nailed down."

A crease formed between her brows. "What if you ask a question I don't want to answer?"

Interesting first thought. "You say red raisin, and I'll ask something else."

Her lips twitched. "Red raisin? Did you make that up?"

"I did. I like red, and I like raisins. Ready?"

"Okay, sure. You go first."

"How long have we been dating?"

Her brows rose. Maybe she'd been expecting a more personal first question. "Two months. But we were friends before that."

He nodded. The woman had put some thought into this.

"Favorite color?" she asked.

"Chestnut." He shot a look into her chestnut eyes and saw her cheeks bloom. "Yours?"

"Blue. But a deep, dark blue, not a pale one. Like the ocean when it's really deep. How old are you?"

"Thirty-three. Why don't you get along with your sister?"

There was an audible shift in her breathing. "I don't know. She's always hated me, and I've never known why. She's five years older than me and just seems to despise my very existence."

What kind of person blindly hated a family member?

"It's her loss," he said quietly, wanting to ease the obvious hurt.

She lifted a shoulder. "I get along with my parents. Really well, actually, and I think that makes it worse for me and Amanda. Like she thinks they like me more than her or something. Which is ridiculous, they love us both. Who's in your family?"

"Just my dad, who lives in Seattle. My mother passed away when I was young, and I don't have any siblings, but I always wished I did. Although, the guys feel like brothers."

One side of her mouth lifted. "That's nice."

"What's your history with the groom?"

The soft smile fell from her lips. "Red raisin."

Fair enough. Although Callum was hoping that, after some time, she'd trust him enough to share. He already knew the guy was an ex. But he was dying to know how long ago they'd broken up and what had led to him marrying her sister.

"Why'd you move to Cradle Mountain?" he asked instead.

"Because it was the perfect distance from my sister and Freddie. Too far to drive regularly, but not so far you need to catch a flight and make it a long trip to visit."

Before he could put much thought into that complicated answer, her next question came. "Favorite food?"

"Apple pie. Favorite day of the week?"

She laughed, and the sound hit him square in the chest like a damn freight train. God, it was beautiful and soft and melodic. And her smile…he had to forcibly shift his eyes away from her and back to the road.

"Funny question, but my answer is probably the same as everyone else's. Sunday, because I get to put my feet up and read my books."

"Ah, yes. Sunday is a common favorite. But it's not mine." He felt her eyes on him.

"What's your favorite day?"

"Definitely Wednesday."

Her brows creased. "What's Wednesday?"

"It's the day the new recommendation tags get put up in the library. Which means I get some awesome new reads, and I also get to see you."

In the beat of silence that followed, her pulse quickened, and when he looked at her, it was to see her lips parted and her eyes on him, brow slightly furrowed, like he was a puzzle she was trying to work out.

"You make it really hard not to like you, you know," she said quietly.

"Why would you want to *not* like me? I'm awesome."

He'd been aiming for humor, but her answer was anything but.

"Because I don't want to be burned again, and you'd be able to do that without even trying."

His hand itched to touch her thigh. Graze her skin. Give her some kind of physical reassurance that he wasn't that guy.

"Are you dating your neighbor?" she asked.

"No." One word, quick and easy. "Kasey's been my neighbor since I moved to Cradle Mountain. Until recently, she was married. Since the divorce, she's struggled being in her house alone. We've also grabbed breakfast once or twice. It's nothing romantic."

"Try telling *her* that."

His lips quirked. She'd muttered the words so quietly under her breath, he was sure she hadn't meant for him to hear them. "I don't feel anything beyond friendship for Kasey. I've had my eyes on someone else for a while now."

Her head whipped toward him, eyes widening.

Yeah, beautiful. That's you.

She opened her mouth to reply, but her phone vibrated in her lap before she could say anything. He put his gaze back on the road, but he felt the shift in her energy the second she read the text. A thick tension coated the air. Then came the quickening of her heart, but he was almost certain it wasn't in a good way this time.

She'd done that before, at the library. "Everything okay?"

She quickly locked her phone and turned it over...because she couldn't bear to look at it? "Of course. Next question?"

ANOTHER MESSAGE. She'd received another damn message.

I'll be watching you, whore.

A shudder coursed down her spine. Were these texts really for her? Was this person really watching her?

"Hey, you sure you're okay? You've gone pale."

Her gaze went back to Callum. They were almost at the hotel, and she was trying to pretend she was okay after receiving the message. Looked like her acting skills were as bad as her don't-let-this-texter-bother-you skills.

The idea of telling Callum *had* crossed her mind...fleetingly. He was a security expert, after all. But for one, it wasn't his problem. The man was already doing her a ridiculously huge favor while asking for nothing in return. And secondly, they were just texts that hadn't even mentioned her name. The chance some weirdo was actually watching her was minimal.

"I'm just dreading the rehearsal dinner tonight." Which wasn't a lie. "And the wedding tomorrow." Big, mammoth, get-me-the-hell-out-of-Twin-Falls dread.

When she felt his gaze on her, she turned. He had that same I-don't-believe-you look on his face. "I read that you can tell when people are lying."

"Afraid so."

Great. One giant, muscular lie detector. "How?"

"Little things give people away. Just now, it was your heart rate. It does this little skip and changes rhythm when you tell me something that isn't true. Your breath also hitches. And if I was looking at you, I may also see your pupils dilate."

Oh, man. "That's not fair."

"If we're both honest with each other, it doesn't affect anything."

"Are you always honest with me?"

"Always." His answer was immediate, and it came out so firmly that she couldn't *not* believe him.

She looked ahead to see they were a street away from the hotel. "Take a right here."

There it was. The hotel where her sister was marrying the man Fiona had always thought *she'd* marry.

"How's it feel to be back?" Callum asked.

Like a bucket of ice water over her head. "My sister used to go out of her way to make sure my life was miserable. Any time she was with her friends and saw me around town, she'd make it a point to harass me. If we were out with our parents, she'd start arguments over nothing. I always tried to keep the peace for my parents' benefit, but she'd always get to me, and I'd argue back."

"Good."

She frowned. "What?"

"You *should* argue. Bullies should be held accountable for what they do and say."

Bully. That was the perfect word for Amanda. "I tried to stay here to be close to my parents, but when they got engaged..."

She'd had to get out. The need had been like a living, breathing thing inside her.

He pulled into a parking space in the hotel lot. "One day, your sister will realize what she lost by not treating you better."

She snorted. "I doubt it."

"I don't."

She gave him a look. "Stop being so nice to me."

"Never." He winked at her before getting out of the car.

She wasn't yet willing to climb out. To touch her feet to the ground of her hometown. Because that would mean she was really back for her sister's wedding, and she'd actually have to accept it, wouldn't she?

Another beat ticked by. Slowly, she moved her fingers to the handle, but before she could touch it, the door was whipped open.

Callum raised a brow. "Come on. You can't hide in there forever."

"Why not?"

"Because then I'd go in and enjoy both my meal *and* yours."

Ha. He was welcome to her food.

She climbed out of the car, grumbling as she went. "You'd still go to the rehearsal dinner without me?"

"Of course. And the wedding. Free food is free food."

Yeah, because Mr. McMansion House needed free food. "You wouldn't know anyone."

"I'd just explain that I'm your boyfriend, and you'd come down with a bad cold. Once I dazzle them with my wit, they'd welcome me with open arms."

The sad part was, he was probably right.

She walked around to where he'd pulled her bag out of the back and grabbed the handle, rolling it forward. "Fine. But only because I don't want anyone touching my salmon."

At least, she'd put salmon on her RSVP. Her sister would probably switch her choice to spite her. She'd then have to switch it back when Amanda went to the bathroom and blame it on Callum.

They crossed the lot and stepped into the reception area of the hotel. Immediately, her feet stopped.

Because there, in front of her, stood not only her parents but Freddie. And he looked exactly the same. His jawline was still chiseled, his brown hair immaculately slicked back, and his Ralph Lauren polo shirt fit perfectly across his thick chest.

Her mother rushed forward. Both her and her father were in their late fifties, with graying hair. She tugged Fiona into her chest. "Baby, you're here!"

"I'm here, Mom."

The second her mother released her, she cupped her cheek. "It's so nice to see you."

Next, her father stepped forward, and she leaned into his embrace. Her father's hugs had always meant safety for her. Warm. Cozy. And that scent...mint and whiskey. She breathed it in. It was the smell of home.

"We've missed you, darling," he said quietly.

She closed her eyes, hugging him tighter. "I missed you too, Dad."

Her parents almost made her forget about the third familiar face standing behind them...almost. They parted, and Freddie stepped forward.

"Hey, Fiona." He leaned in to kiss her cheek, his hand on her elbow, but she moved her head so he kissed air. She *did not* need to feel his lips on her flesh. In fact, just having his hand on her elbow had her fingers twitching to nail the cheating bastard in the gut.

His smile was tight when he lifted his head. But she didn't have time to think about that—because a thick, warm arm slipped around her waist and tugged her against an equally warm body. Freddie's hand dropped. Good.

"Hi, everyone. I'm Callum Thomas. The boyfriend." He said it with all the ease in the world, like a lie hadn't just rolled off his tongue.

Her parents, of course, gushed over him, her mother giving him a kiss on the cheek and her father shaking his hand. Freddie, on the other hand, only managed a bumbled, "Hey."

"Well, we should be getting to our room," Fiona finally said, beyond ready to get the heck away from Freddie and his hard gaze.

But even as they walked away, she felt him staring after her.

CHAPTER 9

Fiona tugged at the hem of her gold dress, staring at her reflection in the mirror of the small bathroom. The garment felt tight and scratchy and uncomfortable. Which was ridiculous because it was the softest dang silk she'd worn in her life. The front fell low between her breasts, while the back was also low cut, and the material hugged her hips.

She looked good. Sexy. Fresh. She ruffled her hair, which fell to her shoulders in loose waves. So why did she feel nervous as hell about stepping out of this bathroom?

Was it because since arriving, she'd felt unbalanced? She hadn't even cared about the one-bed situation when they'd stepped into the room, even though she'd done nothing *but* stress about it since asking Callum to do this with her.

Seeing Freddie had made her feel more than she'd thought it would. Not good feelings, God no. All bad. The way he'd hurt her. Stomped on their relationship like it was nothing. And now, she'd have to go downstairs and see him with her sister, surrounded by her family. The family may not have known that the man cheated on her, but they knew how long she and Freddie had dated. Would they look at her with pity? That I-feel-sorry-for-you expression people wore when they knew you were in the middle of a personal hell?

She just had to accept it. This was going to be god-awful, and there was nothing she could do about it.

Another tug on her dress. All right. Hiding time was over. With a resigned sigh, she turned and pushed into the room.

Two steps, and her feet stopped.

Holy Jesus… Callum stood by the window, buttons of his shirt undone, six-pack on full display. His chest had looked good earlier today, bare and dripping with sweat, but now, beneath an unbuttoned shirt, he looked distinguished and handsome…yeah, *really* handsome.

The chest—wait, no, the *man*—crossed the room, and her gaze met his. Her breath turned sharp as it sucked into her lungs… because his eyes were darker than usual. And so heated, she wondered how she didn't turn into a puddle on the floor.

He touched her arms, and the burn scorched her skin. Then he lowered his head and his breath brushed her ear. "You look beautiful, Fi."

Her brain short-circuited. Beautiful? This god of a man was calling *her* beautiful?

"Thank you." The two words tumbled from her mouth.

Callum straightened. He started to button his shirt, and her gaze caught on those muscular hands. The thick, strong fingers.

Up, Fiona. Look up.

Humor danced in his eyes. "Ready to go?"

Slowly, the bronzed skin disappeared, but that did nothing to take away from everything else. The man was right, he *did* look good in a suit, jacket or no jacket. The shirt was form-fitting, and she could see muscles upon muscles cutting through the material.

Far quicker than appropriate, she turned and grabbed her heels, then sat to put them on. She'd just lifted her second shoe when Callum kneeled in front of her and took it from her fingers. He slipped it over her foot, and after he fastened the strap, his fingers ran up her calves.

Her belly dipped at the contact. At the way his hands skirted right up the outside of her thighs to her hips. "Ready?"

She nodded because she was completely out of words. If he was trying to distract her from her nerves about tonight, he was doing a great job.

It worked right up until they reached the bottom floor of the hotel. The wedding reception would be in the hotel function room, but the rehearsal dinner was in the restaurant.

The second they stepped out of the elevator, he slipped an arm around her waist and lowered his head. "Relax."

Was she as stiff as she felt?

They stepped into the restaurant, and Amanda and Freddie stood right there by the door. Her sister wore a figure-hugging white dress that hit her knees. Her hair was up in a neat bun and her makeup immaculate. She was beautiful, but then, she'd always been stunning.

Amanda gave her a tight smile. "Hi, Fiona. It's good to see you."

Was it? Or had her sister been hoping she wouldn't make it?

Fiona stepped forward and kissed her sister on the cheek. Just like every other time they'd touched in their lives, the embrace was awkward and stilted. She pulled back and gave a fake smile to Freddie. There was no way she was going to touch him again, and certainly not here, in front of a room filled with family.

She turned to Callum. "This is my...boyfriend. Callum."

God, she needed to stop stumbling over the word boyfriend. *Just get the lie out, woman!*

Callum was a lot less awkward. For the second time that day, he shook Freddie's hand, then leaned in and kissed Amanda's cheek. It was a polite kiss, but there was still a zap of jealousy that shot through Fiona.

"Congratulations to you both," he said warmly.

If possible, Amanda's smile grew tighter. "Thank you."

Fortunately, her cousin Stacey chose that moment to pop up and grab Fiona's arm before pulling her into a hug. Hers was a complete embrace. It was warmth and happiness and joy.

She dug her head into her cousin's shoulder in relief. "Hey, Stace."

Stacey pulled back seconds later, gripping Fiona's upper arms. "I've missed you!"

"You have no idea." She turned to look beside her. "This is Callum. Callum, this is my cousin Stacey."

Stacey's eyes grew so large, they resembled saucers. "Holy crack on a cracker. You are *beautiful*!"

Fiona choked on a laugh. Stacey had never been one to hold back.

Callum chuckled. "Thank you. It's nice to meet you, Stacey."

Fiona's calm lasted about two-point-five seconds, until she found her seat beside her nosy aunt and uncle. Damn Amanda— the woman had done this to torture her. At least Stacey sat opposite.

After introductions between her family and Callum, came the questions. Where was she living? How long had she and Callum been dating? How often did she come back and visit her parents?

The second wine was set in front of her, she downed half the glass in one gulp. Thank God for alcohol. It might help her get through tonight alive. She was on her second gulp when her aunt's next words came.

"We were all wondering how you'd handle this wedding after Freddie left you for Amanda."

The alcohol caught in her throat like acid, and she choked. Once she was sure she wasn't about to drown herself in wine, she gave the woman her sweetest fake smile. "Actually, I left *him*."

There'd been no other option after finding the asshole in bed with her sister. Oh, he'd said he was sorry. Said the fling with Amanda hadn't been going on for long and he'd stop sleeping with her...the lying sack of shit. Did he think she had no self-respect?

Aunt Trish's brows rose. "Really? Amanda told us he left you."

Of course she did. She was tempted to tell the woman that the two hadn't actually *waited* for Freddie and her to breakup, but Callum's hand moved to her thigh, and his thumb grazed her skin.

A calm she had no right feeling choked the words back. "Amanda gets confused with details sometimes. Probably all the Valium she takes for her episodes. I left Freddie. And I'm so glad I did. Seeing him and Amanda together, it's like their souls were made for each other."

Her aunt's jaw dropped, words seeming to be lost on her. Well, there was a first for everything.

She sipped her wine again, this time the liquid slipping into her belly with ease. When she looked up, it was to see Stacey biting her lip to stop her laugh. Her cousin leaned in and pulled her aunt's attention away.

Thank you, Stacey.

Her gaze moved down the table—until it clashed with Freddie's. What the...? The man was very obviously staring at her. Which was not a smart thing to do at his own damn rehearsal dinner. Then his gaze shifted to Callum, and just like they had earlier that day, his eyes narrowed.

Callum leaned down, pulling her attention away from Freddie. "I meant what I said in our room. You look beautiful tonight."

There was another swipe of her thigh. She looked up, a real smile curving her lips. And God, did she love the way he said "our room." It felt...intimate. Which it was. She was going to share a room with this man tonight!

She swallowed. "Thank you."

Noise hummed around them as the night proceeded. The chatter of family plus Freddie and Amanda's friends. The dishes were brought out, and for the most part, the evening went smoother than she thought it would. It certainly wasn't the mess she'd been expecting. But then, that had everything to do with Stacey saving her from her aunt and uncle every time their questions got too personal. Which was probably a good thing, because her tongue got a bit looser with each sip of wine.

And then there was the man beside her...touching her leg... making her laugh and smile.

They were just finishing their meals when Callum pulled his ringing phone from his pocket. She saw Liam's name pop up. Callum's finger hovered over cancel, but she touched his arm.

"Take it."

His brows flickered. "Are you sure?"

"Of course. It could be important."

He watched her for one more beat before squeezing her arm and rising. Even that small touch sent her blood roaring through her veins.

She looked up to see Stacey grinning at her. A massive I-see-what's-happening grin, only there was nothing happening.

Yeah, keep telling yourself that, Fiona.

She set her napkin on the table. "I'm just going to the bathroom." Maybe the short walk and separation from Callum would help clear her foggy head.

She rose and moved to the back of the restaurant. Soon it would be speeches, then dessert. She was kind of dreading speeches. Would they talk about how they came to be together? And if they did, would they lie about the timeline?

With a long exhale, she pushed into the bathroom. When she came out of the stall, she was looking at her reflection while she washed her hands, noticing that her eyes were bright and her cheeks flushed. Because of Callum? Or because she'd already had two and a half glasses of wine? Maybe both.

She exited the bathroom—and almost immediately collided with a large chest.

"Freddie. Sorry, I didn't see you." She tried to step around him, but his fingers curled around her arm, stopping her.

His voice lowered. "Hey, I just wanted to check on you. Speak to you alone."

Uh, that was the last thing *she* wanted. Like dead last on the list. "Why?"

"Well, this weekend can't be easy for you, based on our...history."

She could have laughed...or maybe she did a bit, because his eyes narrowed. "We've been over for almost a year, Freddie. I'm happy for you both and looking forward to seeing my sister married."

Well, *that* lie just rolled off her tongue. Thank you, wine. She almost wanted to give herself a little pat on the back.

"What's with your *date?*"

Her brows rose at the way he sneered the word date. "What do you mean, what's with him? He's my boyfriend."

Freddie's light brown eyes sharpened, and he shook his head. "You wouldn't date someone like him."

"Excuse me? Don't assume to know who I would and wouldn't date."

"You and I were together for six years. I *know* you."

She scoffed. "You don't know me. I'm not the woman you cheated on anymore. And even if I was, you barely knew who *she* was. You were always out. Always away for *work*." She barely held back air quotes on that word. Trips he'd labeled as work but probably weren't. "I changed before we ever broke up. And I should have ended things before you showed me the scumbag you really are."

She wrenched her arm from his hold and stepped around him, but he cut her off again. "Freddie—"

"You're in her way."

Callum's low, deep words sounded as he came into view. He stood behind Freddie, towering over him, with fisted hands and a granite jaw.

CHAPTER 10

*C*allum's muscles vibrated with the need to hit the asshole who was cornering his woman. Yeah, he was referring to Fiona as *his woman*, because that's exactly what she was this weekend.

"We're having a conversation," Freddie said through gritted teeth, obviously too damn stupid to sense the danger.

Callum's muscles flexed as he moved closer to Fiona. "She tried to walk away from your *conversation* more than once. That makes it less of a conversation and more harassment. Don't you think?"

Freddie's eyes narrowed. He didn't like what Callum was saying, but then, bullies rarely liked it when they were called out on their shit.

"Move." One word from Callum. But a word so low, and so strongly emphasized, there was no missing the threat beneath it. They might be at the guy's rehearsal dinner, but that didn't change the fact that Callum would knock him out with a single hit if he continued to detain her.

Freddie's chest moved rapidly with his breaths, his cheeks tinging pink.

Fiona's voice was hard when she spoke. "You need to go, Freddie."

He huffed, then finally turned and headed back to the dining room. Callum moved in front of her and touched her arm, right where the asshole's hand had gripped her. He wanted to kick his own ass for not getting here faster. He'd seen the two of them from down the hall. He should have fucking run.

He swiped his thumb over the reddening skin. "Are you okay?"

"Yeah, that was just...unexpected."

Maybe for her. But he'd seen the way Freddie had been looking at her all night. The man was still into her—and it was clear for all to see. Even his damn fiancée must have noticed.

He gave her a gentle look. "It's okay to not be okay, you know."

He wanted to know the history between her, the asshole, and her sister, and he wanted to know it tonight. She'd gotten hurt in the tangle, and it looked like Freddie was trying to *keep* her tangled.

She swallowed. "It's not really the right time to not be okay, is it?"

"I don't care where we are or whose function it is, when you're not okay, I'll take care of you."

There was an audible catch in her breath. "There you go again, being too nice to me."

"Not possible."

Her bottom lip snuck between her teeth, and he suddenly got an overwhelming urge to tug it out.

But before he could, she nodded toward the restaurant. "We should get back."

They should, but telling his feet to move and take him back to other people was harder than it should have been. He forced his hand to slide down her arm and slip through her fingers. Her hand fit in his so well.

Once they were seated again, he didn't need to look up to know Freddie was staring at Fiona. It made him angry as hell.

When Fiona met the other man's gaze, she rolled her eyes before lifting the new wine that had been set in front of her and downing half the glass.

Yeah, Callum was definitely finding out what the hell had happened between them.

Half an hour passed before her father stood and lifted his glass, clinking the side with the flat edge of a blunt knife. "Good evening, everyone. For those who don't know, I'm Mark, Amanda's father, and this is my wife, Edna, Amanda's mother. First, we would just like to say thank you to everyone for joining us this weekend. Tomorrow will be a big day, while we watch her get married." He looked down at Amanda. "Amanda is our first, and she was a bit of a miracle baby. We tried for a long time before she came."

Tears welled in Amanda's eyes.

Mark's gaze shifted to Fiona. "Fiona was our second miracle. So unexpected, but so needed in our family." This time, Amanda's eyes tightened, the smile slipping from her lips. "Together, they were our gifts from God. Two perfect children."

Callum kept watching Amanda throughout the speech. Why did the woman dislike her sister to the extent that their father couldn't even talk about her without clear disdain shading her face?

Mark didn't touch on how Amanda and Freddie had come to be together. In fact, he only spoke about the two as a couple very briefly, mentioning it was a whirlwind romance. There was no talk about one making the other a better person or being meant to be or soul mates.

When he felt Fiona's leg move up and down beside him, he again reached under the table and wrapped his fingers around her thigh. Immediately, her movement stilled.

Touching this woman was starting to feel like second nature. It was something he could get used to.

Once the speeches were done, dessert was brought out, and the rest of the evening went quickly. The aunt kept asking invasive questions, but Fiona held her own.

It wasn't until people started to leave that Fiona rose and wobbled on her feet. He stood and wrapped an arm around her waist. "Hey, are you all right?"

"Yeah, I think I had too much to drink," she whispered, breath smelling of wine.

Callum chuckled. She'd definitely had a few refills. He shifted some hair behind her ear. "Let's get you back to the room so you can sleep."

He was able to bypass most goodbyes on the way out. When they reached the elevator, she leaned heavily into his side.

"Am I a terrible person for not wanting them to live happily ever after?"

The corners of his mouth twitched. "No."

"Good. Because I might even smile if they end in divorce." Her voice lowered, like she was telling him a secret. "I might even hope for it."

"It's hard to root for people who hurt you."

She snorted. It was the least ladylike sound he'd ever heard, and he fucking loved it. "And easy to root for the bride to fall on her face while she walks down the aisle." She quickly covered her mouth like she was surprised she'd said the words out loud.

The elevator stopped and the doors opened. "All right. Come on, you, before you see her and give her a shove yourself."

"Payback for sleeping with my boyfriend."

His muscles tensed, and he almost stopped walking. He waited for the elevator to start moving before he said, "He cheated on you with your *sister*?" What kind of a scumbag did that?

Her face scrunched in disgust. He had his answer before she

responded. "Yeah. I got home early from work one day and found them in bed together."

Asshole.

"I liked that bed too," she continued. "We'd only bought it a month earlier. It was the most comfortable bed I'd ever slept in. Big and squishy. I let him keep it when I moved out."

On their floor, he walked her down the hall, then swiped his card on the door and led her inside. "Did you buy another when you moved?"

"Yes. I wanted different *everything*." She dropped to the bed and closed her eyes. "Amanda didn't even look shocked when I found them. She didn't look guilty or remorseful. In fact, I'm pretty sure I saw just a hint of a smile on her lips. I wouldn't be surprised if she'd set the entire thing up. Asked my boss to let me go early or something."

He sat on the bed and lifted her feet onto his lap before undoing the strap on a heel. "I can see why you moved away from them."

Another snort. "Maybe I should have moved further. There's this town called Svalbard. It's on an Arctic island and close to the North Pole. But I didn't think I could take the months of no sun in the winter."

He switched to her other foot. "I'm sure there are also dangerous polar bears near the North Pole, so Cradle Mountain was a safer choice."

Her smile widened. "You and your team are way more dangerous than polar bears."

"True. But we only pose a threat to bad guys." When her shoes were off, he ran a hand over her calf, loving the smooth skin. "What did Freddie do when you found him with your sister?"

"He begged me to stay, but I just turned and left. I refused to take his calls or texts. I waited until a day I knew he'd be at work, and Stacey helped me get my stuff. The call just a few months later to say they were getting married was the final kick in the gut."

Jesus. "You're better off without people like that in your life. Sister or not."

She pushed on her hands to sit up. It was like watching a baby panda try to sit, slow and uncoordinated. He laughed and tugged her arm to help her up, then she shuffled to sit beside him. "Have you ever cheated on anyone?"

"Never. And I never would." He had too much integrity for that.

She held his gaze for a beat longer before nodding. "I believe you. But Fiona who hasn't drunk her weight in wine might not."

"Well, I'll just need to fill you with wine every time I see you then."

She didn't even smile at his joke. "You're too nice to me. I've been horrible to you about your book returns. And I'll probably push you away again, even though I want to run my hands over your washboard abs while they're oiled and hot."

He pushed that image out of his head, because no fucking way could he get hard right now. It wasn't the right damn time. "Why will you push me away?"

She laid her head on his shoulder and sighed. "Because I'm waiting for Mr. Short, Chubby and Bald."

Callum laughed again, a full belly laugh. Whatever he'd been expecting her to say, it wasn't that. "So I have to be short, chubby and bald for you to trust me?"

"Mm-hmm. Maybe wear one of those tight sleeveless shirts and show some round gut. Because that guy will have less chance of cheating, right? Well, it makes sense in my brain. I haven't looked at statistics or anything, and hell, I might be way off in that assumption, but it just feels safer in my head."

He cupped the back of her head and pressed a kiss to her forehead. "I told you, Fi, I would never cheat, especially not on you."

"That's what Freddie said." She dropped back down to the bed, and he felt the loss immediately.

Slowly, he rose and helped her adjust, then pulled the sheet over her body. She still wore her dress, but she looked on the verge of passing out, and no way was he tackling her clothes when she was too drunk to consent.

"You're sleeping with me, right?" she mumbled, eyes never opening.

His heart gave another massive thud in his chest. "I can if you want." The only other choice was the floor, but he'd sleep there for her.

"I want." She yawned. "And can you turn my phone off? I don't want to get any more of those messages..."

"What messages?"

"The awful ones that call me a bitch and a whore."

Something dangerous ticked in his jaw. "Is that what had you turning pale in the car?"

"Mm." That was all she gave him before she fell into a deep sleep.

FIONA'S EYES popped open at the roll of her belly. She sucked in a deep breath before letting it out slowly. The room was dark, and so quiet that her and Callum's breaths were all she could hear.

She closed her eyes and touched a hand to her stomach. *Please don't be sick. Please don't be sick.*

Man, why had she drunk all that wine last night? She knew she didn't tolerate alcohol well.

On her third inhale, her stomach rolled again, and bile crawled up her throat. She was moving before she could stop herself, shooting out of bed and running to the bathroom. A deep, raspy voice sounded behind her, but she ignored it, throwing the bathroom door closed and dropping to her knees in front of the toilet just in time for the contents of her stomach to empty.

She wanted to groan when she heard the footsteps from the bedroom. There was no part of her that wanted Callum to see her like this.

Do not come in. Do not come in. Do not—

The door opened right as her belly rolled and she was sick again. A second later, fingers threaded through her hair, pulling it back from her face. Then a warm hand rubbed large circles on her back. Those words in her head died at his touch. It was heaven. How did a simple back rub while dying make you feel so much better?

They remained like that for a few more minutes, with her head in the toilet and Callum behind her, comforting. He didn't say anything, neither of them did. They remained quiet while her belly released everything inside it.

When she was finally feeling almost normal, she flushed the toilet, then leaned back against the wall, letting the cool of the tiles seep into her body. That's when she realized she was still wearing the dress she'd had on at the rehearsal dinner. Good God, she was a mess.

Callum rose and grabbed a small towel. He ran it under some water before lowering and pressing it to her forehead. The coolness had her eyes shuttering. "Thank you."

"How are you feeling?"

She peeled her eyes open to find him on his haunches in front of her, concern coloring his eyes a shade darker. Her attention lowered to his bare chest. He only wore pajama pants, which hung dangerously low on his hips, showing those familiar jam-packed abs.

Even sick, she appreciated this man's work-of-art body. "Better. Teaches me to be a more responsible drinker."

Callum reached forward and shifted some hair from her face. Every time he did that, she wanted to melt into him. "Maybe I should have filled your glass with water before the waiter got there."

Her lips curved into a smile. "I might have bitten off your hand. That wine was all that kept my butt in the seat."

"Why are you here?"

Her brows flickered, surprised by his question. "It's my sister's wedding."

"I know. But they hurt you. Badly. No one would have begrudged you for not coming. I'm sure a lot of people expected it."

"Exactly why I'm here." His brows flickered in confusion, so she continued. "I need them both to know that I'm okay. That they haven't hurt me beyond repair. Because *I am* okay. A little battered and bruised but living a new life that I'm happy with."

Understanding lightened his eyes.

"I don't know why," she continued softly, "but that was really important to me."

"I get it."

"Plus, no one knows about the circumstances of my separation with Freddie. Even though my parents would have understood me not coming because he's my ex, me not being here still would have made them worry."

"You don't want them to know about what Amanda and Freddie did?"

She shook her head. "It would kill them. It's not their fault she's the way she is, but they would shoulder the blame. All they've ever wanted is for their kids to be happy."

Something flashed in his eyes. Admiration, maybe? "*Are* you happy?"

Another surprised eyebrow lift. No one had ever asked her that before. Was she? "Most days."

A slow nod from him. "Most days is good."

"Are you?"

One side of his mouth lifted. "Right now? Most definitely."

She swallowed, wanting to drown in those eyes. Drown in his words and gentleness and the way his voice made it seem like he really cared.

But she'd officially embarrassed herself enough for one night. She blew out a breath and went to push to her feet. Callum wrapped his fingers around her upper arms and helped her up.

"I might just brush my teeth and put my pajamas on before heading back to bed."

"You got it." He gave her one of his wide smiles before moving away. "Call out if you need anything."

She nodded and turned to the sink. She had to stop herself from dropping her head into her hands. The man had watched her drink too much, then throw her guts up. He should be running. Jumping in his car and getting away from the mess that was her life as quickly as possible.

Once her teeth and mouth were clean, she went into the bedroom and rummaged in her bag for pajamas. Jeans, shirts, underwear...but no pajamas. She hadn't brought them.

Jesus Christ.

"Everything okay?" Callum asked, making her wonder if she'd said those words out loud.

She scrubbed a hand over her face and straightened. "I forgot my pajamas."

He didn't even blink, just grabbed a T-shirt from his case and passed it to her. "Use this."

Tentatively, she took it, already able to smell his masculine, woodsy scent on the garment. She wanted to say no, but the dress was uncomfortable as hell, and she didn't have any shirts big enough to cover her. "Thank you."

Back in the bathroom, she peeled off her dress. The shirt was huge, reaching her knees. And yep, she smelled Callum everywhere. It was suffocating, in the most torturous, erotic kind of way. She wanted to bathe in it.

She stepped out and moved to the bed. Callum was already

there, lying on his side. His eyes heated as they locked with hers. He almost looked at her with...possession?

Quickly, she flicked off the light and slid under the covers.

"Your stomach okay?" he asked quietly.

"Yes." Her ego on the other hand...not so much.

She was tempted to turn her back to him but didn't. Something stopped her. Instead, she did the opposite. On her side, she scooched closer and touched her hand to his chest. She could feel the thumps of his heart beneath her palm. They were steady and even, almost aligning with her own.

"Thank you for being here with me. I'm not sure exactly why you are, but I'm grateful."

His fingers curved around her hip. "There's nowhere I'd rather be."

Her breath stopped. She told herself to move her hand, to shift away from his touch. But the lull of his pulse beneath her skin was soothing, and the heat of his hand to her hip an extra layer of warmth. So she remained where she was, letting everything that was Callum soothe her back to sleep.

CHAPTER 11

Fiona wasn't sure what she'd expected to feel during the ceremony. Dread? Unease? Definitely a level of discomfort. And sure, there was a bit of that. Tiny slivers here and there. But as she watched her sister marry Freddie, there was something else…something lighter.

Relief. That it wasn't her standing up there.

God, she almost felt happy for her sister. Amanda's dress was beautiful. Her hair, her makeup, everything was perfect. And Freddie…well, Freddie looked like Freddie. He wasn't smiling or tearing up, but he stood straight and looked at her sister head-on.

That could so easily have been her. That had been the plan. After you date someone for so long, a wedding was almost just assumed to take place sooner or later. And she would have said yes.

The thought made a shudder roll down her spine.

Callum's fingers tightened around her thigh. They'd been there the entire ceremony. And she welcomed his touch. Thoughts of last night had been running through her head all morning. The way he'd rubbed her back. Pulled her hair off her face and said all the right words. And this morning, she'd woken to aspirin and water waiting for her.

It wasn't just in her head. He *was* perfect.

Almost without thinking, she placed her hand on top of his. He didn't hesitate, turning his hand over and slipping his fingers through hers.

Her heart gave a little thump. Okay, no, it was a big, this-man's-an-enigma kind of thump. She had no idea where things with Callum were headed, but she almost wondered if maybe everything that had happened was just a culmination of things that *had* to happen to lead her here, to him.

When the ceremony came to an end, Fiona was almost smiling. She was even able to hug and kiss Amanda and Freddie when she congratulated them.

The afternoon involved family photos and returning to the hotel for drinks, then the reception. Callum was by her side every step of the way. Holding her hand. Placing an arm around her waist like it was the most natural action in the world.

It wasn't until she was talking with her cousin in the ballroom that she had a moment away from him. The room was huge and beautifully decorated. Candles and flowers centered the round tables. A band played on the stage and a bar was at the back of the room. Not that Fiona would be drinking much tonight. She'd done more than enough of that last night.

Stacey bumped her shoulder. "Callum's so cute. And *so* into you."

Fiona sipped her juice. "He's just playing the part."

But even as the words left her mouth, they felt wrong. Because things with him *did* feel real. Every time he touched her, his hand felt familiar, like it had run over her flesh a hundred times before. His soft words in her ear sounded like home, and his heat called to hers. Was that even a thing?

"Mm-hmm." Stacey sipped her wine. "Maybe if you say it out loud enough times, you'll actually believe it."

Doubtful.

She observed her sister standing with a circle of friends across the room, her mouth moving a million miles an hour. That was Amanda, though. Always the one to be talking. She'd been the "it" girl in school.

"Careful, you almost look happy for her."

Fiona dragged her gaze from her sister to Stacey. "I am. I'm bigger-personing the shit out of this, actually."

Stacey's brows shot to her hairline. "Really? The woman's been nothing but a bitch to you your entire life. Then everything with Freddie? And you're happy for her?"

"I want her to be happy, but...apart from me. What they both did was awful, but today I'm almost seeing it as a blessing in disguise." At Stacey's confused look, Fiona lifted a shoulder. "I was too comfortable with Freddie. If he'd asked me, I would have said yes and married him. Maybe even had kids if he'd been able to keep it in his pants for that long. I feel lucky that I learned what he's capable of before any of that could happen."

"Well, you are one strong woman, because I would have pounded into them both, then sent their wedding invite to the trash."

Fiona laughed. "Oh, I came close to doing all that."

She sipped her juice again before spotting Callum. He was talking to some of her uncles like he'd known them for years. When his gaze caught hers, one side of his mouth lifted. "Do you think Callum would cheat?" The words slipped into the air before she could stop them.

"No." Stacey said it so firmly, she wanted to believe her. "You can just tell. He's a good man. And a walking heartthrob."

"Freddie was a heartthrob."

"Argh, do not put Callum into the same category as that guy. They're two different species. Yes, they're both tall, dark and handsome. But even though I've only just met Callum, I know he's Freddie's opposite."

"Sometimes it takes six years for the cheating side to come out." At Stacey's frown, Fiona shook her head. "Sorry, that's the damaged, I-saw-my-sister-in-bed-with-my-boyfriend side talking."

Stacey's features softened. "Maybe Callum's your angel and has come into your life to heal you."

"He is *beautiful* enough to be an angel."

Stacey opened her mouth to respond, but whatever she said, Fiona was too distracted to hear, because someone across the room caught her attention. She only caught a fleeting glimpse of their face before they turned and walked away.

Fiona straightened, her breath catching in her throat. The woman almost looked like...

No. *No.* That wasn't possible.

But even though the impossibility of the situation was at the forefront of her mind, her feet still moved across the room. She called to Stacey, letting her cousin know she'd be back, before weaving her way through the crowd, watching the back of that dress. Every so often, a family member or old family friend would touch her arm or say something, but her entire focus remained on the woman in front of her.

She disappeared out of the function room, and Fiona followed her out, stopping at an open hall. Doors were on one side, and one was open. She stepped closer to that door to find an empty terrace. Instantly, her skin pebbled at the cool breeze.

She took two steps forward when the door behind her blew shut. A gasp slipped from her lips and she turned, almost expecting to see the woman there, but there was no one. The terrace was deserted.

Another draft of cold air hit her face like a blast of common sense. It was official. She was crazy. Because if she wasn't, she wouldn't have followed a woman she couldn't have seen out here. It just wasn't possible.

Exhaling a long breath, she walked back to the door and

pulled...but it didn't move. She pulled again. What the hell? Had the door jammed when it swung closed? She tugged three more times before realizing it was stuck. *She* was stuck. Stuck outside in the freezing cold, with no phone to call for help.

～

CALLUM'S GAZE returned to Stacey to find Fiona wasn't with her anymore. He waited for her uncle Burt to finish what he was saying about politics before quietly excusing himself. He only made it a few steps before Amanda stepped in front of him.

"Hi." She tilted her head. "I haven't had a chance to talk to you before now."

Callum tried for a smile. It was tougher than it should have been because of what he knew about her treatment of Fiona. "That's okay, it's your wedding day. You've got a roomful of people to talk to."

"Still, it's important to make sure my little sister's new boyfriend is treating her right."

He had to bite back a less-than-polite response. This woman and her husband hadn't treated Fiona anything close to right. Why would she suddenly care if anyone else did? "Your sister's a very special woman, and I always treat her as such."

Amanda's lips thinned. *Ah, there you are.*

"People do tend to love her." She pursed her mouth. "Have you been dating long? She never mentioned your name until a week ago, and I couldn't seem to get a straight response from Fiona."

"Not long." When he didn't give any more than that, the woman's smile slipped.

"How'd you meet again?"

"I borrow books at the library where she works."

Her eyes lit up like she'd caught him in a lie. "You don't look like a reader."

"Looks can be deceiving. I read a different book every week."

"Fiona always had her head stuck in a book. I prefer reality." She reached out and ran a finger down his chest.

Callum's muscles tightened. What the hell was her game? He immediately stepped back, letting her hand drop. "Books are doors to new worlds. They don't mean a person isn't living in reality. And they connected me to Fiona, so that's a win-win right there."

Amanda's eyes narrowed. He wasn't sure if it was because he'd stepped away or because of his words. Either way, he didn't care.

Edna stepped up beside her daughter. Unlike Amanda, her smile was genuine. "Oh, darling, everything is going so well."

Amanda's lips curved, but the action looked forced. "Thank you." She looked up at Callum again. "I was just asking Callum about his relationship with Fiona. It seems fast, considering we know nothing about him and only learned his name a few weeks ago."

This woman was really trying to get a rise out of him. Maybe she was used to guys falling at her feet and was pissed Callum hadn't done that.

He nodded civilly. "Things have definitely moved quickly. Says a lot about the kind of woman Fiona is. She had me addicted the first meeting."

Wasn't even a bit of a lie.

Amanda's features once again blanked, while her mother's face softened. "Oh, that makes me so happy. I must be honest, I was a bit worried about today, but I'm so glad that both my babies are happy and taken care of."

Callum bit back a laugh at the look of displeasure on Amanda's face. Fiona hadn't been exaggerating.

He cleared his throat and turned to Edna. "Would you know where Fiona is?"

"I saw her talking to her father near the hallway before I made my way over here."

He gave both women an easy smile. "I'll go find her." His gaze stilled on Amanda. "Congratulations again."

"Thanks."

Well, he certainly knew now why the two women had a hard relationship...her sister liked to be the center of attention. Two seconds in her company and that had been clear.

He scanned the crowd and spotted her father. The man was standing with three people, none of whom were Fiona.

Maybe she went to the bathroom? He headed that way but paused when he heard pounding on an exterior door. Then he heard a voice...Fiona's voice.

With a frown, he pivoted, stopping by the door. He tried the handle. Though it wasn't locked, it seemed jammed.

"Can anyone hear me? Can someone open the door?"

Using strength a normal man didn't have, he yanked it open.

Fiona's eyes widened. "Oh my gosh, thank you, Callum! It's freezing out here!"

He cursed at the sight of her almost-blue lips. When he touched her bare arms, they were like ice. "How long have you been out there?"

She shook her head, arms wrapped around her waist as she stepped inside. "I don't know. I don't have my phone. Fifteen, maybe twenty minutes?"

Too damn long. He chafed her arms. "Why'd you go outside?"

"I thought I saw..." She stopped, then shook her head again. "I just stepped out there and the door flew shut."

"It must have flown shut hard."

When a shudder racked her spine, he growled. "Come on. We should go back to the room so you can get warm."

"No. I can't leave the reception. People will talk. I've already been gone long enough."

He cursed again. He wanted to get her into a hot shower, but he understood what she was saying.

"I'm okay," she said softly, as if reading his thoughts.

With a sigh, he tugged her against his side and wrapped an arm around her shoulders, still not fully understanding how the hell she'd gotten stuck outside.

CHAPTER 12

*W*hat the heck had she been thinking? Following some random woman outside and getting herself locked out in the cold.

Stupid.

An hour had passed since Callum had found her, and Fiona was only just starting to feel her fingers again. Of course, his arm around her shoulders wasn't terrible. And the way he intermittently rubbed her bare arm almost made the little ordeal worth it. She should probably tell him she was okay, maybe inch away, but who the hell ever did what they were supposed to do?

She sipped on another glass of juice. She'd been tempted to switch to wine to warm her insides but had decided not to. She did *not* need a repeat of the embarrassing bathroom incident from last night.

Stacey and a couple other cousins sat at the table with them, and Callum fit in like he'd known these people for years. He joked. Smiled. Told stories that had the entire group throwing their heads back and belly laughing. But was she surprised? Nope. She'd already surmised he was the ideal guy, so of course he had to fit in with people he'd only just met.

Her phone vibrated from the table.

Jenny: How's the wedding?

Grinning, Fiona lifted her phone and responded quickly.

Fiona: So much better than I thought it would be. I'd even say I'm almost having fun.

Ha. There was no almost about it. She'd laughed more at this table than she had in the last year.

Jenny: With your hottie date, I would expect nothing less. Make some memories and report back on Tuesday.

Oh, she'd be reporting back, all right. She was just putting her phone down when Amanda took a seat across the table. "What are we laughing at?"

The smiles slipped on everyone's faces. Every. Single. Person. They'd all been subjected to Amanda's cranking bitch too many times. No one as much as Fiona, of course, but still, one time was too many for most. She was less awful to the others and more a naturally self-centered person.

Stacey cleared her throat. "Callum was just telling us a story about his time as a Marine."

Amanda raised a perfectly manicured brow. "What type of Marine were you?"

"Special operations."

"Ooh, dangerous." She cocked her head. "Yet, Project Arma was still able to kidnap and detain you."

Fiona's muscles tensed. Not just because the topic of Project Arma wasn't appropriate to bring up at a wedding, but also because of the way her sister said it. Like she was insinuating he couldn't be *that* badass.

Fiona gave her sister a pointed look. "Amanda—"

"I mean, you were trained to be the best. Wouldn't *the best* be able to protect themselves?"

What the hell? She cast her gaze to Callum, sure she'd find him annoyed or frustrated. He didn't look either of those things. In fact, he didn't seem affected by her words at all. She was about to tell her sister where she could go when Callum got in first.

"I'd just gotten off a fourteen-hour flight after a mission. The men who took me were waiting inside my apartment. There were six of them and one of me. I wasn't armed or expecting an attack. No normal man would be able to withstand that kind of ambush."

Fiona's breath stalled in her chest at the scene he described. At the way his life must have changed after that. One moment, and everything was different. He was held for two years. Drugged. Trained. Altered.

He drew a small circle on her shoulder. "They wouldn't take me so easily today. If at all."

Her sister raised a brow. "Well, *you think* they wouldn't."

"I know."

Fiona cleared her throat. "Your wedding is beautiful, Amanda. Maybe you should do the rounds."

In other words—go.

Slowly, Amanda drew her focus to Fiona. "I should probably be thanking *you* for all of this, shouldn't I?"

Her muscles tensed, and Callum's hand tightened on her shoulder.

This time, it was Stacey who tried to intervene. "Amanda—"

"I *am* sorry about how you found out about us," Amanda cut in, like everyone wasn't staring at her open-mouthed.

Fiona's blood ran cold. Only Callum and Stacey knew the truth about how she'd found out. "Don't—"

"We didn't want you to find us in your bed like that."

There was a collective gasp from her cousins. Fiona's fingers curled into fists, and words tumbled from her lips before she could stop them. "You're not sorry, Amanda. Just like how I'm not sorry about you now being married to a cheating asshole." Fiona's eyes never left her sister's narrowed ones as she pushed to her feet. "If you'll excuse me, I could use a drink."

She moved through the crowd, blinking back tears. The tears were more frustration than anything else. She certainly was not embarrassed. She'd done nothing wrong. But Amanda's words brought it all back. Every emotion she'd experienced that day. The rejection. The hurt. The loss of the future she'd planned in her head.

And the fact her cousins now knew...that burned. Would they tell others? Would the news get back to her parents?

Oh God, please say no.

She stopped at the bar, curling her fingers around the wooden edge. Her chest heaved even as she felt she wasn't getting enough oxygen. Then heat covered her back, and a large hand touched her shoulder.

"Dance with me." Callum's deep, raspy voice whispered over her cheek.

"I don't know if I'm in the mood to dance." Understatement of the century.

"Please."

That one whispered word...it slid over her skin, making every inch of flesh pebble with awareness.

She swallowed. She wanted to say yes. Heck, she wanted this man to take her away from all of this.

It was only when his thumb grazed her skin that she got the words out. "Okay. One dance." Because she couldn't, for the life of her, figure out how to say no.

The hand moved down her arm, and his fingers slid into hers. Then he was pulling her to the dance floor. As she followed, she searched out her parents. They were laughing with her uncles and aunties. Clearly, news hadn't traveled to them...yet. Hopefully Stacey would convince everyone to keep quiet about it, at least for tonight.

Callum stopped in the middle of the dance floor. She expected him to put one hand on her waist, keeping a thread of distance between them. When he curved both arms around her and pulled her entire body flush with his, the air left her lungs.

His mouth neared her ear. "Relax."

"I can't when it comes to her. I don't know why she's like that." She blew out a long breath. "I didn't want people to know."

"Shut them out and don't think about them."

"What should I think about instead?"

His face brushed her hair, and a shudder raced down her spine. "How good I smell."

She laughed. "You do smell nice."

A crisp, fresh, outdoorsy smell. And all masculine.

"How right my arms feel around you," he added.

The smile slipped. His arms *did* feel right around her.

"What we're going to do when we get back to Cradle Mountain."

Her heart thumped, her gaze shooting up. "What we're going to do?"

"Yeah. Where I should take you for our first official date. How I should greet you when I go to the library."

She laughed again. "You say hi."

"With a kiss?"

Her breath caught. "We…we haven't kissed yet."

"That's something we should remedy, isn't it?"

Her lips parted. "You want to kiss me?"

One side of his mouth pulled up. "That's like asking a starving man if he wants food."

She shook her head. "You can't kiss me here."

"Why not?"

She wet her lips, and his gaze flicked down. "Because if we have a first kiss—"

"When."

"Okay. *When* we have a first kiss, I want it to be just you and me. I don't want the eyes of my family on us. I don't want to wonder if my sister's throwing death stares our way or aiming imaginary daggers toward my back. I want intimacy. And privacy. I want…just us."

His eyes darkened, and something hot and unfamiliar flickered through them. Then he tugged her body even tighter against his. "I want those things too, honey."

The pause that followed felt so deep and intense that she looked away. But she didn't separate from him. Instead, she lay her head on his chest like she'd done it a million times before, and just rocked, allowing herself to be swept up in all that was Callum.

CHAPTER 13

Fiona tugged Callum's T-shirt over her head. And there it was again. The smell that was all him. It surrounded her. Consumed her. And she loved it.

She released her updo so her hair fell softly around her shoulders. Then she took a deep breath. She'd already brushed her teeth and scrubbed her face clean of makeup. Now she just needed to step out of the bathroom. But things felt different between her and Callum now. It wasn't only because of the dance or the man telling her he wanted to kiss her. It was the time spent with him. Time that had changed things between them. Twisted the relationship into something more intimate.

A delicious shiver ran through her at the memory of their dance. The feel of his arms around her as he whispered sweet things in her ear. They'd stayed on that dance floor for so long she'd had no choice but to forget there were others in the room. Forget Amanda's words and Freddie's presence.

With a steadying breath, she stepped out to find a shirtless Callum with his back to her as he faced the window. A phone was pressed to his ear as he spoke to, presumably, someone on his team. Words like "security" and "data" flew around. She stared at the deep ridges of muscles in his back. The way his olive skin glowed in the moonlight. The funny thing was, his back was just as spectacular as his front.

Then he turned, and those warm brown eyes darkened.

Suddenly, all ability to think or function fled. She wasn't sure if he was feeling it too, but his words stopped as his gaze brushed over her body.

Holy God, she needed saving from this man.

She swallowed, screaming at her legs to move. When the message from her brain eventually reached her limbs, she made it to the bed, then slipped beneath the covers. But she wasn't hiding herself from him. And more than that, she wasn't running from their attraction.

Nerves almost rattled her teeth as she watched him end the call. Which was dumb, right? Because they'd already slept in the same bed. They'd done this last night. Except that was before they'd danced, and he'd admitted to wanting to kiss her. Oh, and she'd been drunk. Drunk people rarely got nervous.

She cleared her throat. "Everything okay?"

"Yeah, the guys at work need me to look into something. It can wait until tomorrow."

"They can't do it themselves?"

He pulled back the sheets on his side of the bed. "I do a lot of the tech stuff for the company. Finding information. Hacking systems."

So he was smart and gorgeous and sweet and dangerous. *Great.* "Is there anything you *can't* do?"

He grinned. "I struggle to keep my library books in the same condition I borrow them."

She laughed. He was right. His one flaw. "If that's your only problem, you're doing pretty well."

He flicked off the light, and with a small sigh, she rolled onto her side, away from him. She lay there for a full five seconds, wondering if she should—

A strong arm slid around her middle and pulled her back into his front. She bit her lower lip to hold in the groan, because his body just felt so...dang...*good* around her. How the heck was she supposed to sleep without this tomorrow night?

She closed her eyes to the feel of him nuzzling her hair. "Thank you for letting me come this weekend."

She could have laughed. *He* was thanking *her*? "Callum, you have done something for me that I'll never be able to repay. This weekend should have been so incredibly hard, but it wasn't. Because of you."

"Maybe you can repay me by telling me your favorite food so I know where to take you when we get back."

"Vanilla ice cream with crushed Oreos." He laughed, and she quickly added, "But I don't think that's appropriate first-date food, so maybe lamb shanks?"

"Done."

Her breath almost caught, because that was him admitting he'd be taking her on a date when they got home. Had this relationship shifted from something fake to something real? Could they make it work when they got home?

"Can I ask you something?" he asked quietly, his rumbly voice brushing over her skin.

"Anything." Well, anything within reason.

"What did you see tonight before you got locked outside?"

The question had her pausing. Honestly, after everything that had happened with her sister and Callum since, she'd completely forgotten about it. "What I saw was impossible. It was—"

Fists pounding on the door cut off her words. Then a voice. "Fiona? It's me. Freddie. I need to talk to you."

She shot up into a sitting position, Callum's arm falling from her waist. Freddie was here? At her door on his freaking wedding night?

His words had run together, almost sounding slurred. Was the guy drunk?

She was still processing the crazy turn of events when Callum climbed out of bed. Before her slow brain could process what was happening, he was throwing on some pants. She caught a glimpse of the anger on his face before he started toward the door.

He pulled it open, but not enough that she could see Freddie.

"What are you doing here?" Callum's growled words had her falling out of bed and rummaging around in her suitcase for jeans.

"I want to talk to Fiona."

"No. Go back to your *wife*."

The second her jeans were on, she flew to the door, sliding beside Callum. She started to step forward, but his arm came around her waist, keeping her beside him.

"What are you doing here?" she hissed at Freddie.

"I just need to talk to you."

"It's your wedding night, Freddie. You can't be here." The words sounded even crazier out loud than they had in her head. It was his *wedding* night.

He scrubbed a hand over his face. God, the guy almost looked lost. "I know. Just let me talk to you for a second." His gaze shifted to the stony figure beside her, then back to her. "Alone."

Callum growled. "No."

Fiona looked up and down the hall. Where was Amanda? "You need to go back to your room."

"Not until I've talked to you."

Christ, he had that look in his eye. She remembered it well. It was the stubborn, I'm-not-doing-a-damn-thing-until-I get-what-I-want look.

"Shut the door if you want. I'll camp out right here until you agree to talk to me." He scanned the area like he was searching for a good place to sit.

Hell no! Amanda would come searching, and if she found him at her door...

She couldn't believe she was saying this, but… "If I talk to you, will you leave?"

"Yes." The answer came so quickly, she almost didn't believe it. And by the tightening of Callum's arm around her waist, he didn't believe it, either. Or maybe he just hated the idea of her talking to Freddie.

She turned and touched Callum's chest. "We'll just be a second. We won't leave this hall, I promise." Also, he would be able to hear everything, even through the closed door. Still, he didn't look the least bit happy about it.

It took a full three seconds for his jaw to unclench. "Fine. One minute."

She nodded, taking a small step into the hall. She missed Callum's touch immediately. Hell, she even missed the man's body heat. The second the door closed, she lowered her voice. "What's going on, Freddie?"

He ran two hands through his hair, almost looking like he was pulling the strands from the root. "I think I made a mistake."

"You didn't. You love Amanda, and you married her."

He had to love her, right? He'd married her only months after Fiona had left.

He was shaking his head before she'd finished speaking. "No. I was going to leave a month ago, but then she told me she was pregnant."

Fiona stiffened. Amanda was pregnant? She let the information sit inside her for a moment, expecting to feel…something.

Interesting. She didn't even care.

"That's amazing. You're going to have a baby together. Even more reason for you to go to her right now."

His throat bobbed. "We had a fight."

He looked down at his hand, and a gasp slipped from her lips. She grabbed his wrist. "Your palm is sliced open!"

"She threw a vase. I picked up one of the shards and it cut me."

She opened her mouth, almost offering to clean the wound,

but she quickly bit back the words. It was his wedding night. His *wife* should be doing that. "Go back to your room, clean up your wound, and make up with her."

When he was silent, she looked up to see him watching her closely. "I thought I could live without you, Fiona—"

"Don't."

"But seeing you this weekend...touching you..."

"Freddie. You need to go."

He stepped forward. She moved away, her back hitting the wall.

"I still love you."

Oh, no he didn't.

She opened her mouth to tell him that wasn't true. That if he loved her, he wouldn't have cheated, and certainly not with her sister.

But before she could utter a single word, his lips crashed onto hers.

A high-pitched, strangling cry escaped from her throat, and she was a second away from kneeing him in the balls when the door flew open—then Freddie was pulled away from her and thrown into the wall.

CALLUM'S HANDS fisted as he towered over the asshole, blood roaring between his ears. The sound of Fiona's distress played over in his head, fueling him.

"What the fuck are you doing?" he growled.

Freddie scrambled to his feet and shoved at his chest. "Get the hell away from me!"

Callum didn't move an inch. He lowered his voice. "You're drunk and it's your wedding night—those are the *only* fucking reasons you're not on the floor with a broken jaw right now. But believe me when I tell you that if you *ever* do that again, if I ever catch you kissing any woman without her permission, *especially* Fiona, I will destroy you."

Freddie's eyes widened, real fear in his gaze. Yeah, the scumbag might be drunk, but he wasn't so written off he missed the promise of violence in Callum's words.

"Go," Callum ordered.

Freddie swallowed nervously before glancing at Fiona over Callum's shoulder. Then, finally, he moved down the hall. Callum waited until the guy had disappeared around the corner before turning to look at Fiona. Her lips were pink.

His muscles vibrated with the need to run down the hall, grab the asshole, and break his jaw like he'd wanted to do the second he saw the man's lips on Fiona. Instead, he forced his muscles to relax as he stepped forward and ran a thumb over her bottom lip.

"Are you all right?"

"I asked you to wait inside."

His brows rose at her clipped tone, his gaze skirting between her slightly narrowed eyes. "Are you mad?"

"Yes. You took away my opportunity to knee the bastard in the balls." Then she spun and stormed back into the room.

His lips twitched as he followed her, throwing the door closed behind them. "You were going to nail him in the balls?"

She shuffled her jeans down her legs, and his gut rippled at the sight of those creamy, toned legs. The second the pants were off, she spun. "Yes. I didn't get to do it the day I found him in bed with my sister because I was too damn shocked. So that moment just now was my missed opportunity."

"I don't think you need a reason. The next time you see him, you can nail him. He'll know why."

She growled...actually *growled*.

He bit back a grin as he stepped forward, his feet almost propelling toward her on their own. "I didn't like him touching you like that. I'll always help a woman in distress if I can."

"But I didn't need your help. I can fight my own battles. Just because I have breasts doesn't mean I need a knight in shining armor to save me."

His eyes twitched to look down at those breasts. They pressed against the material of his shirt, and the sight damn well toyed with him. "I'm not going to sit back and listen as he manhandles you, Fiona. I'm not that guy."

She swallowed, seeming to notice for the first time how close he'd gotten. This time, when she spoke, her words had less bite to them. "So, block your ears."

That wasn't happening. "How about I just hold the asshole down while you pound him?" That sounded like a compromise to him.

"That wouldn't work."

He swiped her cheek with his finger. "Why's that, honey?"

"Because I don't want him to think I need your help to stand up for myself."

He lowered his head until his lips brushed her ear. "Five seconds. That's how long I'll give you next time before I step in." He wasn't even sure he could give her that much, but hell, he'd try. For her, he'd try.

He touched his lips to her cheek and kissed her, enjoying her jagged breath.

"I can work with that."

His lips stretched into a smile as he shifted his head so his mouth hovered over hers. He wanted to kiss her so damn bad he ached. Her lips called to him, like a fruit that was supposed to be forbidden.

He met her eyes. "It's just you and me."

"It is."

His hands went to her hips, tugging her into him. "Am I allowed to kiss you now?"

Heat blazed in her eyes, and her pulse picked up. She opened her mouth like she was going to say something, but instead, rose to her toes and touched her mouth to his. The feel of her soft lips made his gut tighten and something hot coil over his skin.

His fingers tightened on her flesh, needing to feel more of her against him. Needing her curves to soften his hardness. When her hands moved up his chest and she sighed, her lips parted and he took advantage, sliding his tongue into her mouth to taste her. She moaned, and that moan rippled through his chest.

In one fluid move, he shifted his hands beneath her and lifted her into his arms. She wrapped around him like she'd done it a hundred times. Like they were made to fit exactly as they did.

Needing to feel more of her, he trailed a hand up her thigh, slipping under the shirt and skirting her waist. For a moment, he paused, letting the heat of her skin seep into him. Then her hand covered his, and she whispered, "Touch me," before shifting his hand so he held her bare breast in his palm.

Every rational thought in his head blackened as he kneaded her breast. Her hums turned into moans, and she dug her fingers into his shoulders. He found her hard nipple and grazed it with his thumb.

"Callum…"

His name on her lips was like a breath of life inside him. He spun and lay her on the bed, never separating their bodies as he hovered over her. Then his lips trailed to her cheek and neck. He shoved the shirt up so her breasts were on full display, allowing himself one look at the pink buds before dropping his head and taking one peak inside his mouth.

Her back arched, the action pushing her sweet flesh farther between his lips. He ran his tongue over her, alternating between swipes and circles.

"More," she gasped. "I need more of you."

Hell, fucking, yes, he'd give her more. With his other hand, he trailed down her side before slipping inside her panties where she was warm and wet. She opened for him, her pulse spiking, her fingers tightening on his shoulders. At the first swipe against her clit, she cried out, and that sound tormented him. Twisted and pulled at him.

He caressed again, enjoying every little whimper and raspy moan from her throat.

He switched his mouth to her other breast, devouring her while he continued to play with her. When he slipped one finger down to her entrance, her breaths stalled, then he slid inside. Her gasp cut through the quiet night air. He started a slow rhythm, thrusting in and out, his thumb continuing to run circles over her clit.

When she was trembling on the edge, he shifted up her body and found her mouth, covering it with his own as she broke, her walls convulsing around his finger.

Fuck, she did things to him. Things that made him want to tell the world this woman was *his.*

When she was finally still, a smile slipped across her lips. Then she whispered, "I like you."

His chuckle was low. "Good. I like you too."

She reached for him, but he took hold of her wrist, halting her movement. "Not tonight."

Confusion darkened her eyes. "Why not?"

"Because if you touch me, I'll want all of you." And it was too soon for that. He needed to court this woman first. Make sure she knew she was his.

Her gaze shone with understanding, and he kissed her one last time before straightening her clothes. After turning off the light, he rolled to his back, pulling Fiona close and holding her. Immediately, she softened against him, her cheek resting over his heart.

Yeah. This woman was his. He felt that with everything he was.

CHAPTER 14

The soft beats of Fiona's heart thumped through the air as she slept. The sun was just rising, but he'd been awake for a while, enjoying the weight of her cheek on his chest. The whisper of her breaths brushing his skin.

He wanted to hold on to this moment. Pause it and let it sit in time for longer. Because this place, this hotel room, felt like a bubble, and when they returned to Cradle Mountain, they'd be leaving that bubble. She'd go back to her place, he'd go back to his, and he could only hope like hell this thing between them continued to grow.

Her breathing changed rhythm and her fingers twitched. Then, slowly, her eyes opened. When she looked up, he wanted to fucking drown in those chestnut eyes. They bored into him like they saw deep into his soul.

He shifted a piece of hair behind her ear, making sure to graze her soft skin as he went. "Morning, beautiful."

Her smile was slow. "Morning."

"You sleep okay?"

"I did. It was impossible not to with this big heater beside me."

One side of his mouth lifted. "I run hot."

"You do. Did *you* sleep okay?"

Like a damn baby with this woman in his arms. "Yeah."

She closed her eyes and lay her head back on his chest. It felt so damn natural to have her there.

She made a sexy little hum sound. "This may sound terrible, but I am so glad that wedding's over."

"Doesn't sound terrible at all."

Her long exhale brushed his abdomen, and when she looked up again, she focused on his lips. That one look made his chest tighten and his heart race. "Looking at me like that is dangerous, honey."

A smile teased her lips. "Maybe I like danger."

Fuck. With a short growl, he rolled them over and caged her to the bed, then he kissed her. A long, deep kiss. Fiona hummed as their tongues collided and her hands smoothed over his shoulders.

He'd been wrong last night. That wasn't the moment he needed to pause, it was this one. Because this woman's lips on his made every part of him that he'd thought was put together tug apart and rearrange themselves just for her.

When they eventually parted, he touched his forehead to hers. "God, Fi. I could stay here all day."

"I wouldn't complain," she breathed.

He growled and pecked one more kiss to her lips before rolling over and standing. The morning went quickly after that. They ordered room service for breakfast and packed. Fiona mentioned that some of the family was having breakfast downstairs but said it was nothing formal and she preferred not to go, because Freddie would no doubt be there.

Callum's hands fisted at the memory of the night before. What kind of asshole did what he did? But he already knew the answer to that. The kind who cheated on women. The kind who had no damn respect for anyone but himself.

Packed and ready to check out, they left the hotel room. He

felt the change in Fiona the second they stepped into the elevator. The nerves that made her go quiet. The anxiety that whitened her knuckles on the suitcase handle.

"Hey," he said quietly. "What's wrong?"

"Yeah, I'm just nervous that news traveled to my parents about the circumstances of me and Freddie separating. And nervous that Amanda knows about Freddie's visit last night."

He slid his hand into hers and gave a small squeeze. "It'll be okay. And his visit wasn't your fault."

She snorted. "In Amanda's eyes, it's always my fault. If we had a normal relationship, I'd tell her. But we don't. There's no way I'd get out of that conversation unscathed."

Thank God she didn't live near them. They were toxic. He could see that and he'd only met them two days ago.

When they reached the reception area, it was to find both her parents there. Amanda was there too, but unlike her smiling parents, her face was completely clear of emotion. A breath he hadn't realized he'd been holding released from his chest when he saw Freddie was absent. Thank fuck, because that would just remind him he hadn't punched the guy last night and he'd want to make up for it.

"I'm so sad you're leaving so soon," Edna said, pulling her daughter into a hug.

"I know. I'm sorry, Mom. I'll try to get back soon."

Mark shook Callum's hand. "It was nice to meet you, son. I'm glad to see my daughter's being taken care of."

"Always." He meant that. He planned to date this man's daughter, and he'd sure as hell be looking after her.

Next, Edna pulled him into a tight hug before whispering into his ear, "Thank you. You two are perfect together."

He returned the warm hug, agreeing with her words.

Amanda didn't hug either of them, just offered a tight smile as they left.

The drive home was the opposite of the drive there. Fiona

wasn't quiet. She laughed at his jokes, confirming to him he was as funny as he thought. She told stories about her childhood, most of the good ones just involving her and her parents. She talked about her cousin. About jobs gone wrong at libraries.

It wasn't until they were almost at his place that he brought up the topic he needed an answer to. Fiona had her hand out the window, letting wisps of wind sweep through her fingers. He didn't want to shift her calm, but he needed to know.

He cleared his throat. "The night of the rehearsal dinner, you mentioned some texts you've been receiving."

Her fingers stopped flowing with the wind, and for a moment she was still. Then she turned to him. "Really? I told you about that?" She said it like she wished it wasn't true.

"You did. Can you tell me about them?"

She wet her lips and it was a beat before she responded. "I've been receiving some not-so-nice texts from an unknown number."

His fingers tightened on the wheel. "What do they say?"

"They basically call me a whore or a bitch and tell me to stay away from what's theirs."

What the fuck? "What's *theirs*?"

She lifted a shoulder.

"How many of these messages have you received?"

"I'm not sure. I've lost count. But they don't address me by name, so I'm certain they're a wrong number or something."

The air hissed through his teeth. "Fi, if you've lost count, there have been too many. And just because your name wasn't used doesn't mean they aren't targeting you. Why didn't you tell me? I run a security business."

"Because we weren't close, and you were already doing this massive favor for me, so I didn't want to ask for another." Again, she lifted a shoulder. "And they're just text messages."

"Abusive texts can escalate quickly. As soon as the perp isn't satisfied just texting anymore, they elevate. Do you know who might be behind them?"

She shook her head. "I don't have any enemies." She laughed. "Unless you call my sister an enemy, but it's not really her style to text from a random number. She'd just call me a whore to my face in a roundabout way."

"Tomorrow, I want you to come to Blue Halo so I can see if I can trace the number to its owner."

She was shaking her head before he finished. "You've already done so much for me. I don't want it to take up too much of your time."

"It won't. I'm good with technology." And no way was he just going to ignore this. This woman was *his*, and he took care of what belonged to him.

Fiona got to the bottom of the page before realizing she hadn't taken in a single word. Not one. Zilch. And it wasn't like she was reading a boring story. This was a Lee Child book. He was one of the best thriller writers in the world.

Argh. She couldn't concentrate and there was one blaring reason for that…Callum. Or the lack of Callum. It was almost bedtime, and all she could think about since leaving his place earlier today was that her house felt entirely too quiet and just a smidge too empty.

It was silly. She'd see him again tomorrow, for freaking sake. The man had basically ordered her to go to Blue Halo so he could trace that number, because not only was he perfect, but he was bossy when it came to her protection.

Sigh. She usually loved her own company, but one weekend away with Callum and suddenly she needed him with her? She closed her book with a thud and set it on the coffee table. What she really needed was an early night. Either that, or a good Callum detox.

When her phone rang from the coffee table, she just about leapt for it, desperate for a distraction that would actually, you know, distract her.

She smiled when she saw Stacey's name on the screen. "Hey."

"You left without saying goodbye."

Crap. She had. "Sorry. I was beyond ready to leave and all but ran out of the hotel. Although Amanda and my parents were in the reception area when I got down there, so I couldn't avoid them."

"How was the goodbye? Did sister dearest give you a hug?"

"Nope. I got a tight smile and some side-eye. A pretty narrow escape."

"No Freddie?"

She nibbled her lip. She told her cousin everything, so there was no harm in telling her this. "No, but there's something I should tell you."

"Ooh, gossip. Tell me."

"Freddie came to my hotel room last night and kissed me."

Stacey gasped. "No, he didn't!"

"Oh, he did. And he told me that he thinks he made a mistake and only married Amanda because she told him she was pregnant."

"Oh my fucking God! What did you do?"

She rose from the couch and moved into her bedroom. "Well, I was a second from kneeing him where the sun don't shine when Callum came out and threw him into the wall."

"Oh, Callum. He's such a big, sexy protector."

She was about to pull out a pajama top but stopped when she saw the T-shirt from Callum on her dresser. She *should* wash it and give it back, but...there was no harm in wearing it one more time, right?

She tugged it on. And man... It still smelled of him and the hotel. This was not the Callum detox she needed.

"Are you going to tell Amanda?" Stacey asked.

Well, that would be the normal thing to do. "I would if I thought she'd believe me, but you know my sister. She'll twist it around and find some way to make it my fault. She'll say I encouraged him to come to my room and initiated the kiss."

"You're so right. She'd need to see it to actually believe it, and even then, she'd probably make it your fault."

Of course she would. "My thoughts are she knows who she married. I'm back in Cradle Mountain. I won't have any more contact with him, or at least, not for a while. He'll probably hit on other people, and when Amanda catches him, she'll see he's no good."

Once a cheater, always a cheater. Although Amanda was a cheater too, so that didn't bode well for their future anyway.

"So..." Stacey said suggestively. "What happened after your sexy boyfriend saved the day?"

She nibbled her bottom lip, mouth stretching into a smile. When she took a beat too long to answer, Stacey gasped.

"Oh, it's good, isn't it? Tell me. Tell me now!"

"We kissed, and..."

"And?" Stacey pushed.

"The man gave me the best orgasm of my life."

The groan from Stacey almost sounded pained. "It's like God sculpted this hot as hell man just to shame every other."

Oh, Fiona had definitely been feeling that. She lifted the phone and went into the bathroom.

"So, have you locked him down? Are things official?"

Fiona frowned as she squeezed toothpaste on her brush. "Not official, but he said he wanted to take me on a date. And we're catching up tomorrow to—"

She stopped. She hadn't told Stacey about the messages. She hadn't told anyone until her drunken slip with Callum.

"To what?" Stacey asked.

She blew out a long breath. "I've been getting some messages from an unknown number saying some nasty stuff. He's going to see if he can trace the number."

"Oh my gosh. Really? How long has that been happening?"

"I don't know, like, a month?"

"Why didn't you say anything?"

She lifted a shoulder even though her cousin couldn't see her. "Because they're just texts. It's not like someone's actually threatening me to my face."

"Still, it's a bit scary." She could almost hear Stacey thinking. "I'm glad you have Callum then. If anyone can help, it's him and his team. I don't even live in Cradle Mountain and I hear about how good Blue Halo Security is."

"I'm sure that if this number's traceable, he'll find them." But even that made her nervous, because then the messages would become real, with a living, breathing human behind them.

"You don't think it's Amanda, do you?" Stacey asked quietly.

The same question Callum had asked. "I think if Amanda wanted to threaten me, she wouldn't worry about the unknown number part."

"Yeah, you're probably right."

"Looks like I have a second person who hates me."

"Amanda doesn't hate you. She's jealous."

Fiona scoffed. "Of what?"

"You did well at school. You're independent. You're beautiful."

"Amanda's all those things."

Stacey laughed, but there was no humor. "No. She's insecure, she barely passed her SATs, and she's a fake kind of beautiful. She needs to put in the work. You don't."

Fiona wasn't sure she agreed. She was average at best. "I've never seen her that way, but we can agree to disagree. I should be getting to bed though." Her cold, empty bed.

"Okay, keep me updated on both Callum and the text stuff."

"Of course. Thanks for calling and checking in. Have a good night, Stace."

"You too."

She quickly brushed her teeth before switching off the lights and slipping between the sheets. God, they felt cold. Callum had been a big heater, making the entire bed warm even when she wasn't touching him.

She was just about to roll over when her phone vibrated on the side table. She grabbed it and smiled when she saw the text.

Callum: I'm missing having you in my arms. Sleep well, honey.

Her heart thrashed against her ribs. So it wasn't just her.

Fiona: I miss you too. Good night, Callum. x

She was about to set the phone down when it rang in her hands—only it wasn't Callum. Her smile slipped.

Really? *Freddie* was calling her? Argh.

She canceled the call, then did what she should have done long ago and blocked his number.

Good. Done. She wouldn't be hearing from the cheating scumbag again. Whatever he and her sister decided to do with their lives was on them.

When the phone was back on her nightstand, she flicked off the bedside lamp and snuggled into her blankets.

When the phone dinged with a message a couple minutes later, she groaned. God, if that was Freddie, messaging from another number—

Unknown number: You pretend to be all innocent, but I see what you're doing. Stop! He's mine, and I will go to any length to make sure it stays that way.

She clicked out of the message and dropped it to her bedside table like it had burned her. Suddenly, she was glad Callum was looking into it for her. Because there was something different about that message. Even though her name wasn't mentioned, it felt more...personal.

It took too long for her to feel warm after that, and even longer for her to drift to sleep.

She was finally at that phase between asleep and awake when a noise from somewhere in the house had her eyes fluttering. A shadow stretching into the hallway from the living room made her eyes shoot open wide. She jackknifed into a sitting position, heart pounding against her ribs as she reached for her phone and, on instinct, called Callum. He answered on the second ring, and he sounded completely awake.

"Fiona, are you okay?"

"I think someone's in my house."

CHAPTER 15

*C*allum's fingers were tight around the wheel as he took a hard right. Fiona only lived a few streets away, but it felt too damn far. Someone was in her house? Who? Why?

Another right, this time onto her street. The second he reached her driveway, he slammed his foot on the brake and grabbed his pistol.

The front door opened before he reached the porch.

"I told you to lock yourself in the bathroom," he growled, not feeling capable of soft or gentle right now.

"I *was* in the bathroom, but I didn't hear anyone, and when your car screeched to a stop, I came out."

Fuck. The person could have been waiting for her. He pushed that to the back of his mind as he stepped forward and cupped her cheek. "Are you okay?"

She nodded. And she did look okay too. Damn, she was brave. He entered the house, then stopped and listened. For heartbeats that weren't supposed to be there. Breathing or movement.

When he heard none of it, he closed and locked the front door. "I can't hear anyone, but I'm still going to check the place. Don't move."

Before he could step away, she grabbed his arm. "Callum…be careful."

He forced some of the anger down. "Always, honey."

He moved into the living room, again listening for any sound that didn't belong. There was nothing. Good. But that didn't mean no one *had been* there. He moved around the house, checking every entry and exit point. Everything was locked. Every window, the front and back doors…he even checked the small bathroom windows, which were closed and locked.

When he returned to her, she still looked nervous, but a bit more color had entered her cheeks. "Were there any doors or windows that you closed or locked between waking and letting me in?"

She shook her head. "No, I went straight from the bed to the bathroom to the door."

He let that sit for a moment as he holstered his weapon. "Everything's locked up. What did you see?"

"Just shadows of movement. It shifted down the hall from the living room." She sighed and scrubbed her face. "I'm sorry. Maybe I didn't see *anything*. I was half-asleep and my bed was cold and I was missing you—" She stopped, eyes widening like she hadn't meant to say that.

One side of his mouth lifted. "You already know I was missing you too, honey."

Her hands dropped from her face, but she didn't meet his eyes. "I'm so sorry. I was on the phone talking to Stacey about those texts, then I actually got another text, and it just freaked me out. I shouldn't have called."

She got another text? Fuck, he hated that.

He stepped closer, touching his thumb to her chin and tilting her head until she met his gaze. "I'm *glad* you called me. I want to be the first person you think of when you need help."

"You do?"

"Yes." Absolutely yes. It meant she trusted him to keep her safe.

"Well...thank you." Then she wet her lips, and it took a damn storm of restraint not to look down at those lips. "Now that you're here, you could always stay the night...if you want, that is."

His gut tightened at the thought of another night in bed with her. Holding her. For the first time since arriving, he let himself focus on the fact that she wore his T-shirt. She could have worn anything, but she'd chosen that.

It made every protective and territorial instinct shoot to life. "I'd like that."

"Okay. Good." Then with a nod, she moved around the house, turning off all the lights before surprising him by taking his hand and leading him to her bedroom. He stripped down to his briefs, not missing how she carefully avoided looking at his body, before he slipped into her bed. It smelled of her—fresh and citrusy. Her entire house screamed "Fiona." Her books scattered across the coffee and bedside tables. Little trinkets and photos, and the splashes of blue and purple around the place. It was all her, and he loved it.

She shuffled over so her head rested on his chest. She did it so easily, like this was their place together. He slipped an arm around her waist, loving how she melted against him. He'd been in bed when she'd called, not sleeping, because he'd been missing exactly this.

"Warm?" he asked.

"Toasty. Thank you again for coming. I really am sorry I called you for nothing."

He kissed her head. "It wasn't for nothing. Something scared you. You call and I'll come. Every time."

Her fingers dug into his chest. He held her as her breaths evened out and she fell into a deep sleep. He didn't drift off right away, though. Instead, he listened to the sounds both inside and outside of the house. The whistle of the trees, the odd engine on the road. Because even though it didn't seem possible that anyone could have been in her house tonight, with everything locked up tight, the fact she'd been scared enough to call made every part of him stand at alert.

FIONA ROLLED ONTO HER BACK, scrunching her eyes as rays of sunlight hit her eyelids. Man, oh man, she felt well rested. Like a deep, slept-ten-hours-straight well rested. And she knew exactly why...Callum. His body heat. His heartbeat in her ear. Maybe her tired mind had conjured up the shadowy movement in her head as a means to get Callum here because she'd known he'd come. That had to be it, because every damn window and door had been closed and locked. Thank God Callum hadn't been pissed.

Her eyes opened to find the other side of the bed empty.

Slowly, she pushed into a sitting position, scanning the room as she did. It wasn't just the other side of the bed that was empty, the room was, too. And if the silent house was anything to go by, he wasn't here. She was alone.

Her heart dropped, because the only thing that could match sleeping with the man was waking up to see his beautiful form beside her...something she was not going to get today. Sigh.

Okay, time to get up, get dressed, and go to work like a normal adult who wasn't dependent on a man.

She was just pushing out of bed when she saw the piece of paper on the bedside table. A smile bloomed as she reached for it.

Sorry to run out, I had an early meeting. Come into Blue Halo anytime today and we'll look into that number. Hope you slept well. I certainly did. Cal x

Oh Lord. The man was too good. Ha. Like that word even did him justice.

She spent the next half hour getting ready. She'd just pulled her shirt on when a knock sounded at the door, and she already knew who it would be. Jenny. Her friend only lived a street away, so if they were scheduled to start at the same time, they went into work together. She was a bit early, but at least Fiona wasn't half undressed and running late today. That happened way too often.

She pulled the door open to find a beaming Jenny on the other side, tray of coffee in her hand. "Hey, stranger! I missed you."

Fiona chuckled. "I was only gone the weekend."

"I know. It really made me realize how boring this town is without you." She pulled Fiona into a tight one-armed hug before coming into the house and lowering the coffees to the kitchen island. "I made a trip to that coffee shop you love because I need you to tell me everything before work. How was the wedding? How hot did you look? And did anything happen with you and Mr. Sexy?"

Fiona grinned as she closed the door. "Better than I thought it would, not sure about hot, but decent, and yes."

Jenny's brows rose. "Yes?"

Of course that was the part her friend heard. "Just a few kisses and snuggles."

Jenny's eyes narrowed, and there was a short pause before she shook her head. "Nope. I don't believe you. There was more."

"There was no sex."

Her friend looked like she still didn't believe her.

Fiona grabbed one of the coffees, almost groaning as she sipped. She'd missed The Grind. "He may also have stayed over last night."

Surprise shot Jenny's brows up. "What?"

"It wasn't intentional. I woke up and thought I saw someone in the house, so he came over to check the place."

Concern flittered over her friend's face. "What do you mean, you thought you saw someone?"

"It was nothing. I was half-asleep, and when Callum checked the house, it was all locked up, so I couldn't have seen anyone."

Her fingers tightened on the cup. "I've been getting some offensive texts from an unknown number, and I think that just freaked me out."

"Texts saying what?"

"They're not nice…" When her friend continued to look at her expectantly, she lifted a shoulder. "That I'm a whore. That I need to keep my hands off what isn't mine."

The shock on Jenny's face was almost comical. "Who exactly are you touching who isn't yours? Callum?"

"I don't know. Maybe Callum. Maybe Freddie."

Jenny leaned forward, elbows on the island. "Freddie? Asshole-who-cheated-on-you Freddie? Why on earth would you want him back?"

"I don't." She lifted her coffee, taking another small sip. "He actually came to our room on his wedding night."

"He didn't!"

"He did, and he told me he'd made a mistake and the only reason he married Amanda was because she's pregnant."

Jenny's jaw dropped. "Holy shit. What did Callum do?"

"He stormed out of the room and threw Freddie into a wall. He clearly wanted to punch the guy but didn't, thank God."

"God, your life's like a soap opera. Are you okay? Did you tell Amanda?"

"Nope. And I don't plan to." When Jenny just stared at her, she gave a sigh. "It's complicated."

"Jesus. Well, I don't really feel sorry for her after what she did."

Exactly. "Now that you're all caught up, should we walk to work?"

Jenny laughed as she stood. "Oh, I am far from caught up. There are way too many missing details from that story. But you can share them with me on the way."

"We should go the long route then."

They both laughed as they crossed the living room. She was

locking the door when thoughts of the previous night came back to her. The shadow in the hall. The sound that woke her. It was all in her head…right?

Yes. It had to be.

When they hit the sidewalk, Jenny linked her arm through Fiona's. They'd made it halfway down the street when her phone vibrated from her pocket. She tugged it out, hoping it was Callum, but the smile slipped when she saw the text. Not from Callum. Her pulse spiked at the words in front of her.

"So, tell me more about—" Jenny stopped. "What's wrong?" She glanced down at the phone in Fiona's hand, an audible gasp whipping through the air.

Unknown number: You think I'm joking? Keep your fucking hands off my man, or you'll wish you had.

CHAPTER 16

*C*allum leaned back in his seat behind his desk. It had been a busy morning of meetings with clients and researching information only he could source for the team. It was damn lucky he liked his job, because there was always a lot to do.

His gaze flicked to his phone. Despite being busy, his mind had been a bit...distracted this morning. All because of one woman. Fiona. He couldn't get her out of his head. He was constantly waiting for her call or text. Listening to hear if she'd arrived. She'd messaged earlier that she'd stop in on her lunch break, so he'd been watching the minutes tick by all day.

With a long exhale, he pushed up from his desk and moved down the hall. He didn't just need Fiona here because he wanted to see her. He needed to look into those damn messages.

It had to be the sister, right? Because who else seemed to hate her so much?

He stepped into the kitchen to find Blake lifting a coffee from the machine.

Callum moved to the fridge and grabbed a bottle of water. "Hey, brother."

Blake grinned. "Hey. How was your weekend away with the librarian?"

His entire team knew where he'd been over the weekend and why. They didn't keep secrets from each other. "Her name's Fiona, and it was good."

"Did you break through that tough exterior, or are you still the book killer?"

He grinned. "I haven't damaged a single book since the coffee spill a month ago." Although, he still had one at home, so there was time. "And yeah, I think I had a breakthrough."

He wouldn't be sharing the finer details of his relationship, but he would share the information his team needed to know. He uncapped his water and drank some. "She's coming in today actually, but that's because someone's been sending her threatening text messages."

The smile slipped from Blake's face. "What do they say?"

"Shit about her being a whore and not touching what's theirs."

"From an unknown number?"

"Yep. I'm gonna see if I can trace the number back to a person."

Blake nodded. "Good idea. It doesn't take much for an unhinged asshole to escalate."

Exactly. "How're Willow and Mila?"

Blake's eyes warmed, and that smile returned to his face. "Amazing. Willow's the best mother, and Mila's just…" He shook his head. "She's amazing, man. Being her father is more than I deserve."

Callum was happy Blake was back with his wife and five-year-old daughter. It was all the man had wanted since being forcibly separated from them all those years ago. "That's great."

Aidan stepped into the room and headed for the coffee machine. "Hey."

"Hey. I heard you and Cassie are planning an engagement party," Blake said.

"Sure are. If it was up to me, I'd just marry the woman today, but everyone's convinced Cass she needs an engagement party first, so an engagement party it will be."

By *everyone*, Callum was assuming Aidan meant their friends' women.

Blake smiled. "I remember feeling like that. I just wanted to put a damn ring on Willow's finger. Where will the party be?"

"At the event center."

Callum's brows rose. "So big?"

"We're inviting a lot of people from town. Also, the guys from Marble Protection and their partners."

The men from Marble Protection lived in Marble Falls, Texas, and had also been part of Project Arma. They were actually the ones who'd broken Callum and his team out and ended the project.

"It will be good to see them again," Callum said with a nod.

A distant voice from the reception area hit his ears. Fiona's voice. He didn't try to contain his smile.

"You are so screwed," Blake said with a shake of his head, clearly hearing Fiona too.

He couldn't even argue with that. "See you guys later."

He dropped the empty bottle in the recycle bin and went to the reception area. Cassie was just lifting the phone when he stepped into the room. Fiona looked up at him, and immediately, her throat bobbed.

One side of his mouth lifted. "Hey, Fi."

Memories flashed of waking up with this woman in his arms. Of listening to her soft sighs as she slept and loving the way she clung to him.

"Oh, Callum, I was just going to call you," Cassie said, setting the phone down. She paused, and he felt her eyes jumping from him to Fiona.

Yeah, any person would be able to see what was going on here. Hell, they could probably feel it too.

He dragged his gaze from Fiona to Cassie. "Thank you."

Cassie's grin was wide from behind the reception desk. "You're welcome."

He moved forward and touched Fiona's waist, then leaned down and pressed a light kiss to her cheek. "Thanks for coming in, honey."

He straightened to see her smile wide. "Thanks for offering to help me."

It had been less of a request and more of a demand.

Instead of touching the small of her back or just preceding her down the hall, he skimmed his hand down until he reached hers, then interlaced their fingers. "I'll show you to my office."

He gave one more smile to Cassie as they left the room. She still had that grin on her face, and if anything, it had grown. Yeah, he was making a statement. This woman was his. They may not have discussed the finer details of their relationship, but it was official to him.

FIONA LOWERED into the seat Callum held out for her, almost shuddering when he gently squeezed her shoulder before walking around the desk. She watched as he folded his large frame into his chair. God, the guy even looked hot at work. His dark pants hugged his powerful thighs in the best way, and the tight gray shirt left nothing to the imagination.

"How's your morning been, honey?" His deep, raspy voice brushed over her skin like silk, causing every fine hair on her body to stand on end.

"It was okay. The library was quiet, and Rick was in his good-mood phase."

Callum's brows slashed together. "What does he do on a bad-mood day?"

"Where should I start? He'll tell me I'm late when I get there two minutes past the hour. I apparently catalog books incorrectly, even though it's usually another librarian. And the other week, I left some rotting fruit in the staff fridge, but I'm ninety percent sure that was Elaine, an older and very forgetful coworker."

Okay, maybe eighty percent. She did bring an apple to work nearly every day, and often forgot about them, but she was pretty sure this one wasn't hers.

When the concern on Callum's face deepened, she shook her head. "It's fine. He also has days like today where he's sickly nice. He's harmless. Just a bipolar old man who's been in his job for decades."

She tugged her phone from her pocket and searched for the messages. Without letting herself focus on the latest text, she slid the cell across the desk.

Callum lifted the phone, and the second he looked at the screen, his eyes hardened. Not only that, but the muscles in his arms flexed and the veins in his neck stood out as he continued to scroll up the thread. This guy was definitely not someone you wanted on your bad side. He'd always been kind to her, but he was dangerous. She'd seen glimpses of it around Freddie, but she knew that was barely brushing the surface.

Without a word, he turned to his computer.

She fiddled with the edge of the chair as he typed. The energy in the room had shifted. Thickened. And she almost didn't want to speak and feed into it.

As he worked, a phone rang from the desk, but it wasn't hers. His cell sat closer to her, plus, the man seemed to be in his own little world, so she reached out and lifted it to hand to him. She absolutely was not trying to look at the name on the screen...it just kind of happened.

Kasey. Her belly soured. What did the beautiful bombshell of a neighbor want?

"Thanks." He slipped the device from her fingers, glancing at the screen before setting it down and letting it go to voicemail.

"You can answer that," she said quickly, trying to force a nonchalant tone to her voice. "You don't need to ignore it on my behalf."

"If she needs something, she'll call back."

For some reason, that made the sourness in her gut strengthen. It was stupid. She knew it was. Callum had never done anything to make her question him, but she had trust issues that his beautiful neighbor provoked. And honestly, who *wouldn't* want Callum? The guy was gorgeous, and he was also kind and successful and protective. If she got into a relationship with him, she'd be fighting off competition the entire time.

Callum cursed, and her attention flew back to him.

"What?" A curse was bad, right? Was the number from someone she knew? God, was it someone she trusted?

He swiveled his chair around to face her. "They're using a burner phone."

She frowned. "A burner phone?"

"Yeah, meaning they don't want to be traced."

Crap. That was bad, and it made this so much creepier.

Callum's jaw ticked. "This person bought a phone with the sole purpose of harassing you. It means they've put time and thought into it."

Time and thought into harassing her. Scaring her. Great. "Guess there's not much we can do."

"We can be careful," he said firmly. "Don't go out at night alone. Watch your back. Call me if you suspect anything isn't how it's supposed to be. And make sure you keep everything locked up at home, even during the day."

She gave a slow nod, trying to take in every piece of advice and not let it fly over her head.

"I'd also like to get a security system put into your place."

Her brows shot up. "A security system?"

He rose and moved around the desk before lowering to his haunches in front of her, hands going to her knees. "I know it's a lot. But even if you weren't getting these texts, a security system isn't the worst thing to have."

"What if I forget the code? What if I trigger the alarm and can't get it to turn off?"

"You call the company and they help you."

She nibbled her bottom lip and his gaze followed, darkening.

"Whenever you do that, every part of me wants to kiss you," he said, voice quieter than a moment ago.

Her lip slipped from between her teeth, the security system and burner phone suddenly the furthest things from her mind. Her heart raced in her chest to a new, faster rhythm, and she had to stop herself from inching to the edge of the seat.

"Maybe you should," she said quietly. "Kiss me."

He growled, then his mouth crashed onto hers. She moaned as his tongue swept straight into her mouth and his fingers tangled in her hair.

She almost melted in the chair. This man's kisses were like nothing else. They tugged her away from wherever she was and slipped her into a place that was just theirs.

She ran her palms down the planes of his chest, then bunched his shirt in her fists.

He was just pulling her to the edge of the seat when a knock came at the door.

She gasped and tugged her mouth away, while Callum cursed before shouting, "I'm busy."

She tried to stand, but his hands tightened, keeping her in place.

There was a small pause before a man's voice sounded. "Okay. Just letting you know the one o'clock meeting has been brought forward and starts in ten."

All right, now she really needed to get up. She stood, this time relieved when he let her, standing as well. She went to walk around him, but he snagged her wrist and pulled her back into his body. Then she was in his arms again, his chest warming her.

"Go on a date with me this Friday night."

There was no saying no to that, especially after that kiss and while she still stood in the sanctuary of his arms. "Okay."

The single word was about all she could manage. Then his lips touched hers once more. This kiss was softer. Lighter. It was everything.

"Thank God," he whispered.

CHAPTER 17

$\mathcal{F}$iona's heart sped up at the knock on the door. That was Callum. For a date. Because she was going on her first official date with the man.

Oh, God.

Four days had passed since she'd gone to his office, and in that time, she hadn't seen him once, not during the day or evening, so yeah, her nights had been cold and lonely. They were supposed to get breakfast together yesterday, but he'd canceled last minute. She shouldn't have been as disappointed as she had been.

With a quick breath, she grabbed her phone and keys. The second the door was open, her breath caught in her throat, because there in front of her was a very tall, very nice-smelling Callum in a crisp white dress shirt. It was untucked and the top button undone, showing off just a tease of his muscular chest. Even through the black pants, she could make out his powerful thighs. But the thing that really got her heart stumbling to a new rhythm was his eyes. Brown and intense and beautiful.

"Hey," she said quietly, her voice almost getting stuck in her tight chest.

The corner of his mouth lifted. "Hey, gorgeous."

He stepped forward, wrapped his arms around her waist, and kissed her. The kiss was long and deep, his tongue sweeping into her mouth and tangling with hers. She lost herself in that kiss. Let herself be swept away, not caring if she was ever found. When he lifted his head, it was too soon.

She groaned, and in response, he chuckled. "Let me feed you, woman, then we can keep kissing."

Who needed food with kisses like that?

"Fine," she grumbled, not missing the way his smile widened.

She was about to step out, when Callum glanced at her new alarm system. "Have you switched it on?"

Dang it. She'd almost forgotten. It had only been installed today while she'd been at work. Carefully, she fingered in the code, almost breathing a sigh of relief when she got it right and there were no blaring alarms or sirens. "I did it!"

He touched the small of her back. "You did."

She pulled the door closed and stepped out into the cool evening. "When I got home today, they were just finishing the installation. The guy showed me how it works, then wanted me to do it myself. I like to think of myself as a brave person, but in that moment, there was just a bit of a shake in my fingers."

"I'm sure he gets that all the time. The alarm is loud when it goes off." His arm slid from her back, moving around her waist as he led her to the car.

"Uh, yeah. He showed me that too. I thought my eardrums were going to burst, and my poor neighbors probably had aneurysms." She waited until they were driving to ask, "So, where are we going on this first date?"

"I thought we could try the Cedar Inn. Apparently, they do great lamb shanks. We can then grab some ice cream and Oreos on the way home for dessert."

Her heart gave a little kick at him remembering her favorite foods, something her ex never did, because Freddie only ever thought about Freddie. "Sounds great."

When he reached over and took her hand, she worked hard to silence the sharp inhale of air that slipped through her teeth.

"Now, I need to admit something to you that I don't think you're going to like."

Her belly dropped. Oh God, had he finally realized he was miles out of her league? That he belonged with a model who could also speak three languages and owned an empire? "Okay."

"I may have been reading my library book while I was eating dinner last night and got some marinara sauce on a couple of pages."

She laughed. "Just a couple of pages?"

"Yeah." He cringed. "I thought it was best to come forward now, rather than surprise you with it at the library."

"I thought you were past this hurting-library-books thing?"

"Me too, but all it takes is one slip."

"Two slips. You said there were two damaged pages."

He shook his head. "Nah, just one drop. The sauce went through the page. But to be fair, I was distracted."

"By what?"

"Thinking about you."

She tried to bite back the smile, but it was impossible. "I guess I'll let it slide."

"Thank God. I've been stressing about it all day."

She was still smiling when he pulled into the lot of the restaurant. He slipped his hand into hers again as they headed inside. His touch had become so familiar already, it was almost scary how quickly they'd slotted together, weaving into each other's lives.

The waitress sat them at a table by the window and took their drink orders, then it was just them again.

"So what have I missed in the life of Fiona these last few days?"

She grinned. "Very little. Although, when I asked for the bill from the security company, they got suspiciously quiet."

Callum's face remained unchanged. "We have an account with them at Blue Halo."

"So you guys will bill me instead?"

"Sure."

Why did that sound unconvincing? "Callum, I don't want you or your company footing the bill for my home security because we're...you know."

One side of his mouth lifted. "Because we're what?"

"We're...well, dating."

His grin turned into a full-fledged smile. "I like hearing you say that."

"Well, this is a date so..."

"You're right. This is a date, so we're dating."

She liked hearing him say it, too.

The server returned for their orders. Fiona didn't miss the interest the woman showed in Callum, but to his credit, he barely looked at her. In fact, Fiona seemed to take up his entire attention—right until the restaurant door opened and his gaze caught something over her shoulder. She didn't need to look, because a second later, Kasey stopped at their table.

And Lord, the woman looked beautiful tonight. Her long blond hair fell over her bare shoulders in soft waves, her makeup was perfect, and she wore the most stunning short blue dress that pushed up her ample breasts and emphasized her perfectly proportioned hips.

"Callum, hi, fancy seeing you here."

"Hey, Kase."

Kase? The sexy neighbor had a nickname?

Kasey turned to Fiona and gave her a wide smile. A wide, *fake* smile. "Hi."

Fiona hadn't even returned the woman's greeting when Kasey was already looking back to Callum. Her smile turned sultry. "I'm just here with Gretchen. She's making sure I get out of the house."

"That's nice of her. Have a good evening."

Her smile turned strained. Because Callum's words were kind of dismissive? That brought Fiona more joy than it probably should.

Fiona waited until the woman was out of earshot and sitting across the restaurant to tilt her head. "So you're sure there's—"

"Nothing going on," he finished before she could. "Yes, I'm sure. And the only woman I want to think about tonight is you."

What about other nights? the insecure voice in her head whispered.

Throughout dinner, the man made her smile and laugh more times than she could count. Every so often, she felt eyes on her, but Fiona made an effort to not look Kasey's way.

"How are your lamb shanks?" Callum asked when she was halfway through.

"Amazing. I can't believe I've been living here for eight months and never tried this place." Probably because it was dimly lit and all kinds of romantic, but hell, if Kasey could eat here with a girlfriend, why couldn't she? Maybe she'd bring Jenny, or even Stacey, the next time her cousin was in town.

She looked at Callum's bison steak. "How's yours?"

"Perfect. Everything about tonight is perfect."

Oh, man, this guy... He just had all the right words.

"Any more texts?" he asked, the lightness slipping from his voice.

"Just one yesterday." She'd almost started to believe the perp had forgotten about her. Apparently not.

Callum's eyes narrowed.

When she was well and truly full, she pushed back from the table. "I'm just going to the bathroom."

Even as she walked across the restaurant, she felt Kasey's eyes on her. Was it possible she'd known Callum was coming here? It seemed suspicious the woman had come tonight, while she and Callum were here, and looking as hot as she did.

It was when Fiona was coming out of the stall that the door opened and none other than Kasey herself walked in. Fiona bit back the groan. Instead of walking into a cubicle, Kasey stopped at the basin beside her and began to reapply some makeup. A pointless endeavor. Her face looked perfect.

"You and Callum seem cozy."

Fiona kept her voice even. "He's a great guy."

She grabbed some paper towels to dry her hands with, her gut telling her to get the hell away from this woman.

"I heard Callum accompanied you to your sister's wedding."

Fiona stilled, then turned, watching the other woman in the reflection. "He told you that?"

"Oh, yeah. Over breakfast yesterday. You didn't have a date to the wedding, right? And he felt sorry for you and didn't want you to go alone."

Her lips separated. Yesterday morning? That was when he'd canceled their breakfast.

Kasey swiped lipstick across her thick lips. "Do yourself a favor, Fiona. Don't get too attached. You'll just get hurt."

Her breath hitched. She turned to leave, but before stepping out, turned. No way was she just going to leave, letting the woman get the last word. "In the name of doing favors, maybe you could do yourself one and stop following Callum around like a lost puppy dog. It's a bit pathetic."

Even though her words had some bite in them, and she'd loved leaving an open-mouthed Kasey, she couldn't quite meet Callum's gaze when she sat. He'd had breakfast with Kasey yesterday instead of her. Then why take her out tonight?

She felt his eyes on her before he spoke. "Everything okay?"

"Yes." Shit. Her answer came too quickly and was too curt. She met his gaze for a fleeting second before pushing her seat back. "Should we go?"

"Fiona—"

Whatever he'd been about to say was cut off by the beep of her phone. She pulled it out and gasped, face paling.

"What?" Callum asked.

"It's the new alarm on my house." She clicked a few keys on her phone to bring up the camera. "Oh my God. Someone just used a *key* to enter my home!"

~

CALLUM FOUGHT for calm as he pressed his foot to the gas. It was damn hard. Someone had been in Fiona's house. Someone had a *fucking key* to her house. That meant the other night, there could have been someone in her house while she'd been alone. Unprotected.

Fuck.

He parked in the drive to find the police already out front. He climbed out of the car, moving straight over to Fiona's side. Neither of them had spoken a word the entire drive, Callum too damn angry and Fiona too worried.

Two officers stood on the lawn outside the house, talking.

"Fiona Lock?" one of them asked.

"That's me," she said quietly. Callum wrapped an arm around her waist.

"I'm Officer Hage, and this is Officer Pellet. We got here five minutes ago. The door was unlocked and open, but no one was inside."

She nodded. They both knew that already, because they'd watched the security footage on the way here. The second the alarm went off, the prick had run.

"They drop anything on the lawn on their way out?" Callum asked.

Hage shook his head. "Didn't find anything, although we'd like to watch that security footage."

Callum led them inside. Over the next few minutes, the officers watched the footage and wrote down some notes. "Who has a key to your home, Miss Lock?"

"No one," she said quickly, before shaking her head. "Well, no one that I know of except me and my cousin Stacey. But she lives in Twin Falls."

The officer nodded. "How long have you been living here?"

"Eight months."

"Did you change the locks when you moved in?"

She shook her head.

"We'll look into the previous owners. Anyone you can think of who would want access to your home?"

"No," she said quickly. "Although…"

She took a breath before telling them about the texts she'd been receiving.

"Okay, I'd recommend you get your locks changed as soon as possible," Officer Hage said, closing his book.

Callum was already planning on it.

When the officers left, he closed and locked the door, not that *that* would do much good. Then he turned to see Fiona's eyes darting around the space, like her mind was working overtime.

He stepped in front of her and touched her hip. "Talk to me, Fi. You okay?"

She stepped back, causing his hands to drop. His brows slashed together.

"Yeah, but I think I should stay somewhere else tonight. I might call Jenny and see if I can crash with her."

Her words fell like blows to the gut. Hell no. He didn't intend for the woman to leave his sight. "I'll stay over. You'll be safe with me."

He was better than any locked doors anyway.

He stepped closer, but again she moved back, shaking her head, her voice quiet. "I don't think that's a good idea."

What the hell was going on?

Suddenly, he remembered her face when she'd left the bathroom in the restaurant. He also recalled Kasey exiting the restroom after Fiona.

"What did she say to you?" he asked quietly. He wanted to lash out, but it wasn't Fiona he was upset with.

Her eyes flashed up. "Who?"

"Kasey. She followed you into the bathroom. What did she say?"

She straightened. "She told me about your breakfast yesterday."

He cursed under his breath. He should have told her about that. "She came over just as I was about to leave. Said her ex had come over in a rage and done some damage to her living room. She didn't feel safe waiting for the police on her own, so I waited with her and made her something to eat."

Fiona frowned. "Oh. She didn't tell me that. Just that you had breakfast."

"I did it out of duty, not anything romantic."

She seemed to think about that for a moment. "Why didn't you tell me?"

"I should have. But I know you've been burned before, and I didn't want to say anything to make you question us." He took a small step forward, testing the waters, relieved as hell when she didn't back away. "If it ever happens again, I promise, I'll tell you." He'd made a mistake that he wouldn't be repeating.

She gave a slow nod.

"You thought I'd blow you off for her?"

"It's not hard to believe. She's beautiful."

He could have laughed. "No...*you're* beautiful." She was the fucking definition of the word. At her silence, he raised a brow. "You don't believe me?"

She lifted a shoulder. "I think my self-confidence is a bit low since Freddie."

What he wouldn't do to be able to hit that guy just once. Although, once probably wouldn't be enough.

He took another small step forward, this time grabbing her hips. "Freddie is an asshole and didn't deserve you. I know how lucky I am to have you, and I sure as hell wouldn't do anything to risk losing you."

"Really?"

Did the woman truly not see what he saw? She blew every other woman out of the damn water. "Yeah, honey. Really."

Her chest rose and fell, then she reached for his head and tugged him down to her lips.

CHAPTER 18

The second Fiona's lips met Callum's, she forgot about Kasey and every word that was spoken in that bathroom. She forgot that someone had broken into her home, had a *key* to her home, and allowed herself to get lost in him.

She slid her fingers through his hair, his locks surprisingly soft. Her lips separated and when he slipped his tongue inside, she couldn't breathe. Her lungs refused to cooperate.

A moan sounded from somewhere deep inside her, and the second it reached air, Callum growled and lifted her. Immediately, she wrapped her legs around him, her dress scrunching around her waist. God, being pressed against him, having his warmth blanket her, it was like nothing else. Whenever this man held her, whenever the hard ridges of his body pressed against her soft ones, he felt strong and powerful and just a bit like home.

Their tongues melded together as they tasted each other. There was the sound of steps below her as he moved, the brush of air across her shoulders. She didn't have to open her eyes to know they were in her bedroom.

She reached for the base of her dress and tugged it over her body. All she wore under it was panties, no bra, and the second

134

Callum's gaze lowered to her chest, his eyes darkened to the shade of a starless night sky.

"You're so beautiful, Fi." She didn't have time to respond before his head lowered and he took one of her pebbled nipples between his lips.

It was instant fire. An immediate eruption of desire and need.

She latched onto his shoulders and threw her head back, feeling every flick of his tongue against her peak. Every swirl and suck. It was torture but it was also heaven. An intoxicating annihilation of the world around her. Her nails dug into his flesh. Too soon, it wasn't enough. She ground her hips against him.

"Callum…" Her whisper was more of a plea. A desperate call for more of him.

He released her nipple with a pop and lay her on the soft mattress. Then she watched as he unbuttoned his shirt, so devastatingly slowly that she wanted to squirm. Every inch of bronzed skin that came into view had more heat pooling between her thighs. He was the most beautiful man she'd ever laid eyes on. It was like someone had crafted him with so much attention to detail that no other person could compare.

When the shirt was gone, he moved on to his slacks, first undoing the button, then the zipper.

The beats of her heart stumbled over each other as her nerves grew to an almost violent vibration in her chest.

He toed off his shoes as he pushed his pants down, his eyes never leaving hers. Then he stood in front of her, in only briefs, looking so damn gorgeous it nearly scared her. He hadn't been in the plans she'd carefully crafted for herself when she'd moved here. In fact, he was about as far from them as possible. But here and now, he felt so right.

His knee hit the bed beside her, dipping the mattress. Then he lifted one of her heels and unbuckled it before dropping the shoe to the floor. He did the same to the other, and it, too, hit the carpet with a thud. Then he crawled up her body, every inch aligning them together. On his way, he pressed a kiss to her belly, then to a small oval birthmark on her rib cage.

"What's going on in that pretty head of yours?" he asked, once he hovered over her.

She cupped his cheek, debating whether to give the truth or a pretty lie. "I didn't see you coming."

"Am I a good surprise?"

The corners of her lips tugged up. "The best."

Then she kissed him again, a slow exploration, while lifting one leg and sliding it behind him, urging him closer. He lowered against her, only their underwear separating them. It made her want to arch. To push into him and feel more.

His hand lowered to her breast, and he cupped her, his thumb running over her nipple. She groaned and writhed, impatient. With two hands, she latched onto his wrist and tugged it down her body, guiding it inside her panties. At the first swipe of his finger down her slit, she bowed up. He did it again, and this time a strangled cry cut through the air.

His mouth lowered to her throat and sucked. "Those sounds destroy me, Fi."

Then, with a single finger, he entered her and began to thrust in a rhythm so deep and steady, her entire body moved with him. Her hips rose to meet his hand, her breasts bouncing at the action.

"Yes." She threw her head back and scrunched her eyes, lost in the pressure building inside her. Unable to move or see or breathe.

His thumb worked her clit, his finger continuing its torment while his mouth never left her neck. He nipped and sucked. Pleasure flashed through her from every place he touched.

Then, almost desperately, she slid her hand from his wrist to his briefs and inside to find his cock. It was long and hard, and it pulsed in her hold, making heat flare up her arm.

Callum stilled and growled, but never removed his finger

from inside her. She explored his velvety length, the muscles in his chest bunching and flexing against her breasts at her movements. On every slide of her palm, he grew and thickened. His groans became louder as she became more daring, learning what he liked. What made the muscles in his body harden and his breath shorten.

When a primal growl rippled from his chest, he lifted his head and crashed his lips to hers.

"Tell me you want this," he demanded between desperate kisses.

"I want this," she breathed. She couldn't think of a single thing she wanted more in this moment.

He rolled to the side and she let out a strangled cry that was supposed to be a complaint. He lifted his slacks and pulled out his wallet. When she saw the foil in his fingers, her pulse picked up. Then he pushed his briefs down and her breath caught.

He tore the foil with his teeth and rolled the condom down his length. His fingers went to her panties and, slowly, he slid them down her legs, his hands grazing her skin. Then he was between her thighs, his tip pressing at her entrance.

"Fiona." He said her name so softly, it almost didn't cross the distance. "Say you're mine."

She swallowed, touching a hand over his heart, entranced by the fleck of honey in his eyes. "I'm yours."

His exhale of relief cut through the quiet of the room, then slowly, he entered her. Her legs widened and her walls stretched to accommodate his size, the sensation so agonizingly perfect she could barely get a breath in.

When he was seated completely inside her, she didn't move. She couldn't. This man held her prisoner, caged to him and his body.

He lowered his head and touched his lips to hers in a delicate graze. She wrapped her legs around him and tugged him closer, making him sink a bit deeper.

His chest rumbled, and the second the sound hit air, he lifted his hips before pushing back inside her. She cried out, her heart hammering in her chest. He did it again, another thrust of his hips.

His mouth continued to work hers, and as he thrust, he reached down for her breast, his calloused thumb running over her hard peak. Every fear and insecurity fled from her head, ceasing to exist. Because in that moment, Callum carved himself into her heart, and she knew his imprint was there to stay.

~

CALLUM'S entire body burned for this woman. *That* was what she did to him—set him ablaze without a fucking speck of salvation in sight.

His thrusts were deep and even. Every time he returned to her felt like coming home. A home he'd found in her. A sanctuary. He continued to work her mouth, reveling in the way she tasted of wine and sweetness.

He caressed her tight bud with his thumb, her moans making his chest tighten and his gut twist and turn. He swiped a circle around her pebbled nipple, pushing her to the edge, wanting her as damn insane as he felt.

He knew the exact moment she grew close. Felt her walls tighten around him, heard the racing of her heart.

He feasted on her bottom lip before whispering, "Fall, baby."

It was like his words hit a switch. Her back arched and she screamed as she broke, the sounds like fucking gas on a fire, burning away the memory of everyone who'd come before her.

He kept thrusting as long as he could, but the pulsing of her walls around him was too much. He snapped. Broke so violently and into so many pieces, he couldn't hold back his growl.

He bucked against her until he had nothing left. Until every part of him was hers.

When he finally stilled, he didn't immediately part from her. Maybe he couldn't. He needed to keep her with him for as long as possible.

"That was...amazing," she breathed.

The laugh bubbled from his chest and spilled over. "*You're* amazing."

One more kiss, then he finally slid out of her and dropped to the side. He didn't cut the contact, though, instead pulling her against his chest, needing her as damn close as he could get her.

She yawned as her cheek rested on his heated flesh.

"Sleep," he whispered, pressing a kiss to the top of her head.

"Are you scared someone's going to come in?" she asked, her voice half-asleep.

"No. And you shouldn't be either. I'm better than any lock, and I can go from dead asleep to awake in seconds."

"Mm. You make me feel safe."

His arms tightened, those words making his heart jack-hammer in his chest. He wanted her to feel safe with him. Hell, he wanted the woman to need him like he needed her.

His arm remained tight around her as he waited for her breathing to even out. He wanted to remain exactly where he was and hold her all night, but he also had something to do.

Carefully, he slid out from under her. He spent a few minutes cleaning up in the bathroom and putting his briefs back on before returning to the living room with both their phones.

He rewatched the footage of the person entering her house half a dozen times. Pausing. Zooming in. Changing the angle. They were short for a man or tall for a woman, wearing a cap pulled low over their head. Damn, he wished he could see a face.

His phone rang from the coffee table, Liam's name on the screen. "Hey."

"Hey, brother. How is she?"

He'd notified his entire team of the intrusion. "She's okay. Asleep. Did you get the footage?"

"Yeah. Looks like a woman."

"My thoughts too. Either that, or a small-framed man. They look too tall to be her sister, but I still want to look into the woman a bit more. See if she's made any trips down here to Cradle Mountain this week."

Liam blew out a breath. "You really think this could be her?"

"Maybe. She doesn't like Fiona. I wouldn't put the messages past her, either. And if she found out Freddie kissed Fiona on their wedding night..." A woman so narcissistic could easily turn unstable.

"Got it. Need anything from me?"

"Not right now, but I might put someone on Amanda just to watch her."

"Good idea."

When he ended the call, Callum rose and checked that every door and window was still locked. Not that it mattered, it just added a bit of time if the person tried to get in. Time that would allow him to get up.

Back in the bedroom, he slid beneath the covers and tugged Fiona into his arms. But he didn't sleep right away. He hadn't lied to her—he could go from dead asleep to awake and ready for action in the space of a second, but he also didn't need a whole lot of sleep in general. So instead, he held her. Listened to her breathe, her heartbeat. And he let the silence of the night soothe the storm that raged inside him. Raged because someone was targeting his woman and had breached her home.

One thing he was certain of—whoever this person was, they wouldn't be getting whatever the hell they wanted from her. He'd make sure of it.

CHAPTER 19

*F*iona grabbed her bag from the library staff room. It was late—half an hour past the time she was supposed to finish work, and the library had closed a while ago. Damn Rick and his stupid to-do list. It had been a mile long and impossible to finish. In fact, it still wasn't completed. But she'd decided it never would be, even if she stayed until midnight. Let the man yell at her tomorrow, see if she cared. She wanted to get home to Callum.

Her phone vibrated as she moved around the library. She'd just flicked off the last light when she pulled it from her pocket.

Callum: Hey, I just got to your place, but you aren't home. Everything okay?

Crap. He was early. Only five minutes, but still. Callum had arranged for her locks to be changed the day after the person had broken into her house last week, but he'd still stayed over every night since. Not that she was complaining. Have big, beautiful Callum in her bed every night to keep her safe and warm? Heck yes!

Fiona: Sorry, I had to stay late and do some small jobs. Leaving now.

Small, ha! They weren't small.

Callum: Want me to come over there? It's dark.

She stepped outside and cringed. It *was* dark. She'd been inside so long, she hadn't even noticed. Not that the dark made her nervous. The last week had been fairly quiet. Only a couple of texts, and no home visits. God, what had her life become when she thought a quiet week was only receiving a couple of abusive texts.

She locked the library door, then texted him back as she walked across the lot to her car.

Fiona: I'm okay. Be home in five. X

She slid into her car just as her phone rang. Argh. Amanda. She hadn't spoken to her sister since the wedding.

Maybe she should let it go to voicemail...but then more calls would come. Probably a few texts.

Fine. One quick conversation. "Hey, Amanda."

"I need you to come to a family dinner this Saturday night. I have news to share."

Well, hello to you too. "I can't make it this weekend. I have a shift at the library on Saturday, and it's over a three-hour round trip—"

"So change the shift. And you're the one who decided to move to Cradle Mountain, so you should have expected to do some driving to come home. This is important."

Then Amanda hung up. Just...hung up.

Well, if the woman thought Fiona was going to rearrange her life so she could announce something, she was wrong. Especially after what she'd told their cousins at the wedding.

Fiona: No. I will not be coming this weekend. I have work. You have important information for me? Text it.

She stabbed the send button like it was a weapon. There. Sent. Done.

Heck, after everything, she shouldn't even be talking to the woman!

She was just about to start the car when she realized she didn't have the book she'd promised to bring home for Callum. Crap. Her gaze flicked to the building. She really *did* want him to read it. It was a good one.

Quickly, she grabbed her keys and phone, climbed out of her car, and jogged back to the building. The door unlocked with a click, and she stepped into the library, then ran to the staff room. She was in such a rush, she didn't see the person until she stood in the doorway. Her feet ground to a halt, cementing to the floor, and her breath caught in her throat.

Because there, standing in front of her locker, was a figure dressed in black clothes. It was dark, so they were little more than a shadowed outline, but that outline was clear as day.

Fear washed over her like acid.

Suddenly, the person turned. Fiona only had time to make out the balaclava over their face before the person grabbed something from the table.

It took her brain a second too long to realize it was a heavy-duty stapler.

They turned and hit her so hard, she dropped, her head hitting the doorframe on her way down.

Pain radiated through her skull. The pounding of steps through the back of the library barely registered.

With trembling fingers, she reached into her pocket and pulled out her phone, but her eyes were too blurry to make out the call function.

Nausea crawled up her throat and darkness hedged her vision. When her phone started to ring, she touched the screen, hoping she hit answer and not cancel.

"Fiona?"

His voice sounded distant to her ears. She tried to get out words but barely breathed them. "Callum...help."

~

CALLUM'S JAW clenched with worry as he sat behind the wheel of his car. Where the hell was she? She lived a couple of minutes from her work. If she'd left when she'd said she was, she should be home by now. He looked in the rearview mirror. It was too late and too dark. The woman knew she shouldn't be out alone at night, not with the texts and the perp entering her home.

He waited one more beat, then called her again. The phone rang three times before it was answered...then there was silence, bar some heavy breaths.

His gut tightened. "Fiona?"

One more heavy breath, then two words. "Callum...help."

Callum started the car and slammed his foot on the gas, everything inside him tightening at the pained fear in her voice. "Fiona? Are you okay?"

When there were no more words from her, his muscles bunched, and he forced the car to move faster. "Fi, honey, talk to me!"

Silence. It was so fucking loud, he could have drowned in it. As much as he wanted to stay on the line, he needed to call his team for backup.

"I'm gonna be there in two minutes, honey. Hang on."

He hung up and called Liam.

"Hey, Cal, what's—"

"Fiona's in trouble. She's at the library. I'm driving there now."

There was a rustle of movement over the line. "What kind of trouble?"

"I don't know. She was finishing work so I'm hoping she's still at the library. She may have lost consciousness. She said two words to me, then nothing." Fuck, saying that out loud stabbed at him like a dagger to his flesh.

"I'll call paramedics and alert the team. We'll check the routes between the library and her place too."

"Thank you."

Callum made it to the library in half the time it normally

would have taken him. Her car sat out front, dark and closed. He could only hope like hell that meant she was inside.

He grabbed his Glock and entered the building, scanning the dark library, everything clear to his enhanced vision.

When he saw her on the floor of the office, his heart crashed in his chest. Fiona lay on her side, still.

He rushed over to her and kneeled, gut tightening at the blood that covered her hair and seeped into the carpet beneath her head. A slew of curses flew from his mouth. "Fiona? Wake up, honey."

She didn't, and the only thing that kept him calm was that he could hear the beating of her heart in her chest.

He touched her cheek and lowered his head to her ear. "Fiona, can you hear me?"

A soft groan sounded, then her eyes fluttered. Air whooshed into his chest.

"Callum?"

"Yeah, honey, it's me."

Her eyes scrunched, and she touched her head, letting out another low moan. "My head. Someone hit me."

Her words were like gas on the fire of his rage, but he forced gentleness into his voice as he spoke. "I'm gonna help you up, okay?"

She sucked in a long breath and nodded slowly. "Okay."

Carefully, he took hold of her upper arms and pulled her into a sitting position. Her brows slashed together in pain, and that made the fury barreling through his chest intensify.

"I forgot your book," she breathed, once she was sitting. "I came back in to grab it, but someone was in front of my locker. They…they grabbed my stapler and hit me in the head, then I hit the doorframe when I fell."

So, she'd had two knocks to the skull.

"Did you recognize them?" Callum asked through gritted teeth.

She swallowed and shook her head, then cringed at the movement. "No. They were wearing a balaclava over their face, and it was dark, so I couldn't make out their eyes. They were the same height and frame as me."

His chest seized. Just like the person who'd entered her house. And now they were breaking into the goddamn library to go through her shit?

Engines sounded from the street, then footsteps. Seconds later, Liam stepped into the room, closely followed by the ambulance team.

Callum remained close to Fiona's side the entire time the paramedics ensured she was stable enough to move, then as they treated her in the ambulance while the police spoke to her. In that time, Jason and Tyler arrived. It wasn't until the paramedics were almost done, and the guys were talking at the front of the library, that he squeezed Fiona's arm.

"Is it okay if I go talk to them?"

He didn't want to leave her but needed to talk to his team.

"Yes, go."

"I'll stay close." He gave her one more squeeze before moving to the guys. "What did you find?"

"The back door was unlocked and open," Liam said quietly.

Callum flinched. "Unlocked?"

Jason nodded. "So, either the door was unlocked when she left, or whoever it was had a key."

What the fuck?

When a car drove into the lot, all four of them watched Rick, the library manager, climb out. His eyes shot around the area before landing on Fiona, then he rushed across the lot and stopped far too close to her as she climbed out of the ambulance.

"Fiona, are you okay?" he asked. "I received calls from locals saying something was happening at my library!"

"I'm fine, Rick."

When he got another step closer and touched her arm, Callum was moving before he could stop himself.

"Rick, I don't need your help."

"Fiona—"

"That was her telling you to take your hand off her," Callum cut in, before Fiona could respond.

Rick looked up, his eyes narrowing, hand dropping. He cleared his throat as he stepped back. "What happened?"

"I left but ran back in to grab a book," Fiona said, leaning into his side. His arm went around her. "Someone was in the staff room."

Rick pulled back in shock. "Who?"

"We don't know," Liam said as he drew closer. "You don't seem to have any cameras here."

"Of course not. We've never needed them."

"Well, you do now," Callum said through gritted teeth. "Who has a key to the back door?"

"The back door?" Rick's gaze flashed to the building. "No one. We keep a copy in my office."

Callum frowned. "So no one takes one home?"

"No." It was Fiona who answered. "Staff only have a front-door key. Someone came in through the back?"

He softened his tone. "Yeah. So either it was left unlocked or they had a key."

Rick shook his head. "We never leave it unlocked."

"Then someone has a key." Just like someone had a key to Fiona's damn house. "You need to change the locks and put cameras up. Do everything you can to ensure the safety of your staff."

Rick shot a look at Fiona, then to the library before returning to him. It took the man a moment to give a jerky nod.

Callum turned to Fiona. "How are you feeling?"

"Not too bad. It's just a concussion and some cuts and bruises.

The paramedics wanted to take me to the hospital as a precaution, but I just want to go home."

His jaw clicked. "You sure you don't want to go in?"

She shook her head.

He tightened his arm around her. "Let's get you home."

CHAPTER 20

*C*allum headed into his bedroom, hot coffee in his hand, but he stopped in the doorway at the sight of Fiona in the connected bathroom in front of the mirror.

Fuck, she was beautiful. And after last night, he wanted to hold her tighter and closer. It had scared the hell out of him, knowing she was in danger but unable to prevent it and protect her. The feeling of helplessness was foreign and damn near destroying him.

He needed to figure out who the hell was targeting her and why. He didn't think they were trying to hurt her…yet. It seemed they only hit her last night because she'd caught them red-handed. But the person had been going through her locker, and before that, they'd entered her house. Why? What were they looking for?

She'd just finished applying cream to her face when he stepped behind her and set the coffee onto the counter.

She smiled and leaned against him. "Hey."

"Hey, beautiful." He kissed her cheek, hands going to her hips. "How's your head feeling?"

"Okay. It's just like a dull headache."

149

It shouldn't even be that much. She shouldn't be in any pain at all. "I've got pain meds in the cabinet."

He was about to move away when she grabbed his hands and tugged them around her waist. "Wait, you haven't given me a good-morning kiss on the lips."

He grinned. "You're right."

She turned in his arms and pressed her palms to his chest. "A woman needs her morning kiss to get her day started right."

He leaned down, hovering his lips over hers. His voice quieted. "Big oversight on my part."

"Huge," she breathed.

Then he kissed her, swiping his lips across hers and letting the softness that was Fiona surround him. Her fingers slid through his hair, and when her tongue nudged at his mouth, he opened, tasting his beautiful woman.

His hand skirted down her side, tugging her closer. She hummed, and that sound ricocheted throughout his chest. When she began to push his shirt up, he lifted his head.

He chuckled at her groan. "You have a concussion, Fi."

"I can still kiss you."

If he kept kissing her, it would turn into more than that. "You're spending the day on the couch. Bedrest."

The change was instant. She shook her head. "I have to go to work."

Hell no. "Someone can cover for you."

"No, Callum, it was a mild concussion. I've got a little headache, that's it. I'm fine."

"No."

"Yes."

He bit back a growl.

She stroked a hand over his cheek. "Callum, I don't want to just sit at home all day and think about the fact I'm a target. It will drive me crazy."

"Better crazy at home than passing out halfway through your shift."

She gave him a pointed look. "I'm only on for four hours in the afternoon."

His jaw clicked. "Fine. But no working overtime, and I'm trailing you to work and home, so no driving on your own. And if you're in pain, you call me."

"Done."

He didn't like it. But he also didn't want to get into a fight with the woman after everything she'd been through last night. "And no more late shifts."

"Well, if you're there, we could find other reasons to be in the library after hours."

This time he *did* growl. "You're killing me, woman." He dipped his head and kissed her again. His hand was just skirting up her side when her phone rang. "Ignore it."

She laughed and turned, reaching for her cell on the counter. His chest rumbled with sounds of his disapproval as he continued to kiss the back of her neck.

She groaned. "It's Amanda again."

"Definitely ignore it," he said between strings of kisses to her shoulder.

She did, her lips returning to his. But the second her phone stopped ringing, it started up again.

She groaned and tugged her lips away once more, this time answering the call. "Amanda—"

"Fiona, it's me, Freddie."

Callum's hand stilled on her bare waist and his head shot up. What the fuck was that asshole doing calling her?

Fiona straightened, her muscles going tight beneath his touch. "I'm hanging up, Freddie."

"Wait, please! I just want to talk to you."

"About what?"

"Us."

It took every ounce of Callum's self-restraint to not grab the phone and tell the fucker to hang up.

Fiona blew out an exasperated breath. "There is no *us*, Freddie. You cheated on me, then married my sister. I blocked your number because I do *not* want contact from you. Don't call me again, and certainly not from her phone."

She hung up and turned her phone off.

"Has he called since the wedding?" Callum asked, keeping his voice as calm as he could. It was damn hard.

"Yes. That's why I blocked him, and probably why he called from Amanda's phone."

That little shit.

She blew out a breath. "Well, at least now I won't need to tell Amanda about anything. She'll see it on her call history."

He didn't like that idea or the abuse it would probably bring. "I'm sorry, honey."

"She said there's a family dinner this weekend. I said I wasn't going."

"Well, if you do decide to go, I'll be by your side."

The smile returned to Fiona's mouth. "I'm not, but if I was, you sure as heck would be. Or you'd be dragged along kicking and screaming. I've decided you're the only way I can survive family events with Amanda."

"Wherever you are, I'll be, Fi."

～

"Jenny, you don't need to hover."

Her friend blew out a breath before following her down the library aisle. She'd been no more than two feet away the entire shift.

"I'm sorry, but I'm worried. Are you sure it's okay that you're at work today?"

Fiona grabbed a book from the cart. She'd planned to tell her friend everything when she got to work, but by the time she arrived, Rick had already told everyone…big mouth.

"I'm fine. I've taken my pain meds, my head feels okay, and I've almost survived my four-hour shift." Ten minutes and counting until Callum picked her up. If she was honest, he and Jenny were right. She should have stayed home, but no way would she be admitting that after she'd pushed to come to work.

Jenny lifted a book from the trolley. "Well, good. I'm glad you're okay. And honestly, I'm surprised you chose to come in and not spend the day with Mr. Sexy-pants."

She laughed. "Sexy-pants?"

"Sexy pants, sexy arms, sexy face you want to kiss until the sun goes down. I could keep going?"

"No thanks, I get the gist." She pushed her trolley down the aisle. "And I didn't want to stay home and stew about everything, so here I am."

A shudder she couldn't stop raced up her spine at the memory of the previous night.

"I wonder what the person wanted," Jenny said quietly.

Wasn't that the golden question? She wasn't poor, but she didn't have money or valuables worth stealing. Even if she did, she certainly wouldn't keep them at work.

"And then there's Freddie," Jenny continued. "It's so strange that he's still trying to contact you when he's married to your sister, and you clearly want nothing to do with him."

"Don't even get me started on that guy. I've been so clear with him. I don't understand why he's trying, either." She stopped and slotted a book onto a shelf. "But even if I did still have interest, he married my sister. I just…I can't believe what a scumbag he's turned into."

Or maybe he was always like that, and she'd just been blind to it because she'd been with him for so long.

"You must just have that effect on men."

She snorted. "Yeah, right. I'm in so much disbelief that Callum likes me, I wake up *expecting* him to tell me it's over. That he's going to run away with his hot neighbor, Kasey."

Okay, maybe she wasn't expecting him to say it in those words. He'd probably go with a gentler breakup. *It's not you, it's me* kind of thing.

Jenny gave her a pointed look. "Fiona, you're beautiful. Don't doubt what you bring to the table with that man."

She laughed as she stopped again, slotting another book into place. "I bring a knowledge of books and book categorization."

"You're a beautiful, intelligent, kind woman who has a sense of humor to boot. You bring all of that."

"Uh, I was awful to Callum for months before the wedding weekend."

Jenny lifted a shoulder like it was nothing. "You had trust issues. It's normal after being cheated on. I can't believe you never knocked your sister and that prick on their asses for what they did."

"Not doing exactly that will be a lifelong regret of mine."

Rick moved past their aisle, pausing when he saw them. He opened his mouth, looking like he was about to say something about them standing there talking, but then he snapped it shut again and moved away.

"What was that about?" Jenny whispered.

"He's in an I-feel-sorry-for-you-after-last-night mood. He also knows who I'm dating and what he'll do if he's not nice."

Jenny sighed. "You're so lucky to have him."

"Well, there's still one Blue Halo man who's unattached, if you're interested?"

Her brows pulled together like she was considering it. "Is he hot?"

"Aren't they all?"

"You're right. And tempting, but I'm not dating at the moment."

"Why not?"

She lifted a shoulder. "I don't know, because that would involve talking to a man without freezing up."

Fiona opened her mouth to respond but stopped—because all her attention went to the main door as Freddie stepped inside.

What. The. Hell? She had to blink to make sure she was actually seeing what she thought she was seeing.

"Oh my God," she whispered.

"What?" Jenny glanced over her shoulder, then back to Fiona. "Who's that?"

"Freddie."

Freddie met her gaze and walked straight toward her.

"What are you doing here?" Fiona growled before he'd even stopped.

"I came to see you. I don't have your address, so I was counting on you being at work."

Jesus Christ. She grabbed his arm and tugged him toward the door.

"Fiona—" Jenny hissed.

"I'll be back in a sec."

Rick wouldn't like it, but hell, she was basically done for the day. She waited until they were outside, standing several feet to the side of the library door, before turning to face the guy. "I don't know what the hell made you think driving an hour and a half to see me today was a good idea, but it wasn't. Go home!"

His jaw clicked. "I haven't been able to stop thinking about you since the wedding."

"Since *your* wedding to my *sister,* you mean? God, have you lost your mind? This is so inappropriate."

"I know." He scrubbed a hand through his hair. "But I felt something for you at the wedding. You were giving me mixed signals."

She gaped at the man. "Mixed signals? Are you serious? Freddie, I can only say this clearly so many times. I am *not* interested in you anymore. I am happily dating someone else, and you are *married* to my *sister!*"

God, why did she have to keep repeating that to this guy?

Freddie stepped closer and touched her arm. "Fiona—"

"Hey!"

They both looked up to see Callum walking toward them from the lot. Well, less walking and more storming like he was on a damn mission. She also saw Jenny step outside, arms around her waist, watching with a worried look on her face.

Freddie cursed when he saw Callum. "What the fuck are you doing here?"

"What am *I* doing here?" Callum stopped close and tugged Fiona behind him. "I'm the boyfriend, Freddie. What are *you* doing here?"

"That's none of your damn business." He looked back to her. "I'm staying at the Tamarack Lodge in Ketchum tonight. Please come talk to me."

Her insides rolled. "I won't. You need to go home to your wife."

Callum stepped closer to him. "Go. Away."

"Fuck you!" Then Freddie pushed Callum...or attempted to. Callum moved so quickly, his actions were a blur, grabbing the arm that had shoved him and spinning Freddie around. "Get the fuck off me, asshole!"

Callum didn't. In fact, he shoved Freddie against the wall, lowered his head, and quieted his voice. "You will leave Cradle Mountain, and you will stay the hell away from Fiona. If I see you touch her again or even speak to her, I will break your fucking hand."

When Callum didn't immediately release him, she stepped forward and touched his arm. "Callum. It's okay."

One more beat, and he finally released her ex. Freddie pulled away, straightening his clothes and looking mad as hell at Callum before storming off.

Jenny slipped back inside as Callum turned to Fiona, hands going to her waist. "You okay?"

"You did it again."

He frowned. "What?"

"I didn't need saving just now, Callum."

His gaze shifted between her eyes before softening. "You're right. I'm sorry. I should have let you handle that."

She tilted her head. "Really? No speech about being a protector and how you'll always step in if you can?"

"Nope. I mean, I *will* step in if I think you need it. I can't help my instincts when it comes to you. But I'll try to wait to see if you kick him in the balls first."

Her lips twitched. She wasn't sure she believed him, but she appreciated him saying that. "Thank you."

"Now...are you okay?"

She sucked in a long, deep breath. "Yeah. I just don't know why he won't leave me alone. We're done but he keeps coming back. And he said I was giving him mixed signals at the wedding when I wasn't."

Callum growled. "The guy's delusional. Did he touch you?"

"Not really, just the touch on my arm that you saw." When his features hardened, she cupped his cheek. "But I'm okay. And I would have kneed him in the balls if he did anything else. Although...it was kinda nice to watch him squirm in your hold."

"So my stepping in wasn't all bad?"

"No. It wasn't all bad."

He lowered his head, his mouth hovering over hers. "Good. Because I like being your growly protector."

CHAPTER 21

"*Y*ou sure you don't need backup?"

Callum's mouth stretched into a smile at Liam's words. He was already almost at Tamarack Lodge to make sure Freddie was getting the hell out of town. So no, he didn't think he needed "backup" to talk to the guy.

"He's an accountant. I think I can handle myself."

"Yeah, I was thinking more backup to make sure you didn't do anything stupid."

That was probably a fair call. If he turned up and the guy hadn't packed his bag, Callum might just lose his shit. Not because he was scared Fiona might actually play into his hands, but because the asshole was harassing her.

"I can control myself. I'm also going to ask if he knows anything about those texts."

Liam scoffed. "You think he'll talk to you regardless? You almost broke his arm yesterday."

"Exactly *why* he'll talk to me."

"Fine, but no knocking the guy out or doing anything that warrants me bailing your ass out of jail."

Callum bit back a laugh as he turned onto Walnut Avenue. "You have so little faith in my self-restraint?"

"When it comes to Fiona? Yes."

Fine, he'd give his friend that. "No one's getting knocked out or sent to jail. Hell, I'm hoping he's already checked out and gone home." Fat damn chance, but still. He pulled into the parking lot of the lodge. "Thanks for checking in. Now get back to work."

"If I don't hear from you in an hour, I'm coming to find you."

He almost laughed. He could do a hell of a lot in an hour, and his friend knew it. "Deal."

He ended the call as he turned off the engine. He hadn't told Fiona he was paying Freddie this visit. He would…once it was done. It would be her lunch break soon—maybe he'd pop into the library on the way home, bring her a Reuben sandwich from Bigwood Bread as a way of softening her up so she forgave him.

As he climbed from the car, his gaze shifted around the lot. Unfortunately, the hotel didn't have a high-tech booking system he could hack to find the guy's room number, so instead, he'd have to go the old-fashioned route.

He stepped inside the small reception area to find a wooden counter to the right, and behind it, a middle-aged blond woman who wore black-rimmed glasses.

He plastered a smile onto his face before moving to the desk.

Her eyes widened, and red tinged her cheeks. "Hi, my name's Vanessa. Are you checking in today?"

"Hi, Vanessa, I'm Callum." He stopped at the desk, keeping his body language relaxed. "I'm actually here to see an old friend who's in from out of town. We organized to meet in an hour, but I wanted to surprise him and come by early. He told me his room number, but I can't recall it now and his phone is switched off. I was wondering if you could help me out and tell me which room he's in?"

She swallowed, her mouth opening and closing before she

responded. "I'm sorry, I'm not really supposed to give out guest information. I could call him and ask?"

"That would be great. Freddie Bant."

The woman turned to the screen and began typing. When she lifted the phone, Callum bit back a curse. The asshole was still here. A part of him had been hoping he'd listened to Callum's warning and left.

He watched closely as she typed in the numbers, assuming the last few digits would be the room number. He filed those numbers in his head, then listened as the phone rang. If Freddie picked up and found out Callum was here, he'd come out. If he didn't, well…Callum knew what room he was in now, and he'd already looked over a blueprint of the hotel from the local county clerk's online archives. He knew where each room was located.

Vanessa cringed when she hung up. "Sorry. He's not answering."

Callum straightened, tapping the desk. "That's okay, I'll wait it out. I appreciate your help."

He left the reception area, but instead of walking back to his car, he found a section of fence that led to the courtyard. From his study of the lodge, he knew there was a large grassy common area, and the rooms were built around it. Now that he knew Freddie's room number, he knew the guy was on a ground-floor suite. He may not be there right now, but that didn't mean Callum couldn't wait for him in his room.

He shot one quick glance around before running a few steps and jumping the fence. His feet hit the ground silently on the other side. Orange chairs and pots of flowers were scattered around the space. The second door should be Freddie's room. It was a wooden-framed glass door with a curtain pulled shut over the glass.

He was about to knock when he heard sounds from inside. Deep moans followed by the compression of mattress springs. It sounded like two people making out.

He shifted to carefully glance inside the window beside the door, finding that glass wasn't fully covered.

He frowned at the sight of Freddie leaning a woman back onto the bed. Her head was turned the other way so he couldn't see her face.

Really? The guy came all this way to convince Fiona they were meant to be together and he was already fucking another woman?

Callum was moments from walking away—until the woman's top rode up her waist. His gaze caught on the mark on her rib cage. A small oval birthmark. His muscles tensed. Then he noticed her sweater. It was one he'd seen before.

He stumbled back a step, his skin turning cold. It couldn't be. His eyes had to be fucking deceiving him.

The woman's fingers swept through Freddie's hair while her legs wrapped around his waist, and she ground against him. Freddie kissed her neck, and she tipped her head back and to the side.

This time, his skin didn't go cold—it iced over completely. Something so sickening churned in his gut that it was an effort to not double over.

Because even though the woman's eyes were closed, he could see it was Fiona.

FIONA LOOKED at her phone for what had to be the tenth time that afternoon. She'd texted Callum earlier, and there was still no response. Only two hours had passed, and her text had only suggested what she thought they should have for dinner...it wasn't like she was asking the man to give her a kidney. But still, he usually responded within minutes. Hell, most of the time he texted back immediately.

She nibbled her bottom lip, gaze shifting to the door. He'd be here in an hour to tail her home from work. She should stop being so needy. He was probably busy running his company.

Her phone vibrated and her heart sped up. But when she looked down at her phone, it wasn't the message she'd been waiting for.

Unknown number: You're a whore, and soon, he'll grow sick of you. Then you'll have no one.

Her mouth was opening and closing when a voice sounded from behind her.

"Fiona!"

She jumped, the phone slipping from her fingers and hitting the desk with a thud.

Shit. Rick. *Again*. The man had been on a rampage today. Everything she did was the wrong thing. He'd even criticized the way she interacted with patrons. Told her she took too long on her lunch break and that her dress was too short. Of course she'd defended herself, but that had just led to extensive arguments. It was exhausting.

"I just read one text," she said quickly, pushing the phone into her pocket.

He huffed as he stopped beside her. "I've been trying to give you some leeway because of the incident here the other night."

He had?

"But," he continued before she could get a word in, "if you keep getting distracted by your phone, neglecting your work, and making mistakes, I will have to take further action."

Hang on a second... "Rick, I don't make mistakes, I *never* neglect my work, and what exactly do you mean, further action?"

"You know what I mean, Fiona."

So he wasn't just being an ass now, he was threatening her employment? She crossed her arms and lowered her voice so her words reached only him. "Why do you do this, Rick? This last month, you've had moments where you've been downright awful to me."

His eyes narrowed. "Don't pretend you don't know why."

"What are you talking about?"

"You know exactly what happened. Then you came into work pretending it didn't. That would piss off most men."

Okay, now she was really confused. "I really don't know what you're talking about."

Anger darkened his features. "You're actually playing that card?"

"What card?"

The words were lost in the air because Rick was already turning and walking away from her.

What the hell was that? Good God, maybe she needed to see if there was a librarian position at The Community Library in Ketchum, because working under Rick just wasn't good for anyone.

She blew out a breath and turned back to the computer screen, but the next hour was the slowest of her life. The library was dead, Rick basically ignored her, and Callum never responded.

"Hey, are you all right?"

She looked up at Patricia Edwards, an older librarian. She was nice, but part of that cliquey group of women who'd never welcomed Fiona into their fold. "I'm fine. Almost finished."

Patricia patted her arm. "Good."

Not caring what Rick said, she lifted her phone to send a quick text to Stacey. She needed someone to lift her mood.

Fiona: Tell me something funny. I need to laugh.

The phone dinged almost immediately.

Stacey: Mom got a new alarm system for her house for added security, but then stuck the code up next to the system in case she "forgot." I tried explaining that it wasn't a good idea, but the advice fell on deaf ears. The code is still there for whoever feels like breaking in. That's the level of uselessness I come from.

Fiona laughed out loud. That sounded like Aunt Alison. The

woman was great but didn't always think her plans through. She was still smiling when the door opened, and Liam stepped in.

She frowned as he approached the desk, pushing her phone into her pocket. "Hey. What are you doing here?"

"Callum's going to meet you at your place."

Her frown deepened. Liam's words weren't curt or unfriendly, but they lacked the usual warmth. Plus, why was Callum meeting her at her place? And why hadn't *he* told her?

"Is everything okay?" she asked.

"That's between you and him, Fiona."

She flinched. Not at his words, but at what he *didn't* say. He didn't confirm Callum was okay. He didn't put any warmth into his voice. Hell, he barely met her gaze.

Something was wrong. Had something happened to Callum? Had he changed his mind about them?

Her chest began to rise and fall in quick succession, and she realized she was panicking...because she was falling for Callum. Had let herself fall hard. Given her heart permission even when the rest of her had rebelled against it from the beginning, warned her that it wasn't smart, and she'd be hurt again.

Scenarios raced through her head. Of him telling her it was over. Of her having to live in a town with the man but not be with him.

She was silently spiraling when Liam touched her hand. His eyes softened just a fraction, but enough to pull her back to the present. "Hey. Talk to him."

She gave a quick, jerky nod.

The entire drive home, she had to force herself to breathe. To keep calm. Maybe she was wrong. Maybe the reason Callum hadn't texted back and wanted to speak to her at home wasn't because he was breaking up with her. Maybe she was over-thinking everything.

God, she hoped so.

When she got to her place and saw Callum wasn't there yet,

she wasn't sure if she was relieved or not. She stepped inside, but Liam didn't follow. Instead, he stopped at the door. "I'll wait out here."

Yep, there were those nerves in her belly again. "Okay."

The second she closed the door, she moved to the bedroom and changed into leggings and an oversized sweater. It would be fine. If Callum decided he didn't want to be with her, then she'd be okay. She'd pulled herself out of the deep ditch that was Freddie's betrayal. If she fell into another ditch, she'd pull herself out of that one too.

But this is Callum, a voice whispered. Things were different with him.

Maybe he needed to break it to her that *he'd* cheated.

Her heart skidded in her chest, and she had to remind herself to breathe. To not break down and hyperventilate.

Her phone vibrated, and she pulled it out to see a message from Jenny.

Jenny: So, Rick was on a new level of assholery this morning, wasn't he?

Fiona: Oh, and it continued into the afternoon.

She nibbled her bottom lip before sending her next text.

Fiona: I think Callum's going to end things.

Immediately, the three dots popped up.

Jenny: No way. Why do you think that?

She perched on the edge of her bed, heart pounding in her chest.

Fiona: He didn't respond to my text, then Liam said Callum needs to "talk" to me about something. Now I'm just...waiting.

And man, waiting was the worst part. Her phone rang.

"Am I being crazy?" Fiona asked before Jenny could say anything.

"Not crazy, just reactive. I've seen the way Callum looks at you. He's not just going to end things."

She clenched the edge of the bed, her nails biting into the

mattress. "It's so unlike him to not reply to my texts, and Liam was acting so strange."

"Maybe Callum's just had a long day at work. Maybe something went wrong, and Liam couldn't tell you what it was."

"Maybe..." But her gut told her it wasn't that. That this was more personal.

"Fi, don't stress yourself out. Talk to him."

"You're right." But she was still a nervous wreck.

"Ask him what's going on and take things from there."

Ask him what was going on...without freaking out...she could do that. She could be calm. "Okay. Yes. That sounds smart."

"Of course it does. Let me know how it goes."

"I will. Thank you." The sound of the door opening sent her pulse racing at a sporadic beat, and any thoughts of calm dissipated. "I think he's here. I've got to go."

"Good luck."

She hung up, expecting Callum to walk into the bedroom after hearing her voice. Instead, the sound of his steps moving farther away echoed in the other room.

Another big red flashing sign that things weren't normal.

Chill, Fiona. Ask him what's going on.

Once she was kind of sure she could be calm, she headed out of the room to find him standing by the front window in the living room, hands in his pockets. He was still. So still, he almost looked like a perfectly created statue.

Things weren't fine...

"Callum," she started slowly, "what's going on?"

Two seconds of silence passed before he turned, and when he did, her stomach dropped. There was no warmth on his face. There wasn't anger, either. He just looked...closed off.

"Is there something you'd like to tell me, Fiona?"

Her brows rose, confusion swirling inside her. "Uh, not that I can think of."

Disappointment flashed over his face. Only for a second, then it was gone, replaced by that same stony expression. He almost looked like a stranger.

"I saw you today."

Okay, now she was really confused. "Saw me where?"

At work? Eating her peanut butter and jelly sandwich for lunch under the tree? Getting yelled at by Rick?

When he didn't answer, she moved toward him—but he stepped back. That step was like a blow straight to her abdomen. It hit so deep she almost drew back herself.

Her feet stopped. She lowered her voice, trying to shove down the emotion that was bubbling to the surface. "Tell me, Callum. Where did you see me?"

"In Ketchum, at Tamarack Lodge."

Where Freddie was staying? She shook her head. "No, that's not possible. I was at work all day."

He cocked his head, his eyes squinting as if trying to work her out. "You sound like you're telling the truth, but you can't be, because I saw the birthmark on your side. I saw your red sweater. I saw *you*."

Her heart thrashed in her chest...at the distance between them, the thickness of the air, the words coming out of his mouth. "It wasn't me. Ask *anyone* at the library. I was there all day." When he just kept looking at her with a confused expression on his face, she finally plucked up the courage to ask. "What exactly did you see me doing?"

His jaw clenched. "You were in Freddie's arms, kissing the guy."

CHAPTER 22

*F*iona flinched, and the action had Callum's fingers twitching to touch her. Make sure she was okay.

She stumbled back a step. "I didn't...I wasn't there!"

The truth. The woman looked and sounded like she was speaking the truth. But how the hell was that possible? He'd seen her in that room. "You didn't go to Tamarack Lodge today?"

"No. I've never been there in my life!"

Before he could turn those words over in his head, she spun around, her steps quick. Callum followed into her bedroom, where she was already at her dresser, one drawer open. At first, she just shuffled her clothes around, but with each passing second, her actions became more erratic.

"It's here. It has to be here." Her breath shortened, then sweaters began to fly across the room as she threw them out one by one.

"Fiona—"

"*No*, Callum. It's here. I'm going to show you my red sweater and prove that you didn't see what you think you saw." She slammed the drawer closed, then opened the next one. "Maybe I put it somewhere else. Maybe I was tired and put it with my T-shirts."

She was still speaking the truth. What the fuck was going on?

This time, shirts flew behind her, landing on top of the sweaters littering the floor.

When Fiona cursed, emotion clogging her voice, he stepped behind her and wrapped his fingers around her wrists, halting her movements.

"Stop." The single word was soft but firm. He held her securely enough so that she wasn't able to move, but not so tightly he'd bruise her.

For a moment, she did. Clothes stopped flying, her arms stilled. That only lasted for a second, then she shook her head. "No! I need to find it."

She tugged and pulled at his hold.

He swore. "Fiona, stop."

"You said she was wearing *my* sweater. But she couldn't have been. There can't be a person walking around out there who looks like me and dresses in the exact same clothes!"

She pulled and twisted so hard, he cursed again and released her. But instead of returning to her drawer, she moved to the closet and started pulling clothes from the hangers.

He took a small step forward. "Fiona. Talk to me. If that wasn't you today, do you know who it was?" She had to know something, because the two women were identical.

She kept pushing through clothes, each outfit shoved with more violence. "Things have been happening. Things that don't make sense. And I've been pushing everything aside and ignoring it because there's already too much going on, and I haven't been able to convince myself any of this is possible."

Her hands shook violently, and her chest rose and fell so aggressively he was scared she'd hyperventilate.

"Freddie said I was giving him mixed signals at the wedding, but I *wasn't*. Then today, Rick said something happened between us, but literally *nothing* has happened with him. And at the wedding, I saw..." Her breath caught, her knees shook, and she grabbed a hanging dress for support.

He couldn't keep his distance any longer. He shot forward, wrapped his fingers around her hips, and touched his lips to her ear. "Stop and breathe."

"I-I can't. I don't understand what's happening!"

Her words and the guttural pain in them sliced at him. With gentle pressure on her hips, he turned and lifted her. Immediately, she wrapped her legs around his waist and tucked her head into the crook of his neck.

Some of the anguish left his chest, and he carried her to the bed. The second he was sitting, he cupped her cheek. "What did you see at the wedding?"

She swallowed, her gaze moving between his eyes like she was looking for...something. Answers?

"I saw...*me*," she said quietly.

He frowned, something heavy and uncomfortable settling in his gut. "What do you mean, you saw you?"

"I saw a woman who looked *exactly* like me on the other side of the dance floor. She wore the same dress. The same heels. Even her hair was done the same way. I was in so much shock, that I followed her."

"That's when you got locked outside."

She nodded, her gaze lowering to his shirt as she smoothed out a wrinkle in the material. "When I got locked out, I convinced myself I couldn't have seen what I thought I saw. Because it just wasn't possible."

"It was," he said quietly. "Because I saw her today too."

Her breath stuttered. "And she really looked like me?"

"Exactly like you."

A shudder raced down her spine, and he tugged her closer.

She shook her head. "I don't understand. How could a random person look like me, down to the birthmark?"

"A relative, perhaps?" It was weak, but right now, it was the best he could think of.

"I don't really look like any of my family."

He shifted some hair behind her ear. "Have your parents ever mentioned any relatives you haven't met?"

"No. But I could ask. I could go to that dinner."

"That's a good idea." And even better that he'd be there and would be able to tell if they were lying.

"Freddie will probably be there."

His muscles bunched. "We'll explain to him it wasn't you in his room."

"And we'll have to tell Amanda what he's been doing. That will be fun," she said sarcastically. Her gaze moved to the clothes on the floor. "Someone's pretending to be me, Callum. Someone who has a key to my home. Someone who knows me well enough to know I have a birthmark."

Her breathing increased too quickly again, and he touched his forehead to hers. "Hey. We'll work this out. Together."

She closed her eyes, cupping his head.

He kissed her, and that kiss went a long way in calming the storm of emotions inside him at thinking he'd lost her today. Because he had. For a few hours, he'd had to live with the thought that she'd gone back to her ex. That she was no longer his. And that had almost shattered him.

FIONA ROLLED onto her side and reached across for Callum. When she felt cold sheets, her eyes flicked open. It was the middle of the night, but Callum wasn't here.

With a grimace, she pushed up to a sitting position. They'd eaten a quick dinner and gone to bed early, although it had taken her a long time to fall asleep. Callum had helped, with gentle strokes on her back and whispers in her ear.

Where was he?

A soft sound caught her attention. It was barely a whisper of fingers hitting laptop keys.

Slowly, she pushed the sheets off and rose to her feet. Callum's T-shirt fell to her knees, and her toes sank into the soft carpet as she left the room. She stopped at the sight of Callum on the couch, laptop out. His brows were furrowed, like he was deep in concentration. Then his gaze shot up, and he smiled at her. He was good at that...pretending he was fine so she wouldn't worry.

"Hey, beautiful. Did I wake you?"

"No, I did that on my own." She tilted her head. "Everything okay?"

A bit of the smile slipped, and he held out a hand. She didn't hesitate, crossing the room and sliding into the crook of his arm. "I found something."

She tried not to react to the way he said those words, like he knew she wouldn't like whatever it was. "Tell me."

"I cross-checked the information on your birth certificate and hospital records."

When he paused, she almost didn't want to ask. "What is it?"

"Your birth certificate says you were born at Jensenville Memorial Hospital...but there are no records of you ever being born there."

She shook her head, rolling his words over. "That...that doesn't make sense."

"I know."

"So...my parents lied to me about my birth? Why?" Thoughts tumbled around in her head. She gasped. "Do you think... Could I have a twin sister somewhere?"

That was the only thing that made sense. A woman who looked exactly like her? It had to be an identical twin, right?

"Maybe."

"But why would my parents lie about that? And where has she been all these years?"

Every word out of her mouth had her heart beating faster, the fabric of the life she'd thought she knew being torn apart right in front of her.

"Hey," Callum said, and she looked at him. "Right now, all we know is that your birth certificate doesn't match any hospital records. We'll ask your parents about it, and we'll figure this out."

That required entirely too much patience. She wanted it sorted out *now*. A sister…a living, breathing sister. Someone she'd possibly shared a womb with. God, what had happened? Why hadn't she grown up with her?

As if seeing her slow derailment, he cupped her cheek. "Trust me to help you through this."

She did. She trusted this man with her life, and she was so grateful for him.

Her gaze slid down to his lips, and her belly did a little somersault. Suddenly, all she wanted was something she knew was real—him.

Reaching out, she closed the laptop, lowered it to the coffee table, and climbed onto his lap.

Callum sucked in a sharp breath. "Fiona—"

She kissed him, slipped her tongue between his lips, and let it dance with his. His fingers dug into the flesh on her hips as she ground her core against his hard length. It created an instant inferno in her belly, a storm of need and desire for this man.

Gently, she grazed her fingers down his hard chest until she met the top of his sleep pants. She was just reaching inside when his fingers wrapped around her wrists, halting her.

"Fiona, I don't know if that's a good idea right now."

She slid her tongue over his bottom lip, then whispered against his mouth, "I need to feel you."

There was a small pause as she continued to taste him. Nipped and teased. Then he released her wrist, and she slid her fingers inside his pants and briefs and wrapped her fingers

173

around him. An instant growl tore from his chest, and she let that spur on her own need.

She tugged him out and slid her fingers and palm over his hardness, touching every inch of him, reveling in every groan and ripple from his chest.

"Jesus, Fi. You're killing me."

A strong, warm hand smoothed up her thigh before slipping between her legs. He slid his fingers inside her panties and grazed her clit. Sparks shot through her belly. Her back arched, and she bit back a moan.

"So damn sensitive," he growled.

He touched her again, sliding over her, alternating between firm caresses and circular motions that created waves of sweet tension. Her back bowed again, and he tugged her toward his mouth, wrapped his lips around her nipple through her shirt.

She cried out—a long, anguished cry. He continued to work her clit and play with her nipple, until she couldn't take it any longer. She inched up so his cock sat at her entrance. His fingers gripped her panties, and with one tug, he tore them from her body. Then, slowly, she sank onto him. Her walls stretched, and she had to remind herself to breathe. To allow the air to flow in and out of her lungs.

Once he was seated all the way inside her, she leaned forward and captured his lips once more. "You undo me, Callum Thomas."

The second the words were out, she started to move, rising and falling in even thrusts, allowing him to fill her so completely she felt empty on every rise.

She grabbed his shoulder, trying to anchor herself as he latched onto her hips. He lifted her higher, bringing her down harder. It was different from any time before. More desperate. More intimate. And she loved every second, needing it to be exactly what it was in this moment.

When her shirt was tugged up, air hit her breasts, which bounced with her thrusts. Again, he latched onto her nipple, and every muscle clenched with pleasure. She screamed his name, her voice getting caught on the word. Her body was in turmoil, her blood pumping so fast it roared between her ears.

He released one nipple and moved to the other, while his hand returned to her clit. It was too much, her body was in overdrive. She tried to draw out the moment, to continue to thrust so she didn't lose him, but all too soon her walls convulsed, and she broke around him.

"*Fuck*, I love that sound."

His hand returned to her hip, and he kept lifting her up and thrusting her back down until he growled again, finally coming apart.

CHAPTER 23

he tension rolled off Fiona in waves. They were almost at her parents' house, and her unease had only intensified throughout the drive. Callum reached over and took her hand in his.

"Are you okay?"

She took a moment to answer. "I'm just scared I'm going to learn something today that's going to change everything."

His fingers tightened. "If you do, we'll tackle it together. If there's anything I've learned over the years, it's that it's better to have more information than less."

She frowned. "Did you learn that when you were taken by the people behind Project Arma?" Her words were quiet, like she was unsure whether she should be talking about the horrific project.

"When I was first taken, I didn't know what they wanted. We were put into this big house on a large property, drugged and forced to train. We had no idea what the drugs were until we started feeling the effects of increased strength and speed. I remember being able to hear things I shouldn't have been able to hear, having no idea what was going on with my body."

She swallowed. "I'm sorry."

"When I found out they were turning us into weapons, it was at once a relief and a weight on my shoulders. I was so damn angry that I was being treated as a possession. Turned into a tool for someone else's war." He took his eyes off the road to look at her. "Knowing was hard. But it also took the blindfold off and let me see exactly what and who I was fighting."

She placed her other hand on top of his. "I'm really glad you got out."

"We were lucky that the team in Marble Falls was able to rescue us. Now we try to use what happened to us to help others."

"You're a good man."

One side of his mouth lifted. "Most of the time."

"All the time." He turned right, and her hand tightened on his. "My sister's car is the red Civic. She's parked in front of my parents' house."

He pulled in behind it, but Fiona didn't move to take her seat belt off or get out. "If my parents are keeping some big secret from me...I wonder if Amanda knows, and that's why she's always hated me."

"Maybe. But I have a feeling her issue with you is more an issue of her own. The woman likes attention, and her beautiful sister takes that attention away from her."

Fiona didn't look convinced, but she smiled. "All right. Let's do this."

He kept close to her as they moved up the walk. She took a beat longer than normal to knock, but when she did, the door flew open, and her mother's mouth spread into a wide smile.

"Hello, my darlings! Come in."

She gave them both big hugs, and when they stepped inside, her father moved out of the adjacent hall and enveloped Fiona in a hug before shaking his hand.

Amanda's greeting was more subdued, offering her normal tight smile. "Nice to see you both actually came."

Fiona's muscles visibly tensed. "Just like you, I have things to discuss tonight."

"Well, Freddie was supposed to be here, but he's away for work and hasn't been able to get back."

Away for work? Or away in Ketchum, spending time with a woman he thought was Fiona?

To Fiona's credit, her features didn't change at all. "Guess it's just us then."

"And me!" Stacey said, as she stepped out from the hall.

Fiona's smile returned. "You didn't tell me you were coming."

The women embraced, and Callum was grateful her cousin was there to take the edge off.

The next half hour was busy, with Fiona and Stacey helping Edna in the kitchen and Callum helping her father start a fire in the fireplace. Amanda spent most of the time on her phone. It wasn't until they were sitting at the table that he was with Fiona again. He squeezed her knee, and immediately, her hand covered his.

Callum looked at Edna across the table. "This looks and smells amazing."

The woman beamed at him. "It's just roast chicken and vegetables."

Fiona scoffed. "Just? You do the best roast in the Northwest, Mom."

If possible, the older woman's smile widened. "The secret's in the seasoning."

Throughout the meal, the rest of the family talked while Amanda kept her phone beside her plate. She appeared to be madly texting the entire time. She never looked happy, and every so often, released angry huffs.

Edna touched her arm. "Amanda, dear, please put your phone away. Fiona's come a long way to have a meal with us."

Amanda looked up, but not at her mother. She directed a

furious glare at Fiona. "Well, she is the golden child, so I guess we should put in some effort, shouldn't we?"

Everyone tensed, the smiles slipping from their faces.

"Why do you need to do that?" Fiona asked firmly.

"Do what?"

"Put in snide remarks about me whenever you get the chance. We're having a nice meal, and I've been nothing but kind to you."

Amanda snorted. "Kind? Like secretly seeing Freddie on our wedding night and not telling me?"

Stunned silence thickened the air.

"Who told you that?" Fiona asked.

"*He* did. He said he was going to get ice when you stopped him in the hall. Tried to kiss him."

Callum's muscles tensed. "That's a lie."

Her angry eyes slid to him. "Is it? Or are you just dating a woman who can't keep her hands to herself?"

"Me?" Fiona gasped. "*I'm* the one who can't keep my hands to myself? Are you freaking kidding me?"

Amanda swung a nervous glance at their parents but kept her mouth closed. Clearly, the circumstances of Freddie dating Amanda had never made it back to her parents, and the woman didn't want them to know.

"I do not want him, Amanda, and you need to stop insinuating I do."

Amanda's jaw clicked, and she opened her mouth, but before she could get a word out, Mark cleared his throat. "Amanda, stop it. Your mother has prepared a fabulous meal. I think we should enjoy it."

A beat passed before Fiona wet her lips and turned to her parents. "I actually have a question I'd like to ask you both."

"Anything, dear," her mother said, clearly relieved at any change in subject.

When Fiona paused, Callum put a supportive hand on her thigh.

She lowered her fork to the table. "Some strange things have been happening. Because of that, Callum did some digging...and he's found that there aren't any hospital records of my birth."

He heard it straight away. The shift in breathing from Mark. The speeding up of Edna's pulse, accompanied by the paling of both their faces. He shot a glance at Amanda to see her lips twitching up, almost in a smirk. Stacey just looked confused.

"Why is that?" Fiona asked, when the silence stretched.

Edna and Mark looked at each other, almost like they were silently asking each other what to say.

Fiona touched her father's hand. "Please. I need to know."

"You're not theirs."

Everyone's gaze swung toward Amanda. Edna gasped.

"Amanda, *don't*," Mark said firmly.

"What?" she asked with indignation. "She obviously knows something." Amanda looked back to Fiona. "Your mother was a drug addict friend of Mom's, who left you at our front door and died a week later."

~

Tick, tick, tick.

The ticking of the second hand on the clock was the only sound in the room. It cut through the quiet. The thick cloud of disbelief and shock. The pounding of her heart.

Fiona opened and closed her mouth, not sure what to make of her sister's words. Were they a lie? A means to get a rise out of her?

Her gaze shifted to her parents, begging them to tell her as much. "Is that true?" Her words were almost a whisper.

She'd never seen her mother so pale or her father look so scared. That's when she knew. She didn't need their words to confirm the truth—it was right there on their faces.

Tick, tick, tick.

The clock was too loud. The air too thick. God, she was choking.

She shot to her feet, her chair almost falling backward with the speed of her movement, and without a word, she walked across the room to the back sliding door and yanked it open. Cool air whipped across her face as she stepped onto the deck.

She didn't suck in a single breath until she hit the railing. She curled her fingers over the edge to keep herself upright.

A lie. Her entire life was a carefully fabricated lie. Her parents...her sister...they weren't related to her. Even Stacey wasn't really her cousin. Not by blood. And they all knew. Had Stacey known?

Why hadn't they told her? Why hadn't they let her in on the huge secret that was her life?

Little things started to piece together. The way her sister shared her mother's blue eyes and her father's dark hair, but she had neither of those things. How Amanda and her parents were short, yet she was tall.

Her chest tightened again, holding in the air. Her birth mother was a drug addict?

The door opened behind her, but she didn't turn to see who it was, just tightened her fingers around the railing as if that would stop her from falling while the ground beneath her disintegrated.

"Darling..."

Tears welled in her eyes at the sound of her mother's soft, gentle voice.

"Why didn't you tell me?" she whispered, swinging around to look at the woman who'd raised her.

Her mother's eyes became watery too. "We meant to. We always planned on telling you. But we just kept making excuses that it was never the right time, and then you grew up and we just...left it. We didn't want you to feel less like ours."

"It wasn't your information to *leave*. I had a right to know."

"You did." A tear fell down her mother's cheek, and she scrubbed it away. "It was selfish of us. It just got to the point where too much time had passed, and I thought you'd hate us for not telling you sooner."

She dug her fingers so deeply into her palms that her hands ached. "Tell me how this happened."

"It took us a long time to conceive Amanda. When she was two, we started trying for a second. We tried for years but couldn't get pregnant. We were going to give up." She paused. "Candy Holder...she was an old friend of mine from college. She got herself on a bad track and had issues with drugs. I didn't even know she was pregnant. I hadn't seen her for over a year. Then, we just woke up one morning to crying at the front of the house." Her mother swallowed. "Your father went outside, and there you were, so little and wrapped in a tattered blanket in an old bassinet."

Her heart turned at the thought of the person who gave her life just leaving her like that. "Did you try to find her?"

"We did. I tried reaching out to mutual friends. Looking into where she used to live. But I never shared with them why I was looking because a part of me knew, if I gave you back to her, you wouldn't have a good life." She paused, looking over Fiona's shoulder, like she was searching for answers. "By the time we'd exhausted all avenues to find her, a couple of weeks had passed, and we'd already fallen in love with you. So we...we found someone who could forge a birth certificate. Fortunately, we were living in California at the time and hadn't seen either of our families in months, so they didn't know that I was never pregnant. We moved back home to Idaho and raised you as our own."

Every word her mother spoke revealed a new layer of a life she'd never known about.

"It was when you were five that we searched for her again,"

her mother continued. "That's when we learned that she'd died a week after she left you with us."

So many emotions flickered inside her. Grief that her birth mother was gone. Relief that she'd lived a better life than she was born into. "Is that why Amanda hates me?"

Sadness, deep and pained, carved into her mother's face. "She was five, honey. Old enough to understand a baby had shown up on our doorstep. We pulled her away from her home and forced her to lie to everyone about who you were. I also think she struggled to share us with someone else."

She nodded. Her sister's hate ran deep, but maybe it was always just her own selfish belief that she should have been an only child. "Did I have a biological sister?"

Her mother jolted. "No. Not that we ever knew about. It was only you left at our door."

She studied her mother's eyes, looking for any signs of deceit. A day ago, she would have thought her mother could never lie to her. Today, that trust was fractured. "There's someone out there who looks like me. I think they've even pretended to *be* me a couple of times."

Her mother gasped and covered her mouth. "Candace never had a baby before you, unless…"

Her mother didn't finish, but she knew they were both thinking the same thing. Unless there was another baby, one who was left with someone else…a twin.

"Really? You're blaming some sister for your behavior?"

Fiona swung around to see Amanda in the open doorway. "What?"

"Are you going to tell me it was *her* who's been coming on to Freddie since I married him?"

She swallowed and stepped closer to Amanda. "I *never* came on to him. And yes, I think this woman did. Callum saw her making out with Freddie in his hotel room in Ketchum."

Anger, so dark and ravenous, washed over her sister's face. "He was making out with you?"

"*No*. Not me."

Amanda shook her head and stepped back. "You never deserved this life. It wasn't yours to have. And now you're trying to take my husband too, and blaming it on some fictitious sister? You're a piece of fucking work, Fiona."

Fiona took a small step forward. She was done with Amanda. Done with her callous words and inability to see past herself. "Actually, Amanda, I was at work at the time Freddie was making out with this woman. There are eyewitnesses of me at work, and Callum saw this woman with Freddie. As I can't be in two places at once, it couldn't have been me."

Amanda's jaw tightened and she opened her mouth, but Fiona got in first.

"And the only person who stole anyone is *you*. You slept with my boyfriend, behind my back, while I was still with him."

Her mother gasped from behind her, but Fiona kept going, the emotion taking root inside her.

"You and Freddie had no respect for me, whatsoever. In fact, you've never had any respect for me. You've treated me terribly for something I had no control over. And now, I'm done, Amanda."

Amanda's jaw dropped, but Fiona didn't wait around for any words she may come up with in response. She moved into the house and grabbed her bag.

Her dad touched her arm. "Fiona—"

"I just need time, Dad."

The hurt that crossed his face cut deep into Fiona. But she did need time. To come to terms with everything she'd learned. To accept this new reality.

Stacey pulled her into a hug, then whispered, "I didn't know. I swear."

Thank God. She didn't think she'd be able to handle everyone lying to her.

The second the embrace ended, Callum was there, slipping an arm around her waist, and his strength was everything. She leaned into him, letting him be her support as he led her away from the home she'd grown up in.

CHAPTER 24

*T*he smell of coffee was strong and had Fiona's eyes shooting open. Last night had been rough. She'd barely said two words on the drive home, then she'd gone straight to bed.

Shock. She'd been in complete and utter shock, barely able to process everything that had been revealed to her. Her family wasn't related to her by blood. Her birth mother was a deceased drug addict. And she possibly had an identical twin sister impersonating her for unknown reasons.

God, her life was a mess.

She groaned and closed her eyes, rolling to her side. Maybe if she kept her eyes closed long enough, reality would shift back into something familiar that made sense.

Footsteps sounded in the hall. She popped one eye open to see Callum stepping in. The other popped open at the sight of the coffee in his hands. Thank God. There was no getting through this day without caffeine.

He didn't smile as he set the coffee onto the bedside table and perched beside her. He just studied her like he was worried she'd have a mental breakdown or fall into a heap on the floor…neither of which were out of the realm of possibility.

His hand went to her hip. "How are you feeling?"

"Confused. Angry. Like I woke up a completely different person from who I was yesterday." Which she kind of had. She wasn't Fiona Lock, not genetically.

"I'm sorry."

She found a crease in his jeans and traced it with her finger. "I feel bad that I left my parents in such a rush."

Yes, she knew her actions were warranted, but the sadness in their faces, and fear, as if they thought they were going to lose her… They weren't. They should have been honest with her, but she still loved them.

"It will take time to mend things," he said quietly.

She wrapped her fingers around his powerful thigh. "Thank you. For being with me. For not making me talk about any of it last night."

His silent companionship had been everything she'd needed.

"I'm here for whatever you need." He tilted his head. "Are you going to work today?"

"I texted Rick last night that I was sick." She wasn't one to call in, but she'd regretted not taking time off the day after the incident in the library, so today, she was doing the right thing for her mental health. The man had been far from happy, but she barely used her sick days, so he'd have to deal with it.

Callum watched her carefully. "I was going to go into the office for a quick meeting, but—"

"No, no. If you need to go to the office, you go."

"Are you sure?"

"Of course. You've got top-notch security and locks. Besides, I've been eyeing your huge bathtub since I first saw it. I could use a little time in there to digest it all."

Ha. Like she could do that in one bath. She'd probably need a few years' worth.

"A bath?" His hand slid up her thigh. "Maybe I should come home early and join you."

She chuckled. It felt good to laugh. "I don't think any digesting would happen if you did that."

He would be one big, hard distraction.

She swallowed. "Hey, I've been thinking that maybe those texts I've been getting are from this…sister?" God, that was hard to say. "I mean, if she's been impersonating me, she's clearly got issues."

Maybe she was even insane?

He slid some hair from her face. "Yeah, I was thinking the same thing."

"Well, at least that's just one person gunning for me instead of two!" She meant to inflect humor into her words, but Callum didn't even smile.

"I'm going to look into your birth mother today," he said slowly. "See if I can find anything about a second baby."

Her belly gave a little turn. "Okay. Thank you."

"I won't be long." He leaned down and pressed his lips to hers. She wanted to pull him into bed, still the moment and make it last a bit longer, because around him, she still felt like herself. Too soon, he straightened. "Call if you need anything."

She didn't get up as soon as he left. Instead, she grabbed her phone to see a string of messages. From her mother and father. There were also some from Stacey.

Lying back, she sucked in a long breath before responding to each text, telling everyone she was okay. That she had Callum to help her through it and just needed some time to process. And that she loved them. Because she did. Her parents had risked a lot to keep her. If they hadn't, what would have happened to her? Would she have been tossed into the foster care system? God, she would have lived a completely different life.

The responses were instant, which told her they'd been sitting on their phones, waiting for her to reply. She'd already texted

Jenny that morning to let her friend know she might get a call from Rick to fill her shift. She hadn't shared why she wasn't coming in, just that she wasn't feeling the best and was staying with Callum, both of which were true.

When her phone finally stopped buzzing, she pushed up, her gaze catching on the coffee.

Hello, how did I forget about you?

Almost desperately, she reached for the mug and basically inhaled the stuff. Yep, it was exactly what she needed.

In the bathroom, she turned on the tap. While the bath filled, she pulled her hair up into a bun. The bumps on her head felt better every day, but there was still a slight ache there. At least she couldn't see the damage.

What would Callum find today? That she *did* have a sister? A sister who looked exactly like her?

A twin...that was like having half of yourself exist in the world, one that you knew nothing about. But if this woman was impersonating Fiona, then what was her end game? Why hadn't she just come and spoken to her?

Those were questions she needed answers to.

She tugged Callum's shirt over her head, then slid into the tub. The water was warm on her cool skin, and she instantly sank deep below the surface. Heaven. Well, as close to heaven as she was going to get today.

Grabbing her phone, she turned on some music, then just relaxed, giving herself permission to not think about the train wreck that was her life.

She lay there so long, the water was cooling when the door-bell rang downstairs. She planned to ignore it, but a second later, the pounding of a fist on wood started—followed by the distant screams of a woman.

She jackknifed into a seated position, water splashing out of the tub onto the tiles. Jesus, who was that?

Quickly, she climbed out of the tub, dried, and threw pants

and a top from yesterday over her damp skin. The pounding continued the entire way down the stairs.

She looked through the peephole to see the neighbor, Kasey, on the other side of the door. Her eyes were wide, and she was holding her stomach. Fiona's gaze lowered.

*Oh God...*was that *blood* seeping through her fingers? And through her fingers, Fiona could see what appeared to be the handle of a knife still penetrating her flesh.

Without thinking about anything but the injured woman, she tugged the door open. "Kasey!"

The woman's eyes flashed up. "H-help!"

The second the word was out of her mouth, something hit Kasey in the neck.

A dart.

The woman dropped, then a person—dressed in black and wearing a balaclava—flew into view from the side of the house.

Fiona screamed and tried to slam the door closed, but they got their foot in before she could. She attempted to kick the foot away, but the person threw their body weight into the door, making Fiona stumble.

The second the person was in the house, she realized the attacker was female. The woman raised her arm. The metal of a gun, presumably the one she'd used to shoot Kasey, flashed.

Fiona reacted on instinct, grabbing the woman's arm and shoving it to the side, pushing her back into the wall. Her wrist hit the wood so hard, the gun dropped.

Immediately, the attacker threw her head forward and hit Fiona in the temple.

Pain blasted through her skull. She fell back, stars dancing across her vision. She blinked them away as the intruder lifted the gun again and took aim.

Fiona's heart pounded against her ribs as she kicked her foot forward, catching the intruder's leg and sending her to the ground. She kicked again, this time hitting the woman in the stomach.

The attacker let out an *oof* as Fiona rolled over and pushed to her feet. Her knees trembled, threatening to buckle beneath her. She forced them to hold her upright as she threw herself into the office to the left of the hall and slammed the door closed.

When she saw there was no lock, her heart slammed in her chest. *Dammit!* She needed something to keep the door closed. Desperately, she cast her gaze around the room, spotting the wooden chair by the desk.

With legs that still weren't steady, she ran toward it, groaning at the weight as she lifted it. When she reached the door, she tilted the chair at an angle and wedged it under the handle. It had just been set in place when a body hit the wood. Fiona fell back, tumbling to the floor, more from shock than anything else.

Her throat closed at the groan of the wood. At the screech of the chair as it moved just an inch across the floor

Would they get in? She couldn't just sit here and wait. With limbs that felt too weak, she rose and raced back behind the desk, opening every drawer, pulling out the contents. *God, Callum, you have to have a gun in here somewhere.*

Bang.

Something—maybe the woman's body—collided with the door. The wood of the chair groaned and inched forward.

It wouldn't be long. She'd get in. And when she did, Fiona would need a weapon.

She reached the last drawer, crying out when there was no gun. But she didn't stop. She checked under the wood of each drawer, then under the desk itself—that's where she spotted the pistol, strapped to the underside of the desk's surface.

Thank God. She tore it off and took aim right as the chair fell and the door flew open.

The woman stopped, her gaze colliding with the gun, which was now pointed at her head.

"I know how to shoot," Fiona said, voice as steady as it was going to get. "And I *will* shoot you if you don't leave."

But God, she hoped she didn't need to. She was almost certain the gun in the person's hand only held tranquilizers. So if it was a competition of whose weapon could do more damage, she'd win.

The woman's gaze shifted to hers, and it almost stole Fiona's breath. It was the first time she got a clear look at those eyes. Eyes that were familiar—because they were *hers*.

"You're my sister," Fiona breathed.

The woman's eyes narrowed, like the truth in that statement made her angry. She stepped back, and Fiona stepped forward. "Please! I don't know why you're doing this, but you don't have to. We're...we're *family*. It doesn't have to be this way!"

Rage—it swirled through those chestnut eyes. "Fuck you!" The two words were hissed so quietly, and with so much hate, that Fiona flinched.

Then the woman turned and ran. Fiona raced to the window and watched as the woman ran from the house, down the street, and eventually disappeared from view. But still, Fiona's fingers remained firm on the gun. She was frozen, unable to move, barely breathing.

The hate...it had been so thick, Fiona could practically feel it.

She wanted to keel over. To let the depths of that reality take her down. But then she remembered Kasey...

God, Kasey! She ran to the door and dropped to the woman's side, lowering the gun to the ground. Her chest was moving, but blood soaked her top. And the dagger...

Phone. She needed a phone to call for help.

Lifting the pistol again, she ran upstairs and grabbed her cell from beside the bath. There were three missed calls from Callum. She had to call him—but first, she needed to call 911.

CHAPTER 25

*C*allum's eyes moved over the information on his computer. Candace Holder gave birth to identical twin girls on December fourth at the Community Regional Medical Center. Fiona and Olivia Holder.

He clicked over to a news article dated a week later. Candy Holder was found dead in an alley due to an overdose, and her babies were declared missing.

Callum ran his hands through his hair.

Fiona was a twin.

God. To find out so late in life would be like a kick in the damn gut. What kind of life had that sister led? How had she come to the point where she'd not only found Fiona but felt the need to *impersonate* her? Stalk her?

If Fiona had kept her name, maybe Olivia had kept hers too. He could ask Fiona's mother if she knew any of Candy's other friends, but there was another route he wanted to try first.

His fingers returned to the keyboard, moving quickly. He spent the next hour hacking into government systems he had no business hacking into, but hell, when it came to Fiona and her safety, he'd do whatever it goddamn took.

When he finally found it, he leaned back in his chair.

On the same day Fiona was left on Edna and Mark Lock's doorstep, a baby by the name of Olivia, no last name, was placed in government care. She became Olivia Cohls, and she remained in foster care, moving from home to home until she aged out.

He kept digging and found a police report for what looked like her first misdemeanor for possession. The photo popped up —and he blew out a long breath. She had the same eyes as Fiona, but that was where the similarities ended. The woman was thinner, like she'd used too many drugs in her life. Her hair was bleach-blond, and she wore a pound of makeup.

He dug up a few more misdemeanor charges. Drunk driving. Vandalism. Resisting arrest. And in each photo, she looked the same, just older, her makeup a bit heavier.

Fuck.

Footsteps sounded down the hall moments before Tyler appeared in his doorway. "Hey, I just came to tell you—" He stopped when his gaze hit Callum, his brows tugging together. "You okay?"

"No." He couldn't lie to his friend if he tried.

Tyler came farther into the room. "This about the woman who's been stalking Fiona?"

He scrubbed a hand over his face. "It's her biological twin sister."

Tyler frowned, and Callum gave his friend the CliffsNotes version.

He looked as shocked as Callum felt. "Whoa."

Callum almost laughed. "Yeah, my thoughts too. I found all this information, but I can't find a current address."

Tyler was just opening his mouth to say something when Callum's phone went off. He looked down—and cursed when he saw it was the silent alarm to his house.

He shot to his feet and grabbed his keys, calling Fiona as he ran out of the office. When she didn't answer, he cursed and tried again.

Tyler followed closely behind. It wasn't until Callum slid behind the wheel of his car that she finally returned his calls.

"Are you okay?"

"Kasey was stabbed!" Her voice was panicked, her words high-pitched.

Callum stepped hard on the gas. "What happened?"

"She was banging on the door, and I saw she was bleeding, so I opened it. Then someone shot her with a dart and attacked me." Every word rushed into the next.

He took a hard right, his gaze shooting to Tyler in the rearview mirror. "Are you hurt?"

"No. I ran into your office and found your gun. When I pointed it at her, she ran away, but Kasey's not opening her eyes, and her chest is barely moving! I've called the paramedics but... God, what if they're too late? What if she's lost too much blood?"

"Do you still have the gun?"

"Yes."

Good. She had something to use to protect herself if the person returned. He pressed his foot to the floor, pushing the car as fast as it could go.

When he arrived minutes later, the ambulance was pulling up, too. His gut clenched at what he saw—Fiona, on her knees on his front porch, face pale and a trickle of blood running down her head.

His hands fisted as he climbed out of the car and ran toward her. She was hunched over Kasey's body, crimson soaking through her fingers as she pressed at the wound.

He lowered beside her. "Fiona—"

"I can't move my hands—there's too much blood."

He touched her wrists. "Paramedics are here."

On cue, the paramedics dropped beside Kasey. He pulled

Fiona up and away, grabbing the pistol from beside her as he did and handing it to Tyler.

Fiona's hands shook and her breath heaved. "It was *her*."

Callum cupped her cheek. "Who?"

"The woman who looks like me. She wore a balaclava again, but her eyes...they were *my* eyes."

Fuck. He tugged her into his chest, not caring about the blood that soaked his shirt, just the need to hold and soothe his woman.

"You're okay," he said quietly, for his own damn benefit as much as hers.

"I'm okay," she repeated, her voice muffled against his chest.

"Excuse me, ma'am, are you hurt?"

Callum's gaze caught on the bruise and small cut just visible in her hairline. The reason for the blood on her face.

"Yes."

"No."

They both answered at the same time.

Callum's fingers tightened on her arms. "Let them check that your head's okay, Fi."

She sucked in a shuddering breath, her gaze skirting to Kasey, who was being loaded into an ambulance. Then she nodded. "Okay."

Fiona watched the water in the shower run from red to clear as the blood on her hands washed away. Kasey's blood. She still didn't know if the other woman was okay. Had Kasey only been hurt as a way to get Fiona to open the door?

Of course she had. Fiona didn't need to hear the story from the woman's mouth to know that. And the guilt of that sat so heavy on her chest it was like an immoveable weight.

She scrubbed at her hands, attacking the dried blood under her nails.

Once the paramedics had cleared the bump on her head as superficial, she'd spoken to the police and described her attacker as best she could, knowing she'd sounded crazy. She hadn't stuck around as Callum had spoken to the officers. She'd needed to get away. Wash the damn blood off her hands.

When the blood refused to budge, she scrubbed harder, the flesh on her fingers aching at the action.

A knock on the door sounded, and she sucked in a sharp breath. "Yes?"

"Fi? You okay?"

She swallowed, forcing her lungs to accept air they felt too damn tight to let in. "Yes. I'll be out in a second."

There was a small beat of silence before Callum responded. "Okay, honey. Shout out if you need anything."

She nodded, even though he couldn't see her. Then she closed her eyes and let the water fall over her, hitting her skin like small drops of fire on icy flesh. She'd made the water as hot as she could, needing the heat to help her feel clean. She remained under the stream until her skin was red and her fingers wrinkled. Then, finally, she stepped out and wrapped herself in a large towel.

She couldn't get those eyes out of her head. So similar to hers but so filled with hate. Why? What had she ever done to warrant such rage?

Swallowing, she stepped out of the bathroom to find Callum by the window, phone to his ear. His gaze met hers, and his eyes...they seared her. Her brush with danger had probably scared him. He didn't have to say it out loud for her to know.

Quickly, she pulled on some panties, a bra, some leggings, and an oversized tee. She was just sitting on the edge of the bed when Callum ended the call and sat beside her. Then he surprised her by lifting her from the mattress and pulling her onto his lap so she was sitting sideways. Gently, as if he was scared he'd hurt her, he grazed her forehead with his lips.

"How are you feeling?"

"My head's fine, just another headache." It wasn't exactly what he was asking, but it was easier than trying to make sense of the mess that was her thoughts. "Who was that on the phone?"

His jaw clenched. Yeah, he saw right through her.

The hand around her waist moved below the material, and his fingers touched bare skin. "Tyler. He followed the paramedics to the hospital. He was in the hall when Kasey woke and spoke to the police. He heard her recount everything."

"She's okay then?"

"She lost some blood, but she's stable."

The air ran out of her in a rush. Thank God.

His gaze moved between her eyes. "Kasey was coming over to talk to me. She'd just reached my porch when someone stabbed her from the side."

His thumb swept up and down Fiona's ribs.

"My best guess," he continued, "is the woman saw me leave and was either waiting for you to come out or looking for a way in. Kasey gave her that opportunity."

She shook her head. "I feel terrible."

"It's not your fault."

She studied his eyes before asking the question she needed to ask. "Did you find any information on her?"

Something passed over his face, giving her an answer before he spoke.

"Yes." The way his eyes darkened almost made her not want to know. "Her name is Olivia Cohls, and she's your twin."

Fiona nodded, a slow, trying-to-take-it-in nod. Callum's fingers tightened on her ribs. She'd known as much, but hearing it confirmed...it made it so much more devastating. "Identical?"

"I saw a few photos of her and, apart from her eyes, she didn't look much like you, but that could be because of the bleached hair and the ton of makeup."

"You saw photos?"

He paused before saying, "Mug shots."

Her heart dropped. So she had an identical sister who was a criminal.

"Olivia grew up in foster care," he said slowly. "She was bounced around the system until she aged out. She was charged with a few misdemeanors, but as of a few months ago, I haven't been able to find any more information on her."

Fiona's mind raced, piecing the information together. "Maybe she got left with another family, but unlike my parents, they didn't take her in?"

"That's what I'm thinking."

A tightness seized her chest before she whispered, "That could have been me."

"What?"

"My mother leaving me with my parents was no doubt random. So, me having the life I lived rather than growing up in the system was completely by chance. As simple as her grabbing me to leave with Edna instead of Olivia." Her next breath was more of a gasp of air. "That's probably why Olivia's doing this. She found out about me. Knows I got a better life. And now hates me for it."

The realization was like a kick in the gut. Could she even blame the other woman for that? Maybe she'd hate her twin too, if the situation was reversed? "If I'd grown up like her and realized what she'd been given and I hadn't, I could be doing exactly the same thing."

He shook his head. "You wouldn't."

"How do you know?"

"Because I know you."

She held his gaze for a full five seconds, letting the intensity in that look anchor her. Then she dipped her head to his chest. "You always have all the right words, Callum."

But even though he said the right things, she wasn't sure she believed him.

CHAPTER 26

Callum leaned against Aidan's kitchen island. His team stood around him, pizza and beer in hand, while the women sat in the living room with cocktails. Everyone was here tonight bar Tyler, who was in Salinas, California, searching for any information he could get on Olivia. It was the last town where Callum had found a record of Fiona's twin living. Tyler was there to ask questions. Find out what they could about the woman.

As for him, he just wanted to be present with the rest of his friends and have a night off the threats. And more than that, give Fiona a night off.

"It was fine," Liam said, giving them a recount of his date. "There were definitely lulls in the conversation during dinner, but she was nice."

"How'd you say you met her?" Logan asked.

Liam lifted his beer to his mouth. "Grocery store. She bumped me from behind. We started talking, she asked me out, she was cute and sweet, so I said yes."

"Second date?" Callum asked.

"I don't think so."

Not a surprise. Liam rarely dated, and when he did, the relationships didn't last long. Callum wasn't sure what kind of woman it would take to lock the guy down, but whoever it was, he hadn't found her.

Callum nudged Aidan's shoulder. "You all set for the engagement party?"

Aidan laughed. "Well, I'm responsible for drinks. Pretty sure I'm nailing it with the beer and wine."

"Anything we can do to help?" Jason asked.

"Nope. Those women are a well-oiled machine. Watching them plan a party is almost scary. I think they could join the Special Forces and organize a raid better than any of us."

Callum's smile widened as Mila ran into the room. Blake lifted his daughter into his arms. "Hey, baby girl. The women get too boring for you?"

"Mama said I had to ask you if I could have a hot chocolate." She yawned. "It's to help me stay awake."

Callum's heart fucking melted at the exchange. The two of them were damn cute. On instinct, he swung his gaze to Fiona in the living room. She sat cross-legged on the couch, smiling at something Courtney was saying.

A week had passed since they'd learned the truth about her birth mother and sister. Every day seemed to help her come to terms with it a bit more. She'd even had a few long chats with her parents on the phone.

The text messages had continued, each one as awful as the last. He fucking hated it.

When her eyes met his, his gut tightened. Because this woman owned him. Without even trying, she'd claimed him, and in return, he'd claimed her. Forgotten how to damn well survive without her.

One side of his mouth lifted, and he winked. Her smile softened and widened. Then Grace touched her arm and said something, pulling her gaze away from him. Still, he didn't look away.

Because as well as falling for this woman over the last few weeks, he'd also become scared as hell of losing her. At the danger they were largely blind to, with no idea where Olivia was at the moment.

"How's she doing?" Flynn asked quietly.

Callum forced his attention to his friend. "Well, considering."

Damn well. The woman was as strong as they came.

Flynn nodded as he watched the women also. "No more news on the sister?"

"I found her apartment in Salinas. She left without paying rent and hasn't used a credit card or any form of ID since."

"So she had a fake ID made and ran with cash?" Flynn guessed.

"That's what I'm thinking. With her past, it's not a stretch to think she'd know people who could do that for her."

"We'll find her," Flynn said quietly, his hand going to Callum's shoulder. "A person can only stay hidden for so long."

Callum nodded, fingers tightening around his beer. They would, but he could only hope they did so before she made another play for Fiona. His gaze shifted back to her, only to find her looking at her phone. The carefree expression on her face was gone, and in its place, unease. Strain.

He straightened. What was she looking at? Was it another message from the unknown number?

He started toward her but stopped when his phone rang in his pocket. He pulled it out to see Tyler's name on the screen. Dammit. He had to take this.

He moved into the hall. "Tyler. What did you find?"

"Nothing that will tell us where she is. But I can see why she left. She owes some bad people a lot of money down here."

Callum's brows tugged together. "How much?"

"More than she'd be able to repay. She apparently took the loan, then up and disappeared on them. They're not happy."

Shit. He ran a hand through his hair.

"One thing I found interesting," Tyler continued, "is the timing of her disappearance. It was right after the incident in the bar with Levi. Remember how that story went viral on social media? Hell, the story was even picked up by a couple of major news stations."

Callum let that sink in. "You think Olivia saw Fiona, saw that they look the same, and figured it out."

It wasn't a question. Still, Tyler answered. "Yep."

He blew out a long breath. "Okay. Thanks for going down there and investigating. You doing okay?"

"Yeah, wore a semi-disguise and blended in as much as I could."

"Watch your back."

"Always."

He hung up, letting the information sink in. Olivia had needed an out from her problems, and when she'd learned about Fiona, her sister had *become* that out. Now she was here, in Cradle Mountain, impersonating Fiona, while dangerous people were looking for her. It all put a sour fucking taste in his mouth.

FIONA TRIED to smile at the women who spoke around her. This was her first time meeting all the partners of the Blue Halo men, and they were wonderful. Friendly. Kind. Welcoming. Grace, Courtney, Carina, Cassie, and Emerson. There was also Willow, who had a gorgeous daughter named Mila. She'd been enjoying her night...then the messages from her sister had started.

Is Freddie with you?

Where is he?

Tell him to get his ass the hell home!

The women were talking about Cassie and Aidan's upcoming engagement party. Everything had been organized, and now they were discussing outfits, Cassie currently describing her tight white dress, which was shoulder-less and knee-length.

"You're going to look amazing," Carina said with a smile on her face.

Fiona's phone vibrated again.

Amanda: I'm not kidding around, Fiona. I want him home. Now!

Good God, had the woman not understood Fiona's last words to her?

Fiona: Stop! He's not here. Leave me alone. I have enough to deal with.

Seconds after she hit send, her phone vibrated and Amanda's name came onto the screen.

She was calling her now?

She gritted her teeth, debating what to do. Her sister was clearly spiraling, and there was every chance if she didn't answer, the woman would either call her parents and harass them, or she might actually drive down here.

Nope, she did not want that, so it was time to take this outside. She could feel eyes on her as she walked to the back door, primarily Callum's from the kitchen, but also a few others. She stepped outside onto the deck, then finally answered.

"Amanda—"

"Is he there? He is, isn't he? He's with you!"

She closed her eyes, praying for just a shred of calm. "He's not here."

"But he's still there in Cradle Mountain, isn't he?"

"I don't know."

"What have you said to him? How are you keeping him there?"

She massaged her forehead, where a tension headache throbbed from behind her eyes. "I have been *very* clear with Freddie that things between him and me are over. It's *him* who's been persistent about wanting me back."

"You're lying!"

Fiona clenched the phone so tightly her hand shook. When she spoke, her voice was tired. "This is the last time I'm telling you this, Amanda. We're done. I can't do this anymore. Freddie cheated on me with you. *You* took what used to be mine. Something you've never shown a shred of remorse for. I was a mess, so I moved away, and I've moved on. I can't control his actions any more than you can. I honestly don't know what you want from me."

"What I want from you is to get the hell out of my life."

Amanda's words sliced like a knife across her skin. "Because I'm not really your sister?"

"Because you were their damn *miracle* child left on their fucking doorstep, and from that point on, I became irrelevant."

"That's not true. Mom and Dad have always loved us equally."

"They shouldn't have! *I'm* their child, not you!"

Her breath cut short.

"You came into my life, uprooted me from my home, made me leave everything I knew. I had to lie to people about who you were. And you became Mom and Dad's whole world. The golden child. Good at everything. Kind to everyone. And I was almost insignificant to them, when I was their own flesh and blood!"

She'd been right. This woman, the older sister who grew up and was supposed to love her, didn't because of simple jealousy.

She swallowed the lump in her throat. "Have you been texting me from a burner phone? Calling me a whore and telling me to stay away from what's yours?"

"What? No. But if someone else has, I'm not surprised."

Fiona's jaw dropped at the ugliness of her sister's words. The utter lack of empathy. She straightened her spine as the hurt twisted into anger. As the years of unfair treatment and blatant hate smacked her right in the face.

"You will stop all contact with me. I will be civil while in the company of our parents, but other than that, we won't speak. I don't want Freddie, and we both know he's a cheating asshole and a scumbag, so anything he does is *solely* on him and between the two of you, seeing as you were dumb enough to marry him. I will not allow you to hurt me anymore. Stay away from me."

She hung up and pulled in a breath so deep her lungs ached. A part of her yearned for a sister who loved her. Who would show her kindness and affection. But that was never going to happen. And it had nothing to do with her and everything to do with Amanda.

"Are you okay?"

She whipped around so fast she almost lost her balance. "Callum. I didn't hear you come out. How long have you been standing there?"

He took a small step forward, his fingers circling her hips. "I didn't want you to be outside on your own."

Long enough to hear everything.

She swallowed. "So you know I have one sister I grew up with who hates me enough to think I deserve being called a whore, and a biological sister who has been impersonating me and tried to...I don't know. Hurt me? Take me?"

Man, that sounded even worse out loud than in her head. Maybe she would have been better off with brothers.

Callum lowered his head. "They have some deep issues. Both of them. Their inability to love and be good people has nothing to do with you."

She knew that. Still, it was hard to accept. He reached up and swiped a tear from her cheek with the rough pad of his thumb. She hadn't even realized she was crying.

"Freddie isn't home."

Callum's eyes steeled. "I heard."

Had he remained in Cradle Mountain this entire time? Or had he gone home, then left again? What the hell was he doing?

"My team will do a search for him."

"And if you find him?"

His eyes narrowed. "We'll make sure he leaves."

God, she wasn't sure she wanted to know the finer details of that plan. She sighed and leaned her head on his chest. "Sometimes I just feel like running away with you."

A kiss pressed to the top of her head, and she felt it swirl right down to her chest. "Anytime, anywhere, honey. You're all I need."

CHAPTER 27

"*I* need you to go get plastic cups and drinks for the author reading." Rick didn't even look at Fiona as he spoke.

She turned from the front desk computer. "The reading isn't until next week."

He blew out an exasperated breath like he was frustrated by her very existence. "We're going to have a lot of organizing between then and now. I have a checklist, and this is the next thing on the list."

The first part of that was true, at least. A well-known author was coming in to do a reading next week, and based on the excited questions from their patrons, a lot of the Cradle Mountain community and those of surrounding towns were coming.

Fiona cleared her throat. "Rick, I'm not supposed to leave work without Callum or another of the Blue Halo guys."

His eyes narrowed. God, if looks could kill. "Fiona. You're going to the grocery store, not some dark alley with criminals hiding around the corner. I don't think someone's going to attempt to kidnap you at the store."

Well, she hadn't thought she'd be attacked at work or at Callum's house either, but both had happened.

She opened her mouth, but Rick spoke first.

"I didn't want to have to pull this, but your job is on thin ice."

Really? This again? "You don't have the power to—"

"I have pull, and your recent string of days off combined with your refusal to do particular tasks isn't helping the team."

Her brows rose to her hairline. Her days off had been after her almost-kidnapping, and the only tasks she refused to do was stay after close on her own and take the trash to the dumpster out back.

"Rick—"

"I'll go," Jenny interrupted, touching her arm from behind. "It's a one-person job. I can handle it."

"It's not. Not with the number of cups and cases of water we need." His gaze hit her like he was daring her to refuse. Then he held out the library credit card.

She snatched it from his fingers. "Fine." She'd tell Callum about her little excursion when he came to tail her home, and maybe he'd go all G.I. Joe on Rick and this would be worth it.

Jenny slipped her hand into Fiona's and they headed outside. "I'll drive. We'll be back before you know it."

Fiona's jaw was tight as she crossed the lot and got into Jenny's car.

Her friend must have sensed it, because she touched her thigh. "Guess you have me for a bodyguard, and I'm the definition of tough."

Fiona chuckled, taking in her friend's large frames, cute bob, and colorful polka dot dress. "You are?"

"Oh yeah. People have gone so far as to say they'd fear the day they meet me in a dark alley."

"Who's said that?"

"Let's not get caught up in details." Jenny's grin widened

before her expression turned serious. "How are you doing with everything?"

That was a good question. How *was* she doing? She didn't even know. "I'm scared, but that's more because I don't know what Olivia's plan is. She must look exactly like me to have people so fooled."

Jenny nodded. "That is scary. It's like the woman's been watching and studying you."

A shudder rippled down Fiona's spine. "Yeah."

Seconds later, Jenny frowned at the rearview mirror—then sped up.

"What is it?" Fiona asked, looking over her shoulder. A breath whipped through her lips at the nearness of the car behind them. Then her gaze caught on the man behind the wheel…

Freddie. God, what the *hell* did he want? And why was he so close? If Jenny stopped suddenly, there was no way he wouldn't hit them.

"It's okay," Jenny said calmly. "We're almost there, then there'll be people around and he won't be able to do anything."

Freddie beeped at them, a loud, keep-the-hand-on-the-horn-for-as-long-as-possible beep.

She reached for her pocket, then cursed when she realized she'd left her phone at work. "Did you bring your phone? We could call Blue Halo Security."

"Um…" Jenny touched her pocket, then shook her head.

Crap.

Before she could fully process what he was doing, Freddie pulled into the oncoming lane before swerving and cutting in front of them. Jenny cried out and pulled to the side of the road, narrowly missing his rear bumper.

Oh my God. Fiona was going to kill him. Murder the cheating stalker asshole on the very spot.

She reached for the door handle, but Jenny grabbed her arm. "Don't. He looks dangerous."

Jenny hit the locks just as he reached her door. When he tried the handle and realized he wasn't getting in, his fist hit the glass.

"Open the damn door, Fiona!"

Anger lit her spine. "No. Go away."

His face reddened, but instead of banging again, he moved around to the other side and hit Jenny's window. Her face paled, and she flinched back at each punch, like she expected his fist to go through the glass. Then he started pulling at the handle.

"Stop!" Fiona yelled.

"I need to talk to you. Unlock the damn doors!"

When he kicked the car, Fiona had had enough. She unlocked her door and shot out. "Stop it!"

Freddie moved around the car and grabbed her upper arm. "Why are you doing this?"

"Let go of me!"

"You come to my motel room, you have *sex* with me, then you refuse to answer my messages? My calls don't even connect. You're making me fucking crazy. Making me want you, then icing me out like I'm *nothing*."

She studied him, noticing for the first time that the normally pristine, put-together Freddie was completely disheveled. Wrinkled, dirty clothes. His hair was a mess. Dark circles under his eyes.

"It wasn't me," she said slowly.

His eyes narrowed. "What the fuck are you talking about?"

"That person who went to your room? It wasn't me."

Jenny's door opened and closed, and she moved toward them, but Fiona shook her head at her friend. She didn't want the other woman getting caught in this, possibly hurt.

"It was *you*."

She tried to twist out of his hold. When that didn't work, she attempted to bring a knee up, but he was too close. "*No*. My parents aren't my biological parents. I have an identical twin sister I didn't even know about. She's been impersonating me. It was *her*."

"That's not true."

"It is."

"No!" His shout was so loud, it made her ears ring. "It was you. You told me you love me, and I fucking love *you*, Fiona!"

"Love me? Freddie, you were having sex with my *sister* while we were together, then you married her. That's not love."

"I told you, it was a mistake. And I only married her because she said she was pregnant, but the bitch fucking lied."

Her sister lied about being pregnant? It shouldn't surprise her, but it still did. She lowered her voice. "Freddie, I'm sorry that she lied to you. But that doesn't change anything. You and I are over. Done. I'm with Callum, and you and I will never be together again. That woman who had sex with you *was not me*."

She said the words slowly, needing him to understand.

"You don't have a twin, Fiona." But this time, his voice held less certainty.

"I do. Ask Amanda. My parents. They all knew, and they didn't tell me. I'm sorry that she went to you pretending to be me. I really am."

Freddie frowned, his gaze still incredulous. "It really wasn't you?"

She shook her head.

He stumbled back a step, his hands dropping from her. "I thought...she looked and sounded *exactly* like you. She told me that she forgave me..."

Even though this man didn't deserve her sympathy, she couldn't help but feel just a drop. Maybe because of the devastation on his face or the disbelief in his eyes. Either way, a woman had tricked him, had sex with him, and played with his head.

"I don't know why she did that," Fiona said quietly. It was all she could offer.

A car pulled up behind Jenny's, and her lips parted when she saw Callum and Liam climb out. Both looked ready to kill.

"SECOND FIRST DATE in two weeks and still no connection?" Callum asked Liam as he took a right turn. They were on their way to grab some stuff from the grocery store for the kitchen at work. Cassie usually went, but she'd taken a few days of leave.

He chuckled. "Nope. I should give up while I'm ahead, shouldn't I?"

Callum's lips twitched. "No. You should stay out in the dating pool until you find a woman who makes you want to go on a second date."

"I don't know, Cal. I don't know if that's in the cards for me like it is with you guys."

Callum laughed. Women fell all over themselves for Liam. No way was he getting away with *not* dating. "You just haven't found her yet."

"I'm not in a rush." Liam leaned his head back against the headrest. "You and Fiona are doing pretty well."

More than well. He loved her, and he was well and truly ready to tell her. "I feel so damn lucky to have met her."

The chances of meeting a woman who just got you and made you feel as much as Fiona did were slim. For him, anyway. Yet it had happened. Luckiest man on the damn planet.

"I'm happy for you."

Callum turned the corner...and his eyes narrowed at the scene halfway down the road. A car was parked almost on the sidewalk, and another sat on an angle in front of it.

It took him another second to realize the couple outside one of the cars was Fiona and Freddie.

"What the *fuck?*"

He slammed his foot on the brake behind what he now realized was Jenny's car and jumped out. Before he could reach Freddie, Fiona stepped in front of Callum and touched his chest. "It's okay."

"What did I tell you about staying away from her?" Callum shouted. He should have broken the fucker's arm the last time he'd pulled a stunt like this.

When Freddie didn't respond, didn't even look at him, Callum tried to sidestep around Fiona, but she mirrored him, keeping her palm on his chest.

"Callum. I'm okay," she said quietly.

A beat of silence passed before finally his gaze shifted down to her. "You sure?" He scanned her body, checking every inch he could see.

She nodded.

His gaze shifted to Jenny, who stood to the side of the road, arms around her waist in a defensive gesture. "Are *you* okay?"

She nodded.

Fine. The asshole would live another day.

Fiona turned back to Freddie. "You need to go. Leave Cradle Mountain and return to Twin Falls."

Freddie held her gaze for what felt like an eternity, and it made Callum's blood boil. Then the guy stormed back to his car.

"What did he want?" Callum asked, trying and failing to keep his voice calm.

She exhaled loudly as she turned back to him. "Olivia had sex with him. Told him she loved him. He thought it was me, and he didn't understand why I would forgive him, then ice him out again."

Callum cursed, ready to find this damn woman and take her down.

"So that's all he did?" Liam asked from behind Callum. "Talked?"

"Yes."

Liam looked at Jenny with obvious concern. "You sure you're okay?"

She gave a sharp nod, her bangs bouncing into her eyes. "It was just all a bit of a shock."

Liam stepped forward. "I can drive your car back to the library if you want."

Jenny frowned. "Oh…you don't have to—"

"I know. I want to."

Color tinged her cheeks, and she handed her keys to Liam.

"We'll go get the cups and water," Fiona said to Jenny, who gave another small nod before getting into her car.

The second Jenny and Liam were gone, Callum stepped forward and cupped her cheeks. "Why did you leave the library?"

She scowled. "Rick told me in no uncertain terms that I had to."

"I'm gonna kill him."

"I wouldn't stop you."

He swiped some hair from her face. "I hate that Freddie had you alone out here."

"I know. But now that he knows it wasn't me in that hotel room, I'm hoping he'll leave Cradle Mountain."

He'd better. If not, he'd get a little nudge from Callum and his team.

"I'm putting a man on you at all times," he said firmly. He'd already offered it to her, but she'd declined. This time, he didn't care if she didn't like it. Her safety came first.

She shook her head. "No one will attack inside the library. This was my fault for leaving. I let Rick bully me into it. I won't do it again."

"Not taking the chance."

"It's a waste of your resources."

He wanted to growl. "Your safety is not a waste of resources. This is non-negotiable, Fiona."

She must have heard in his voice that he wasn't backing down on this. She sighed. "You're probably right. Thank you."

His deep chuckle had her looking up. "Probably? I'm definitely right."

"Don't let it go to your head."

Callum lowered his head until his lips hovered over hers. "You don't go anywhere without me or my team on you. I mean it."

"I know. I screwed up. I'm sorry."

He tugged her into his arms and held her close. He needed to keep this woman safe. There were no ifs, ands, or buts about it.

CHAPTER 28

*C*allum pushed his body to the limit, his feet pounding the pavement in a fast, even rhythm, air rushing through his lungs. He'd always been a good runner. And he enjoyed it. The freedom it gave you. The way it blurred the world and the problems within it.

Liam was at Callum's house with Fiona. He'd needed to get out and move. The run certainly wasn't what it used to be, though. Before Project Arma, he'd been able to exhaust himself, mind and body. Push himself so hard that he could numb his thoughts.

Now, it felt so much fucking harder, and his problems so much heavier.

He loved Fiona. The emotion had snuck up on him. Hit him in the damn chest while he'd been busy getting to know her. He welcomed it...but the danger that surrounded her scared him.

He rounded a corner onto his street, spotting Liam's car halfway down in front of his house.

Fiona was officially on lockdown. Where she was, he or someone from his team would be. He'd made a mistake not sticking someone on her twenty-four-seven earlier. He wasn't making that mistake again, not when Olivia and Freddie were still out there. She was still getting those damn texts too, which were likely Olivia. He was leaning toward just blocking the damn number.

Too many possible threats coming from too many directions.

When he entered his house, Liam was standing by the window, arms crossed.

Callum closed the door. "Everything okay?"

Liam took a moment before dragging his gaze to Callum. "She's okay. Went up to the bedroom to lie down."

He slid his shoes off and crossed the room to stand beside his friend. "You thinking about how quiet it's been, too?"

"Yeah," Liam agreed. "Calm before the storm?"

Fuck, he hoped not. "All the pieces are telling us she wants to take over Fiona's life. Hide from the people who are after her."

"The perfect out," Liam said quietly. "Which would mean, she'd need Fiona—"

"Gone." Dead. It would be the only way to assume her life. Callum's insides rolled at the thought.

Liam finally turned to look at Callum. "You want me to stay?"

"Nah. I'll call if I need you. Thanks for coming over while I got out for a run."

"Hope it helped."

When his friend left, he closed and locked the door, then alarmed the house. The alarm was more for his team. If it went off, they'd be alerted.

He grabbed some water from the fridge and downed half the bottle before moving upstairs. He wasn't sure if he was expecting Fiona to be asleep or just resting, but she was doing neither of those things. Instead, she sat cross-legged on the center of the bed. An open book sat to her right, but it looked like she'd deserted it. Instead, photos and printed information were spread around her. It was everything Callum had been able to find on her birth mother and twin sister that he'd printed off for Fiona.

She ran a finger over her mother's face, like she was trying to become familiar with someone she'd never met.

"She missed out on raising a hell of a woman," he said quietly.

Fiona's gaze swung up. "Mom said I looked only a day or two old when I was left at their front door. And I can't help but think that she never even tried. To get clean. To be the mother Olivia and I needed her to be."

He crossed the room and sat on the edge of the bed. "Your mother was an addict. From what I found, it looks like she had no family. No one to lean on or to help her get clean. In leaving you at a friend's home, she probably thought she was doing her best by you."

She stared at the photo of her twin sister. "I'm not sure it was best for Olivia." She shook her head. "Since we found out about her, I've just been feeling so guilty. Like I somehow *took* the better life."

Callum cupped her cheek. "Hey. Look at me, Fiona." It took a beat, but she finally did. "You got the better life, there's no questioning that. But that was by chance. You had no hand in that, you didn't *take* anything. And I said it before, but I'll say it again, if situations were reversed, you would not be doing what she's doing."

"How do you know? I've had privilege and safety and love. She's had none of that."

"Because I know your heart." He touched a hand to her chest, felt the thumping beneath his palm. "You are inherently good. You did not have a choice in your upbringing. And her adversity does *not* excuse her trying to hurt others."

A small hint of a smile touched her lips. Then she cupped his hand, which still held her cheek, and rubbed the soft pad of her thumb over his skin. "You continue to be my knight in shining armor, pulling me back when I'm right on the edge."

"I'll be whatever you need me to be, honey."

His gaze caught on something on her arm, and his eyes

narrowed. Were those fucking bruises? She followed his gaze, and when she saw what he was looking at, she covered her arm with her hand.

"That asshole bruised you." It wasn't a question. She'd been wearing a sweater earlier today, so he hadn't seen the marks. Fuck, he wanted to murder the scumbag.

"I'm okay. And with some luck, he might leave town now. In fact, he said it was over between him and Amanda, so he might be out of my life for good."

Callum's jaw clicked. He'd seen the way Freddie looked at her today. Like she was *all* he saw. He wasn't so sure getting rid of the asshole would be so easy.

He shifted his hand from her cheek to her arm, gently brushing her hand off the marks before grazing them with his thumb. Then, slowly, he leaned down and kissed the bruises, one at a time, making a vow that no man would ever hurt his woman again.

Her breath hitched. Slowly, he trailed his kisses up her shoulder, then her neck. When he reached her cheek, she sighed and tilted her head.

"Callum..." His name came out throaty and raspy, and so damn sexy, he wanted to replay it over and over again.

Her hands went to the base of his shirt and tugged it over his head, then she grazed her fingers down the planes of his chest, leaving a trail of fire in her wake.

"I've just been on a run, Fi. I need to shower."

She chuckled, and the sound dug into his chest, laying its claws into his damn heart. She kissed his cheek, then his ear before whispering, "You could have been dragged through mud and I'd still want you. Every. Time."

Her words blazed through him, decimating every other thought.

His lips crashed to hers, his tongue sweeping inside her mouth. One arm swept around her waist, while the other shoved aside the papers on the bed. Even the book thudded to the floor. Then he lay her down, his body pressing hers into the mattress. She was soft against him, and each touch felt like silk to his fingertips.

His lips left her mouth but never her skin, trailing down her chin and neck before reaching her top. She wore a button-up white shirt that fucking toyed with him. One button popped open, then another. One by one, he bared her skin, his kisses trailing down the center of her chest as he went. When he saw the bra had a front hook, he wanted to groan.

He unlatched it, freeing her perfect tits, then swooped, wrapping his lips around one tight bud. Fiona cried out, the sound slicing through him, cutting into his damn heart. He swiped his tongue over that perfect nipple, finding the other with his fingers and thrumming.

She writhed and arched below him, clenching and tugging his hair. Every movement was torture. He switched to her other breast while he reached down and undid the top button of her jeans before unzipping her.

He slipped inside her panties, and her breath stopped. At the first stroke of his finger over her clit, she arched, and the sounds she made were pure music. Perfectly tuned beats of moans and groans made just for him.

He played with her clit, his mouth never leaving her breast. She was close, exactly where he wanted her.

"Callum...I need you!"

Best damn words he'd ever heard. In under a second, he had her jeans and panties off and his own shorts and briefs removed. Then he was between her thighs, loving how she widened for him. Welcomed him.

He held her gaze as he slowly pushed inside. Stretching her. Stealing the breath from both their lungs. When he was seated deep inside her walls, he took a moment to watch the woman, almost in awe.

Beautiful. So damn beautiful. He cupped her cheek, his thumb swiping the delicate skin beside her eye.

"I love you, Fiona." The words slipped from somewhere deep inside him, accidental yet perfectly placed. Because those words had been tormenting him. Clawing at his throat, needing to get free.

Her eyes widened, tears filling them as her heart sped up.

"I've loved you for a while," he continued in her silence. "So much that you're all I think about. You've become my world. Wherever you are, I need to be."

She swallowed, a single tear slipping down her face. He caught it with his thumb and wiped it away.

"Callum...I love you so much that I can barely think about my future without thinking of the life I want to live with you. The life I crave because I crave *you*."

Each word dug deeper inside him until she was all he could feel. His head dropped and he kissed her. Drowned in her. Then he moved, lifting his hips before thrusting back inside.

Fiona whimpered, and he did it again, starting a long, rhythmic series of thrusts, each one bringing them closer, chaining them together.

He never separated his lips from hers, never wanting to be apart from her. She'd become such a key element of his world that he had no center without her. No damn strength to go on. To continue. To survive without her.

Fiona's fingers dug into his shoulders, her leg curving around his hips, urging him deeper. Faster.

He reached for her breast, rolling her bud between his thumb and forefinger.

Her nails bit into his skin, her back arched, then she broke, her long, passion-filled screams cutting through the air. Callum wanted to hold on, but at the feel of her walls pulsing around him, he growled and his body shattered. For her. Always for her.

CHAPTER 29

"Oh my freaking God, this room is packed."

Fiona chuckled at Jenny's words, her gaze sweeping over the mass of bodies in the library. "It really is."

There were people everywhere, of all ages. Mostly women, all fans of the historical romance author who stood at the front of the room, but some obvious husbands who'd been dragged along. It was actually pretty special to have the author in a small-town library like Cradle Mountain.

Her gaze flicked to the back door. She could just make out Liam through the crowd. Callum stood at the front entry point, and she was pretty sure they had a third man roaming around outside. No one would be getting her out of this place except the guys.

It would have been easier to just take a day of leave, something she'd mentioned to her favorite boss, but Rick had insisted they needed all hands on deck. And actually, seeing how many people had turned up, he wasn't wrong.

"Why are you two just standing there?"

Fiona jumped and spun at Rick's voice. God, was he hearing

her thoughts now too? Was she not safe anywhere? She cleared her throat. "We're just making sure everyone has a seat."

"By standing and watching?"

"Well, no—" Jenny tried, but Rick cut her off.

"Go." Then he blew out a breath like he was trying to calm himself. "I'm sorry, I'm just...stressed. Please help people to their seats so we can get started."

She'd told him about the twin sister and the danger. He'd looked shocked and gone really quiet. Since then, he'd been making an effort to be less of an asshole. He still was an asshole, of course, just a bit less. Even now, as she watched the back of him as he moved away, she knew if she ever got him alone in a room with a bat in her hand—

"You fantasizing about his death too?" Jenny asked.

"Baseball bat and an empty room."

"Baseball bat? Ha. My fantasy has a torture chamber and a vat of acid."

Fiona laughed before splitting off from Jenny and moving through the crowd. She spoke to a few people, helped a couple get to their seats, but intentionally beelined for the outer edge of the crowd near the front so she could see Callum. When her eyes landed on him, it was to see him at the door, talking to Tyler, who she guessed was manning the exterior of the library.

It all felt a bit like overkill. Even the craziest psychotic wouldn't attempt to kidnap her in front of all these people... would they? If this sister *did* want to take her place, she wouldn't very well kill her in front of everyone. That was just stupid.

But she hadn't argued with Callum's plan, because she knew he was nervous. He'd barely been himself for days, his gaze continually scanning every place they went, double-checking the locks and alarms at home, calling for backup on most of their outings.

As if he felt her gaze, his eyes shifted to her, and his deep frown eased, replaced by one side of his mouth lifting. Then he winked.

He'd also been doing *that* a lot—trying to hide how anxious he was by erasing it from his face when he looked at her. She returned the smile and walked over to him, not caring if Rick saw.

Immediately, his arm swept around her waist, and he kissed her. "You okay?"

"Mm-hmm." She wet her lips, gaze skirting his face. "Are you?"

"Yeah, we got it all covered out here."

Not really what she was asking. "I've got to get back before Rick sees me. But I was thinking Chinese takeout for dinner."

His smile broadened. "Can't wait."

One more kiss, then reluctantly, she moved away. Wow. She'd actually gotten a kiss in without Rick popping out from the crowd and berating her.

Once this was over, she'd reach out to the Ketchum Library and see if there were any available positions. She'd be sad about leaving Jenny, but honestly, there was only so much Rick she could take.

She helped a few more people find seats, passed a couple of the librarians who looked as excited as the visitors, then reached Jenny again, who blew out a breath.

"Christ, I didn't know this many women lived in Cradle Mountain."

"I know, it's like they magically materialized just for today."

Jenny was just opening her mouth to respond when an exasperated sigh sounded to her right.

Good God, was he just watching them? Waiting for them to find their way back to each other?

"Seeing as you two are stuck at the hip," he said, "I need you to get more paper plates. People are eating more snacks than I thought."

Fiona's gaze swung to the table, and sure enough, all the plates were gone. *Crap.* "I don't think we have any more, Rick. Everything we bought was put out."

He opened his mouth, presumably to chew her head off, when Jenny linked their arms and quickly said, "It's okay. I think I saw some in storage."

Her friend pulled her through the crowd toward the back. Fiona lowered her head and whispered, "Storage?"

Once they were in Rick's office, Jenny moved to his desk and opened the top drawer, pulling out a small key. "Yeah, Rick keeps a few things down there. He's made me get stuff before. It's like I'm his slave some days."

Jenny moved to a door at the side of the office, a door that was always kept locked.

"Uh, I've never seen that opened." Granted, she didn't go into Rick's office much, but still...

"Like I said, Jenny equals slave." She laughed and unlocked the door before stepping forward. Fiona craned her neck and saw... Holy heck, a staircase. There was a *basement* down there?

Jenny moved confidently down the stairs, and Fiona followed into the dark basement.

CALLUM WAS ready for this to be over. Hell, he'd been ready all damn day. There were too many people, and the crowd made him anxious as hell. The author was done with her reading and seemed to be at the tail end of signing books.

His gaze found Fiona for what had to be the hundredth time that day. She was smiling and helping some readers in the line. When she caught Callum's gaze, her features softened. Rick moved over to her, and Callum's muscles tightened. He fucking hated that guy.

Fiona nodded at something he said, then moved toward the

staff room just as his cell rang. He tugged his phone out, watching as Fiona left the staff room with her bag, surprised as hell that Rick was actually letting her leave.

He answered the call. "Logan. Hey."

His friend had gone down to the lodge today to check that Freddie had left.

When Fiona reached him, he touched a hand to the small of her back and led her outside, nodding at Tyler as he went. Tyler would also let Liam know they were done.

"I'm just leaving the lodge," Logan said.

Callum scanned the lot as he walked, not wanting any surprises. When he reached the car, he opened the passenger door and guided Fiona inside. He waited until the door was closed to respond. "Was he there?"

"Nope. Room is empty and he's checked out."

Thank fuck. The asshole was finally getting the damn picture. He slid into the car. "Thanks for checking for me."

"You got it."

He hung up and started the car. "Happy with how it went?"

"Yes," she said with a smile, pulling her seat belt across her body. "It was great. And even better that it's done now."

Yeah, exactly how he felt. He pulled out of the lot. "I'm surprised Rick didn't make you wait until everyone was gone."

"He's been kind of okay since I told him about my twin…for Rick standard. Plus, he had big, intimating men at the door watching him."

Good. Whatever the hell got her out of there was fine with Callum.

As he drove, he continued to shoot his gaze between the road and the rearview mirror. He didn't want any surprises.

The drive home was pretty quiet. It wasn't until they were a street away from his place that she touched his thigh. "Hey. You okay?"

Shit. He was doing a bad job at hiding the unease swimming through his gut. "Yeah, just worried."

"You know, this twin hasn't said or done anything for a while. Maybe she's given up. Realized I'm too well protected."

Callum's brows twitched. In a perfect world, that might be true. Unfortunately, he'd seen too many messed-up people who didn't give up on a cause so easily. "Maybe."

He covered her hand with his own and squeezed it before pulling into his garage. When they stepped inside, he got her to wait by the entrance as he checked that every window and door was still locked.

"We're clear."

Fiona smiled. "Perfect. I might go and have a shower if that's okay? It's been a long day."

She was just moving away when he grabbed her wrist and frowned. This was the first time he was getting a proper look at her, and there was just something...different. He frowned. "Is everything—"

His words were cut off by the ringing of his phone. He cursed and pulled it out to see Liam's name flash on the screen.

"Take it," she said with a smile. "Then we can talk dinner."

She headed up the stairs, and he waited until he heard her step into the bedroom to answer. "Hey."

There was the rumble of an engine in the background. "Hey. I've been thinking about something throughout the day..."

When Liam paused, Callum urged, "Tell me."

"Have you seen the way Jenny looks at Fiona when Fiona's attention is somewhere else?"

He paused. "No. How does she look at her?"

"I don't know if it was just today, but there was an...intensity in her gaze. Like she was, I don't know, studying her. I caught it a couple of times before the reading began, but I didn't see Jenny after."

Callum moved to his office, dropped into his chair, and cracked open his laptop. "I haven't noticed, but then, I'm usually looking at Fiona or for an outsider to attack."

"I was also thinking," Liam continued, "we've assumed this person's been watching her at a distance. What if they haven't? What if they've been in her life this whole time but dressed in disguise?"

Callum's stomach clenched at the thought. He put the phone on speaker and set it on the desk. "Give me a minute, Liam." Then he started looking into Jenny, searching for information he shouldn't be able to find.

It took him a couple minutes, then—

"Shit."

"What?" Liam asked.

He leaned back in the seat, scrubbing his hands over his face. How had he not looked into this earlier? "The woman's a fake," he said, almost not believing his own words. "I can see from a time-stamp that her driver's license was created three months ago. Whoever did this for her did it illegally, using a back door."

"So Jenny—"

"Isn't Jenny," Callum finished. "But she can't be Olivia. She doesn't look anything like Fiona. They have different colored eyes. She has a mole on her cheek. Hell, she even has a small scar beside her right eye. The only thing they have in common is their height and build."

"Maybe she's the person behind the texts," Liam said quietly.

It was possible. They'd assumed Olivia was behind the texts, but maybe not.

Fuck. Fiona had been working with that woman, a fake, hanging out with her, all this time… "Have you left the library?"

"Yes. But before I did, I checked for Jenny and she was gone. She must have gone out the front after you."

His gut tightened. "Can you go to the woman's house?"

"On it. Send me the address."

Callum dug until he found the rental in the name she was using. He sent it to Liam, all the while berating himself for his huge fucking oversight.

CHAPTER 30

$\mathcal{L}$iam took the stairs two at a time. Jenny's apartment building wasn't just in the worst part of town, it was also the worst fucking building amongst the dumps— peeling paint, a musty, moldy smell thickening the air. Tyler was on his way as backup, but Liam was impatient. The second that address had come through, he'd wanted to check it out. If the woman was targeting Fiona, he needed to know now.

When he reached the third floor, he moved down the hall. Sounds pricked his ears from behind closed doors. TVs. Dishes clattering in water. A person in the shower. Behind one door, he heard the raised voices of a couple arguing.

He ignored all of it, stopping in front of Jenny's apartment and knocking. He waited exactly five seconds, listening for any movement on the other side. When there was nothing, he pulled a glove from his pocket and slid it over his hand, then turned the handle, easily breaking the lock.

He stepped into a dark apartment. Every curtain was pulled closed, every light switched off. The space was small, with a kitchenette to the left, a couch and TV to the right, and a small dining table separating the two spaces. The musky smell didn't end in the hall. If anything, it was thicker in here.

Damn, the place was a mess.

Dishes were piled up in the sink. The carpet was riddled with stains and appeared to have not been cleaned for months. There was an open door that he could already see led to a bathroom at the end of a hall, and two closed doors on either side.

He was just closing the door to the hall when his phone rang. He already knew who it would be. Callum was anxious to learn what he'd found—as he should be.

"I'm in," Liam said quietly, scanning the messy kitchen counter. The scurry of movement from inside a cupboard had his head shooting around. It sounded again, and he looked away. A rat or some other rodent.

"See anything?"

"The apartment building's a dump and her place is a mess." He shuffled around the stuff on the table. There were a lot of takeout coffee cups and paper bags. Napkins. He paused on a couple of printed receipts, eyes narrowing. "There's a receipt for a tattoo."

"A tattoo?" Callum sounded as confused as him.

Liam lifted another two receipts. "There's a receipt for a lock-smith, and she also paid for some online acting courses."

"The key…" Callum breathed. "If she was the one who entered Fiona's house, it could be for that. She'd have access to Fiona's bag all day. Maybe she made a copy of the library back door key too. And *acting* classes?"

Yeah, sounded fishy as hell. A bad feeling began to churn in Liam's gut. "I'm going to check the bedrooms."

He moved to the room on the left to find a large bed centered the space, but similar to the living room, there was shit every-where. The bed was unmade. Clothes covered every inch of the floor. And there were more takeout containers.

He moved to her dresser, checking each drawer but finding nothing that shouldn't be there…until he reached the last drawer.

"Did you say it was a red sweater Olivia stole from Fiona and wore with Freddie?"

"Yeah, why?"

Liam's fingers tightened on the material. "I found it in her dresser."

There was a long, thick silence, then Callum let out a string of curses.

It was pretty good evidence that this woman was involved, but it also wasn't enough. Fiona and Jenny were friends. Lots of women bought similar clothing. "There's one more room. I'll see what's in there."

He moved out of the bedroom and tried the last door. His brows slashed together when it wouldn't open easily. She'd locked it? A room in her own apartment? He gave the knob one sharp turn, breaking the lock as he'd done to the front door.

The second he flicked the light, every muscle in his body turned to stone.

It took a lot to surprise Liam. You didn't go through deployments, then Project Arma, without seeing a shitload of messed up. But this?

His inhale was sharp.

"What?" Callum growled.

"It's her. It's fucking *her*, Cal. Jenny is Olivia."

Another thick, dangerous beat of silence. "What do you see?"

He ran his gaze over the images plastered on every inch of the back wall. All of Fiona, and all in different places. In some she was alone, in others she was with Callum. Some of the photos had notes on them.

Right side of mouth higher than left.

Squint eyes when smiling.

His gaze shot to the closet to the right of the back wall. It was open, with women's clothing inside. Fiona's clothing? Or replicas? There were also wigs and makeup. Boxes of contact lenses.

His blood burned through his veins like acid as he moved to a computer that sat on a small corner desk. "She's taken photos of Fiona and stuck them on the walls. There are hundreds of them, Cal. Clothing, contact lenses, and wigs too."

"I want to kick my own ass. She's been under our damn noses this entire time."

Liam lowered to the seat in front of the laptop and tapped some keys. He expected to be stopped by a locked screen, a password he didn't have. Instead, the computer woke to what she'd last been doing.

Two images sat side by side. At first glance, they looked identical, but on closer inspection he saw slight differences. The whites of the eyes in the photo on the right weren't quite so bright, and there were darkish circles that shadowed those dark eyes.

He moved the mouse, minimizing the photos and finding a folder full of images, some labeled "Fiona," the others labeled "replica."

He scrubbed a hand over his face and leaned back. "She's been practicing Fiona's expressions."

"I'm gonna kill her," Callum growled.

Liam clicked into another folder, his chest tightening when he saw videos inside. He opened the first one and his stomach soured. "She put cameras in Fiona's house. They date back to a couple months ago."

This woman hadn't just been studying Fiona. She'd put all her time and resources into *being* her.

THE SECOND CALLUM HUNG UP, he wanted to punch something. Throw his fist through a damn wall and let the pain drown out the frustration. The raw fucking anger.

She'd been right there the entire damn time, and no one had suspected her.

He scrubbed his hands over his face as he heard the shower turn off upstairs. Now, he had to go tell Fiona that her best friend was actually her twin sister. Was attempting to steal her damn life. Hell, the tattoo was likely the damn birthmark.

Fuck.

He shoved his phone into his pocket and moved up the stairs. His steps were slower than they should be because he was dreading the coming conversation.

He stopped at the closed bedroom door, frowning.

Fiona never closed the door.

He turned the handle and stepped inside to find Fiona pulling a shirt over her head. She looked up and smiled at him. "Hey. What should we have for dinner? I'm starving."

He frowned in surprise. "You still want takeout?"

She paused. "Oh, yeah, of course. Sorry, I'm exhausted."

He took a couple more steps into the room. "I need to tell you something, and I think you should sit down while I do."

Her brows rose. "Oh, um. Okay."

She moved to the bed and perched on the edge, and again, he was hit by that feeling he'd gotten downstairs. Like something was different about her.

"Jenny's not who you think she is," he said quietly.

There was a beat of silence, where Fiona's lips parted, and she just looked at him. She finally shook her head. "What?"

"Liam didn't like the way she was looking at you today, so I did a search on her and found she's been using someone's else's identity. Liam then went to her place. He found pictures of you and surveillance videos. Even acting-class receipts."

Fiona covered her mouth. "Oh my God!"

Callum studied her. Was it just him, or was there something almost...disingenuous about her reaction?

A bad feeling began to churn in his gut, something he had no fucking clue how to even navigate. She looked and felt...different. And now her reaction didn't feel authentic.

"I don't know what to say," Fiona said, shaking her head.

"Did you suspect anything?" Callum asked carefully, studying every part of the woman in front of him as she answered.

"I mean, I've only known her for a few months, so it shouldn't surprise me. But she was my friend."

Her voice...that was different too. He heard it now. He'd been distracted before, with the phone calls and the need to get home away from the crowd, but now that he really focused on her, it was like each word was carefully said in a certain tone. Too carefully.

"Well, at least I have you guys to protect me," she said, before touching the bridge of her nose with her forefinger.

It took him half a second to realize what she'd just done.

She'd tried to push nonexistent glasses up the bridge of her nose. Only, Fiona didn't wear glasses.

Jenny did.

His stomach dropped, his skin turning stone cold in utter disbelief at having his suspicion confirmed. The woman's hand lowered slowly, like she realized her mistake.

He took a step forward to grab her, but she quickly pulled a gun from beneath her discarded towel on the bed. She stood and aimed it at his chest.

"After the way you looked at me downstairs, I knew I needed to keep this close. Just in case."

Her voice was different now. Raspier. Colder.

"Where the fuck is Fiona?" Callum growled, the shock now twisting into a suffocating mix of fear and rage. Fear for his woman. That she was somewhere else. Possibly dead already. That he'd figured this out too late. And rage that this fucking imposter had done something to her.

"He would have taken her by now. Doesn't really matter, though. Soon she'll be dead—just like you."

His hands fisted. "Where. Is. She?"

"It's a shame I have to kill you. You would have been a fun boyfriend. For a while."

"You have five seconds to tell me before I force the words out of you."

He'd never hurt a woman in his life, but this person wasn't a damn woman. She was a fucking monster. And she was the only thing standing between Fiona and safety.

"I'm holding the gun, Callum, so I'm in charge. But if you really want to know, I have enemies. And they may have received a *tip* on Olivia's location. Maybe even a photo of her new appearance..."

He was so fucking close to snapping, his muscles twitched, but first he had to get information from her. "So you sent the assholes you stole from to the library?"

She scoffed. "You think I'm that stupid? I couldn't have the bitch dying here in Cradle Mountain and exposing me. I was actually going to drive to a location the other day, when I convinced Rick to send her to the store. Then that idiot Freddie followed us. And of course *you* found us and ruined everything by refusing to leave her side. So, I had to get creative. Decided Freddie could be useful. I went to visit him at the lodge. Told him who I was, that I planned to kill Fiona. Him too. But if he agreed to help me, I'd let him live instead, and in addition, he could take Fiona and keep her for himself. Win-win."

If there was anything that could put even more gas on the fire of his rage, it was the knowledge that Freddie had agreed to take part in this.

"He's totally obsessed with her, if you haven't guessed. Of course," Olivia continued, "he doesn't know that the second he reaches the little house he's rented, he's going to get a not-so-friendly welcoming committee."

Callum took a small step forward, not caring about the gun pointed at his chest. "Give me the location of the house."

She laughed. "Why? So you can know where she's going to die? I don't think so. Any last words?"

"You messed with the wrong fucking guy, Olivia."

"Did you forget what I said? I have the—"

He dropped and kicked a leg out. The second she hit the floor, he rolled her to her stomach, grabbed the gun, and pressed it to her head, her own hand still on the weapon. "Give me the location."

Her breath wheezed from her chest. "*No.*"

He grabbed her other hand and pressed the muzzle of the gun to the center. "One fucking second. That's what I'm giving you to tell me before I shoot. And believe me when I tell you, I will *keep* shooting until I have the information I need."

CHAPTER 31

"*N*o. We're over."

Pain thrummed behind Fiona's eyes so fiercely, they refused to open. The person's voice was doing nothing to help her. Each word pinged her skull harder, like a perfectly placed blow.

A pause, then, "And I told *you* that we were temporary."

She bit back a groan, needing the noise to stop.

She tried to lift her hand, wanting to massage her temple, but something stopped her. It almost felt like...rope? She tried again, this time tugging harder, but was met by the same resistance.

Small flickers of awareness came to her. The hard surface under her. The crick in her neck, like her head had been at an odd angle for a long time. And tightness around her ankles. With each realization, her pulse beat faster, and her breath shortened.

Finally, she pieced it together...she was tied to a chair. The realization was both terrifying and infuriating.

Slowly, she forced her eyes open. Everything was a blur. No distinct shapes, just outlines and fuzzy movement. She blinked. Once. Twice. On the third, the shape in front of her began to come into focus. The lines turned into a pacing body...and that body was familiar.

Her lips parted, a gasp inflating her chest.

Freddie?

"I know, Stacey. But I'm going away and I'm not coming back. Deal with it."

Fiona's breath caught again. "Stacey?" The word felt dry and scratchy in her throat.

Freddie hung up and stopped his pacing to turn and look at her. His gaze whipped to the stairs and back, like he was...afraid? That she'd call for help? God, was there someone up there?

"You're awake," he said quietly.

Really? That was all he had to say?

Her brows scrunched as she tried to tug back her last memory. She'd been at work for the author reading. Rick had asked her to get some plates, and Jenny had gone with her to the office. Then...the key. Jenny had pulled out a key for a door, which had revealed a basement. She'd been walking down the stairs, then nothing. She couldn't remember a single thing.

Was she still in the basement?

"How did I get here?" It was an effort to make her voice work.

He swallowed and took a small step forward. "I'll tell you, but I need you to listen before you say anything. Okay?"

Her stomach rolled. She wasn't agreeing to anything. With an aggressive tug, she pulled at the bindings on her wrists, suddenly finding a small scrap of energy. "Tell me what's going on, Freddie! *Now*. And how do Jenny and Stacey fall into this?"

"Stacey doesn't. After you left me, she and I had a thing, but I ended it for you."

She balked. "You and Stacey got together?"

"Yeah. And I'm sorry about the messages she's been sending you. She got it in her head you'd want me again and it was her job to somehow stop that from happening. When I found out, I told her to stop."

Fiona opened and closed her mouth. *Stacey* had been sleeping with Freddie? And was responsible for those awful texts?

"But she's not the reason I'm here, tied to this chair?" Fiona gasped.

"No. She knows nothing about this. Jenny came to me last week with...an offer."

"Jenny? As in my *friend* Jenny? Jenny who works at the library?" Disbelief coated every word from her mouth. Because it was a lie, right? It had to be.

"Jenny isn't Jenny." He ran a hand through his hair, and there was a visible tremble in his fingers. "Her name's Olivia. And she's your twin."

Fiona's breaths stalled entirely, an icy layer of shock coating her skin. "That's not possible."

"It is."

His eyes shifted to something in the corner. She followed his gaze to a small pile of material. A wig...the outfit Jenny had been wearing at work...even her glasses.

She shook her head more vigorously, ignoring the jolts of pain it brought to her head. "I don't believe it." She couldn't. She knew Jenny. They saw each other almost every day.

"I thought you'd say that. So, I filmed her today. She didn't even see my phone sitting on a shelf, but I wanted it in case you thought this was all my doing."

He took out his cell and fiddled with it. She stared at it like it was a bomb about to detonate. When he crouched in front of her and placed the screen before her eyes, she almost didn't want to watch, but at the same time, she couldn't tear her gaze away.

The video showed the dim basement. Freddie stood beneath the stairs. There was the sound of a door opening, then footsteps. Jenny stepped into frame first, and Fiona followed. The second her feet hit the floor, Freddie raced forward and stuck something in her neck. A syringe.

She gasped as she watched herself drop, Freddie catching her before she hit the floor and laying her down gently.

"I'm sorry it had to be this way."

Her gaze flicked to him, anger like a living, breathing beast inside her. Like *hell* it had to be this way!

Her gaze returned to the screen, and she watched as Jenny removed her wig, revealing hair exactly like her own beneath it. She removed her glasses, then a pair of contacts, and grabbed a makeup wipe to scrub away a mole on her cheek and a scar beside her right eye.

Every move made by the woman had her looking less like Jenny and more like...Fiona.

No. No, no, no! This had to be a bad dream. A nightmare that felt so real, she couldn't wake up.

She did her makeup perfectly. When Jenny began taking off her clothes, and Freddie's hands went to Fiona's unconscious body, she wrenched her gaze away from the screen to look down at herself, seeing a plain black T-shirt and jeans. Oh God. She wasn't wearing the shirt and slacks she'd put on this morning.

Her gaze flew back to the screen to see Freddie had undressed her and was now redressing her in the clothes she currently wore. A disgusting, overwhelming feeling of being violated ran through her body.

Jenny was donning Fiona's clothes when Fiona noticed the birthmark on her side that looked exactly like hers. *Oh, God.*

Freddie took the phone away and pushed it back into his pocket. "She came to my room at the lodge. Took off her disguise and showed me who she was." He swallowed. "She told me she was going to kill you...but that I could save you."

"Save me?" Her gaze flicked around the basement. "Is *this* you saving me, Freddie?"

Please, God, let him say no. Let him say he'll take me to the police. Or better yet, to Callum.

"I've rented a place. Paid in cash. We're going to live there for a bit. Together. Just you and me."

Nausea crawled up her throat. "That's not saving me, Freddie. That's kidnapping."

He swallowed, guilt flickering in his eyes before he blinked it away. "It might take time for you to adjust. I screwed up, I know I did. But we were good together, and we can be good again. And this way, Olivia won't kill you."

"So, a woman comes to you, tells you she's going to kill me and assume my life, and instead of going to the police or, hell, going to me or even Callum and telling us, you agreed with her fucked-up plan and decided you're going to kidnap me and force me to live with you?"

His eyes narrowed, his voice hardening. "Like I said, it will take you some time to adjust."

"This is crazy. You see how this is crazy, don't you, Freddie?"

"What I see is the woman I love! The woman I'm a fucking shadow of a man without. The woman I need to win back. When the opportunity arose, I took it. Jesus, Fiona, I *saved* you! That woman was going to kill you."

She could have laughed at his earnestness. "If you really believe that, you're lying to yourself." She tried to calm her voice. "Let me go, and I won't tell anyone what you did. I'll pin it all on her."

It was a lie. She'd scream to anyone who listened about what this man had done, but her desperation made it sound true enough.

"No." The word came quickly, with no leeway.

Shit. Shit, shit, shit.

Her gaze went to the stairs. Were there still people in the library? Was Callum, Liam, or Tyler still up there somewhere?

She opened her mouth and screamed—a long, loud wail.

But Freddie didn't even flinch at the sound. He just shook his head. "They're gone. Which means we'll be gone soon, too." He glanced at his watch. "Five more minutes."

She tried to swallow her panic, her mind scrambling to come up with something to get her out of this. "Freddie, look at me."

He'd started that pacing again. It was his nervous pacing. She'd seen it many times before. But he did as she requested and stopped to look at her. She forced her features to soften. "You know this won't work. You can't abduct someone and expect them to love you. Things will never be like they were between us ever again."

And why did he even want that? They weren't good for each other. He'd been having sex with her *sister*. Maybe even her cousin at the same time, for all she knew.

Betrayal pressed on her chest. If the situation was different, she'd allow that betrayal to choke her. But it wasn't different. She was here, bound. She didn't have the luxury of feeling sorry for herself. She had to focus on getting out.

Freddie moved forward, once again crouching in front of her, hands on her knees. "I know. Things will be even *better* this time. I didn't appreciate you before. I got engaged to Amanda because she told me she was pregnant. Then I tried to fill the void with Stacey once you left. But neither of them were *you*. I won't hurt you again. We'll disconnect from our families. From Cradle Mountain. It will just be you and me, living on a big property I purchased for us in Utah." He cupped her cheek. "It will be an adjustment for you, but I'll look after you."

It took everything in her to not pull away from his touch. To not flinch or dry heave. He was taking her from her life, and he expected her to be...what? Excited? Grateful?

God, he was crazy. Just as crazy as Olivia.

Words tried to crawl up her throat. Words about Callum finding them. Saving her and murdering this man. But what would that achieve? It would cause him to restrain her even tighter. Possibly knock her out again so he could get her to the car.

She swallowed the words she wanted to say and whispered words that sounded sick to her own ears. "I *have* missed you." Her voice trembled with the force of the lie, the strength it took to release it into the air.

Hope danced in his eyes—but only for a moment, then it was replaced by suspicion. "You've missed me? You were just calling me crazy."

She wet her dry lips, using the fleeting moment to scrounge more lies. "Because you drugged me and tied me up, Freddie. My head, wrists, and ankles hurt. But...yes, I missed you. You cheated on me, so I had to try to learn how to live life without you. But if you can promise that you won't cheat again..."

"I won't. I swear on my life."

Ha. Like she'd believe anything this lying sack of shit said. "Good. Because I don't want to be cheated on again. I need to be able to trust you."

That's it. Make him work for it.

That hope returned to his light brown eyes. "You'll be the center of my world, Fiona." He nodded and stood. "Good. See? This is good. We can start a new life together." When he looked at her again, his gaze lowered to the rope around her ankles.

"I can walk, Freddie. I won't run." She was impressed by how the lie came out with such ease.

He ran a hand through his hair, the tremble in his movements becoming more violent. "I need to keep your wrists bound, but I'll untie your ankles. Getting out of here will be easier if I don't have to carry you."

Her stomach dropped, but she was careful to keep her features clear in case his tenuous trust snapped and he decided to knock her out instead. With unbound feet, she could run. With nothing over her mouth, she could scream. There was hope.

Her heart thumped when Freddie lifted a small knife from a

table against the far wall. He used the sharp blade to cut through the rope on her ankles.

"Once it's safe for her to do so, Olivia will return here and clean everything up," he muttered, almost to himself, like he was reminding himself of the details of the plan. When her legs were free, Freddie pulled her to her feet. Her head swam and her knees almost buckled.

Concern skittered over his face. "Are you okay?"

No, asshole, you drugged me. Oh, how she wished she could say exactly that.

"Yes," she said quietly. "I'm a little dizzy. I think I just need to lie down."

"You can sleep in the car. We'll only be driving about forty-five minutes tonight, just far enough to be safe. Then we'll do the rest of the drive tomorrow."

He lowered the knife to the table beside her, then looked around the room. When he stepped away from her to lift a back-pack, she quietly shuffled in front of the knife and grabbed it, attempting to hide it between her hands. It was small, so it wasn't hard. Thankfully, he didn't look for the weapon again, just grabbed her elbow and tugged her up the stairs.

Every step was an effort and had her head throbbing more. God, what had he given her?

When they stepped into the office, Freddie released her arm to close and lock the basement door. The second he turned his back, she used the knife to saw at the rope on her wrist. It was slow, but the blade was sharp. Twice, she nicked her skin, feeling a slice of pain.

"How long were you waiting in there before we came down?" she asked, keeping her front toward him, trying to distract him in case he noticed the movement of her hands behind her back.

He moved to Rick's desk to deposit the key. "Olivia let me in an hour before the library opened, and we went through everything."

Her chest tightened at the use of Jenny's real name. He'd used it in the basement, but with every passing minute, the reality of the situation sank just a little deeper.

Jenny was Fiona's twin sister. She'd been "friends" with her twin for months and hadn't even known it.

She hadn't fully cut through the rope before Freddie once again grabbed her arm and tugged her forward. The movement jolted her and caused another slip of the blade. She cringed but was careful to hide her pain as they exited the office and crossed the library to the back door. Everything was dark, and every so often, her head swam again, and she blinked her vision back to clarity.

He stopped and unlocked the back door, pulling it open. They shuffled through, then he tugged it closed and locked it. At every stop, she used the knife to slice at the rope. She was so close. She could feel the rope hanging on by a thread.

Instead of pulling her to the parking lot, he tugged her toward a side street. When he finally stopped beside a dark Ford, she vigorously used the knife to slice a few more times. The car door opened, and she gave her hands a violent tug.

The rope came apart just as Freddie turned.

In a desperate move, she swung her hand forward and dug the knife into his side.

At the sight of the blood, her belly coiled, but she ignored it, turning and running down the street of closed businesses. She made it half a block before thick arms wrapped around her and tugged her off her feet.

"No!"

She opened her mouth and screamed, putting as much volume behind it as possible.

Freddie's curse was a rumble against her back, then something cracked against her skull.

CHAPTER 32

*E*very muscle in Callum's body was tight as Flynn drove. He couldn't believe he'd driven home with Olivia and not known she wasn't Fiona. Yeah, he'd been distracted, but that goddamn distraction could cost Fiona her life.

His insides rebelled against the thought.

His entire team had gotten to his place within minutes of him calling. Now, Jason, Liam, Aidan, and Logan drove in cars behind him and Flynn, while Tyler waited for the police at the house so they could arrest Olivia. She'd be driven to Fiona and Freddie's first stop by the police, just in case they weren't there.

Blake had gone to the library to make sure Fiona wasn't there. Olivia had told them Freddie had already taken her, but he needed all bases covered. It hadn't taken him long to get the information he needed. A few bullets to the floor beside her head and hand and she'd cracked.

The entire team was working on this. Eight former soldiers. Eight men who were the equivalent of an army. But their skills would all be for nothing if they were too late. If the loan sharks who were after Olivia got to Fiona first.

His cell rang and Blake's number came up on the screen. He answered on the first ring. "Is she still there?"

"No."

Callum cursed. He'd known the chance was low, exactly why he was going to the house Freddie had rented for the night, but there'd been that dim hope.

"I checked the basement and found drops of blood by the door in the office," Blake continued. "Then more by the back door."

Callum's chest tightened. "Blood?" The fucker had hurt her?

Flynn pressed his foot harder to the gas.

"It's not much, just a few drops here and there." Wind blew over the line. "I'm going to head to the location now."

"We're half an hour away," Callum said through gritted teeth. Too damn far.

He hung up, clenching the phone so tightly in his fist it was close to being crushed.

Flynn looked at him. "We won't be too late. He would have gone the speed limit to avoid detection, so we're going to make up ground."

"If I'd just realized earlier—"

"Don't do that to yourself. She spent months making sure she was a perfect replica of Fiona, even going as far as to practice on people she knew. She would have fooled anyone."

He should have paid closer damn attention.

Flynn shot him a glance. "We have to be smart when we get there."

"You think I won't be?"

"I think if we find Fiona in a dangerous situation, you might put yourself at risk to save her."

Damn straight he would. There wasn't a chance in hell he'd watch her die to protect himself.

The gun felt heavy in his harness. If they'd harmed a hair on her head, he wouldn't use it. He'd tear the assholes apart with his bare hands. No pause. No hesitation.

"We remember our training," Flynn said quietly. "And we get everyone out alive."

They sure as hell better.

~

FIONA FOCUSED on deep breaths to keep from being sick. She'd come in and out of consciousness for a while, the consistent hum of the engine continuing to pull her under. The ache in her head combined with the drugs still flowing through her system was unrelenting. It stole almost all her energy.

She didn't know how long had passed before she finally turned to look at Freddie. He hadn't bound her wrists again, but she knew that if she tried her door, it would be locked. He looked so calm now. Because he thought he'd won? God, she wanted to hit the smugness out of him. The asshole really thought he could just keep her? Hell no.

Her gaze lowered to his side, where she'd stabbed him. He'd wrapped some gauze around his waist and the blood on his shirt was now dry.

"Are you okay?" he asked, his voice cutting through the silence.

Was he serious? "No, Freddie. I'm not *okay*. I've been drugged, hit on the head, and kidnapped while another woman takes my life!"

Only a freaking psychopath would think she'd be okay after all of that.

He swallowed, his knuckles whitening on the wheel. "You stabbed me and ran, Fiona. You should consider yourself lucky that all I did was hit you."

A low laugh that was the furthest thing from humorous escaped her lips. "You're right. Thank you for hitting me over the head and kidnapping me, Freddie. Thank you for deciding this was the better option than going to the police when Olivia told you what she planned to do."

His sharp breath was audible in the car. "Sarcasm isn't attractive on you. And I'm doing what I think is best for us."

"No. You're doing what you think is best for *you*." She sucked in a long breath in an attempt to keep the nausea and light-headedness at bay. Then she straightened and touched his arm, needing to convince him to turn this car around. "Freddie. You need help. I'm not sure when this spiral in your mental health started, but normal people do *not* kidnap women."

His chest rose and fell so heavily, she wondered if maybe she was getting through to him. "It started when you left me. When Amanda started criticizing every aspect of my life. Wanting to know where I was every second of the goddamn day. When she started shopping for cribs when there was no fucking baby!"

He slammed his fist against the wheel, and she jumped, snatching her hand back.

"It started," he continued, "when I tried to replace you with Stacey. But she wasn't you. Not even close. It started when I saw you with another man. When you teased me with the idea that we could be together again, then pulled away. When we had a blissful night together."

"Freddie, that wasn't me," she stated firmly, suddenly seeing more pain in his gaze than anything else. "You already know it wasn't."

"It was. In my head, it *was* you." He swallowed and straightened, seeming to get a hold of his emotions. "And it will be again."

Jesus Christ.

He pulled off the main road onto what looked like a dirt driveway. "We're here. Tomorrow morning, we'll drive to the property I bought."

Okay, this wasn't terrible. She had a night close to Cradle Mountain and the house was near a semi-busy road. If she could get away from Freddie and back to the road, she might just be able to flag someone down to help her.

Different escape plans ran through her head. She'd have to get a look at the house. See what she could use as a weapon.

Her mind was moving a million miles a minute when a car suddenly pulled out from behind some trees into the drive, right in front of them. Freddie slammed his foot on the brake and cursed.

Another car pulled out from the other side of the house. Both had their high beams on.

When lights shone from behind, Fiona swung her head around to see two more cars.

"What the hell is this?" Freddie gasped.

Dread clawed at her gut. It dug so deep, she struggled to get air. "Freddie…did you tell Olivia you were bringing me here?"

His gaze swung to her. "Yes. She asked what my plan was, so I told her."

Her heart started to pound to a new rhythm, loud and hard in her chest.

"What?" Freddie asked.

"Olivia stole money from some really bad people, then she ran. If she took over my life, she may have put me into *hers* to get them off her back."

All the color drained from Freddie's face.

The doors of the cars in front of them opened, and big men in sleeveless shirts, all of them riddled in tattoos, stepped out, two from each car. The guns in their hands made a new wave of terror weave through her belly.

"Get out," one of the men yelled.

For a moment, Fiona was still, not because she was intentionally going against the order, but because she was utterly paralyzed. Unable to move. Unable to speak.

The same man lifted his gun and aimed for their windshield. "Get out now, or I'll shoot you through the glass."

Move, Fiona.

The shout in her head had her trembling fingers reaching for the door. It opened, but when she turned, she saw Freddie was still sitting there, so pale she wondered if he'd pass out. She shoved his shoulder.

"Freddie, we need to get out or they'll kill us."

Her words seemed to pull him out of whatever trance he'd been in. He undid his seat belt and climbed out with her. She turned to look behind them, spotting an almost identical scene of four men standing in front of two cars.

Eight men in total surrounded them, all armed. Unless she could talk her way out of this, she was screwed.

She lifted her hands and opened her mouth, but before she could speak, Freddie did.

"She's not Olivia! And I'm not part of this. We can tell you where the real Olivia is, but you need to let us—"

The bullet cut through the air, hitting Freddie between the eyes.

Fiona's heart stopped, her world almost fading to black. She covered her mouth with one hand and grabbed the car with the other to keep herself upright.

Freddie…dead. The two words together didn't compute in her head.

Before she could completely fall apart, her arm was grabbed from behind and she was shoved forward. The fingers were tight and punishing, and she stumbled so many times, she wasn't sure how she made it in front of the car. But when she was, the man who'd done the talking came forward, only stopping when he was right in front of her. Then he studied her. Her eyes. Her face.

"You killed him," she whispered, the words tortured. She hadn't liked Freddie. Hell, the man had been planning to keep her hostage. But she'd known him for so long…dated him for six years. She hadn't wanted him to die.

"You look different, Cohls. I almost thought it wasn't you. You clean up good." He tilted his head. "If it wasn't for the eyes, I'd assume that tip-off was wrong."

She swallowed, terror stealing her voice. She wasn't sure if speaking or not speaking was better. These men obviously killed without hesitation.

"Freddie was right," she whispered, unable to stop herself. "I'm not Olivia. I'm her twin sister."

The men around her laughed. Even the man in front of her cracked a smile. "You forget, Cohls, I've known you a long time. You have no twin. No fucking family. I must admit, this sweet-girl act is convincing, though." He cocked his head. "You've done a good job, creating this little...disguise."

"My name is Fiona Lock. Olivia went into foster care, but I was adopted. I can take you to her."

The smile dropped from his face, and suddenly, the muzzle of his gun pressed to her forehead. "You know how much I hate your lies. I've heard them too many fucking times. And you know what else I hate? That you took money from me. Money you had no intention of paying back. You should have been smarter than that. No one steals from me and lives."

A tear fell from the corner of her eye, and the only thing she could think about in that moment was that she hadn't had enough time with Callum. To love him. To know him. To belong to him, and for him to belong to her.

The man's lips twitched. "Think about that while you rot in hell, Cohls."

The sound of a gunshot exploded.

It stopped her heart. Her breath. Her entire world. It made every emotion inside her heighten and sharpen.

It took her a fraction of a second to realize she was still standing and another to realize the man in front of her was on the ground.

Her lips parted, her gaze flying around her to see the other men shifting their focus to the trees, cursing as they aimed their weapons. A new gun was pressed to her head by a man behind her—but then another shot rang out, and he dropped as well.

The men suddenly took cover behind cars. Fiona wasn't sure if she should be running or hiding. She did neither. Because yet again, she couldn't move. She couldn't believe she was still standing.

Suddenly, bodies flew out of the trees, attacking the remaining hiding men so fast she *almost* couldn't track them.

But she did.

She spotted Liam and Jason. Then Callum and Flynn. They killed with precision, their speed and strength far greater than those of the other men.

The ease with which they took them out made her knees weak and her lungs seize.

She watched as Callum snapped a man's neck like it was a twig. Then his gaze found her. He blurred in front of her as the lack of air and the throbbing in her head caused the little energy she had left to disappear.

Fiona began to fall, but Callum's body became a blur again—this time as he raced toward her, grabbing her waist moments before she crumpled.

She leaned her head to his chest, breathing him in. "Callum."

"I'm here, honey. You're safe."

She closed her eyes and let him hold her, the night around them going silent. The violence was over.

She wasn't sure how long she stayed buried against his chest. She only pulled away when sirens sounded. She knew she'd have to talk to people, but she had no energy and her head was killing her.

Doors opened and closed, then a voice sounded. A familiar voice.

"Why am I fucking here?"

Fiona turned her head to see a woman who looked exactly like her, standing in cuffs.

Callum's mouth went to her ear. "They brought her in case we didn't find you," he whispered. "So she could help us."

Finally, the woman looked at her—and her eyes narrowed.

Like her feet had a mind of their own, Fiona tried to move away from Callum.

"Fiona—"

She turned to look at him, his arm still firmly around her waist. "I need to talk to her."

His chest moved up and down, then his jaw ground before he reluctantly moved forward with her.

"*You*," Olivia growled. "They were supposed to fucking kill you!"

There was so much hate in her voice that each word hit harder. But Fiona's voice was surprisingly calm. "You could have just come to me, explained things and asked for help."

Olivia laughed, the sound filled with scorn and bitterness. "I came to Cradle Mountain thinking I'd find a woman who'd experienced the same shit life I had. You know what I found instead? The sister who was given *everything* I wasn't. Opportunity. Love. Privilege. You got it all, and I got *nothing*!"

"That wasn't my doing."

"You think that changes anything? No. It was *my* turn to have it all."

Tears pressed to Fiona's eyes, but she didn't let them fall. Instead, she shifted further into Callum's embrace. "I would have loved you. And I would have helped you. I wish you'd chosen differently."

Then Fiona walked away from the sister she'd never known, the sister she never *would* know, ignoring her curses and angry shouts, understanding with everything she was, that if their situations had been reversed, she would have chosen differently.

CHAPTER 33

*C*allum's fingers tightened around the glass as he listened to Fiona in the bedroom. They were both still coming to terms with everything that had happened last night.

Paramedics had checked Fiona out thoroughly. She had another damn concussion, but other than that, she was fine. He'd wanted to go to the hospital, but she'd argued that she wanted to go home, for the night to just be over.

Seeing her surrounded by those men, the muzzle of a gun pressed to her head...

His chest tightened, and he had to physically force the air into his lungs. He'd never experienced that kind of fear in his life. The panic and rage and every other hell that could be experienced, all at one time.

He set the full glass of water onto the counter and grabbed the pain meds as memories of the night before continued to torment him. He'd been too far away when he'd taken that first shot—so deep in the woods, he shouldn't have hit his target. But he'd taken it because he'd had to. Because *not* shooting would have meant certain death for her.

He lifted the pills and moved to the stairs.

When he reached the bedroom, he found Fiona sitting in bed, sheets around her waist and phone to her ear. She looked so sad, and he fucking hated that. She was talking to her mother, telling her about Freddie and Stacey.

He set the pain meds and water onto the bedside table and sat on the edge of the mattress.

"I need to go," Fiona said quietly. "I love you too, Mom. Bye."

He wrapped his fingers around her thigh over the top of the sheet. "How'd it go?" He'd tried like hell not to listen to the entire conversation, but it had been hard.

She nibbled her bottom lip. "They're in shock. They're going to check in on Amanda today."

"And did you decide what to do about Stacey?"

He tried to keep the anger out of his voice, but it was damn hard.

Fiona blew out a breath. "I know you want me to press charges against her for those texts."

Fuck, yes, he did. The woman had put Fiona through a shit-load of emotional and psychological trauma. She should pay for that.

"But I just can't." She touched his chest. "Please understand. The family knows what she did, and I know my parents will rally against her."

It still didn't feel enough to him, but he could see the conflict in Fiona's eyes. The hurt.

Everyone in Fiona's life had gone about everything the wrong way. Olivia. Freddie. Amanda and Stacey. Hell, even her parents should have told her about the circumstances of her coming into their life.

He was going to make damn sure she was treated the way she deserved from now on.

She sighed and met his gaze. "I was honestly hoping to wake up and find everything from last night was a dream."

He cupped her cheek, needing to touch her. "I know. There's no more danger, though."

No one gunning for her or the sister who looked like her.

She swallowed, her eyes flicking between his. "When he pressed that gun to my head, I thought I was going to die."

Pain slashed through his chest, like a blade cutting his heart out. "I've never moved so fast in my life as I did in that moment."

"Do you know what went through my mind?"

"What?"

"That I wanted more time with you. I missed you already, and I wasn't even gone yet." She wrapped her fingers around his wrist. "I missed the time we were supposed to get. The things we were supposed to do."

His hand remained on her cheek, his thumb grazing her skin. "I felt the same things when I thought I was going to be too late. Like our future was about to be taken from us."

"But you weren't too late. It was your bullet that hit that first man, wasn't it?"

"Yes. I'm a good shot, but I was too damn far away, and I had no business making that one."

"But you did," she whispered. "You saved me." Water shimmered in her eyes. "Thank you."

He shook his head. "Don't thank me. I left the library with a woman who wasn't you. What happened is on my shoulders."

"No." The single word was said so firmly, he almost believed it. "She looked like me. She put months into studying *being* me. In your eyes, and in Freddie's, and in Rick's...she *was* me."

He shook his head. "I should have known. I wasn't looking at her properly. I was distracted by the crowd, by watching for an enemy. I almost cost you your life."

"None of this is your fault, Callum. You believed what she wanted you to believe. And she was good. Smart. She had to be to pull off everything she's done." Fiona shook her head. "The woman was my identical twin, and I was friends with her for months, and *I* never realized who she was until she wanted me to."

He could hear the pain in her voice. Because instead of giving Fiona a biological sister, the woman had tried to take everything from her.

"I'm so damn sorry," he said quietly.

"I wasn't lying last night. I would have done everything I could to help her."

"I know. Unfortunately, I don't think there *was* any helping her."

She leaned forward, her forehead touching his. "I love you so much. If I didn't have you—"

"You do. I love you too, Fiona. And I can't wait for us to have that future that was almost stolen from us."

Tears swam in her eyes once more, but they didn't fall.

"Move in with me." The words were out before he could stop them. He wanted this woman with him. In his home. By his side as much as damn possible.

"You want me to live with you?"

"There's nothing I want more."

A tear finally spilled over her cheek. He leaned down and kissed it. He was just straightening when she nodded and whispered, "Yes."

Yes…the woman was his. She'd live with him. He growled and kissed her on the mouth, her soft lips swiping against his. He needed to let her take the pain meds, but he couldn't make himself stop. Couldn't back away.

Something told Callum he'd be holding her close for a long, long while.

FIONA TIED the helium balloon to the lantern. The balloons were gold and heart shaped. As jobs went, this one wasn't terrible.

Two weeks had passed since the kidnapping, and tonight was Cassie and Aidan's engagement party. The entire Blue Halo team was here helping with setup. She'd been assigned to tie three balloons to each black lantern, then divide the lanterns over the tables.

Her gaze wandered around the room. It was busy with movement, everyone with a job of their own—even Willow and Blake's daughter had the task of coloring some of the signs.

The women had been amazing since the attack—stopping by Callum's house with meals and treats, calling and texting to take her mind off everything. Not a day had passed in the weeks following the attack that she hadn't had a visitor. And the men had been as protective as ever, always checking in on her when they came around.

She was so lucky to have everyone.

She moved on to the next lantern.

Fiona hadn't spoken to Stacey, and honestly, she didn't know if she ever would. Trust had been fractured, and they'd never again have the relationship they used to. Stacey had always been the one family member she was closest to.

Callum had pushed for her to press charges a couple more times, but Amanda had already ratted Stacey out to the family, telling everyone what she'd done. It was an attempt to get sympathy for herself but had also made everyone turn against Stacey. That was enough punishment.

"You're doing an awesome job," Cassie said from behind. "Thank you so much for helping."

Fiona straightened. "Of course! I wouldn't want to be anywhere else. All ready for tonight?"

"Yes." Her eyes softened as they moved across the room. Fiona didn't need to follow the woman's gaze to know she'd found Aidan. "Honestly, I just can't wait to marry him. Every day brings us that much closer."

Oh, that was so sweet. "Well, I think tonight will be perfect. A beautiful pre-wedding celebration."

Cassie's gaze moved back to her, then she reached over and squeezed Fiona's arm. "Thank you. And remember, if you need to sit down and rest, or go home to lie down—"

"I'm okay. I want to be here, helping."

"Thank you."

"Cassie, how do you want these?" Courtney yelled from the flower display.

Cassie had just moved away when warm, muscular arms wrapped around Fiona's waist. She leaned back into Callum, humming when he kissed her cheek.

"You sure you don't need a break?" he asked.

"Well, I *was* sure, but if my break involves your arms around me, I'll take one."

Another kiss, this one closer to her mouth. "If my arms are enough to make you take a break, I'll keep them around you all damn day."

"Don't tease me." She turned in his hold. "But also, I've been resting for two weeks. I'm okay. It was only a concussion."

"A second concussion in a short period of time." The anger in his words was as fierce today as it had been two weeks ago.

The smile slipped, and she gentled her words. "I'm okay."

"Good."

"So…" She ran a hand down a crease in his shirt. "You sick of me yet? Living together. Home most days together. Your friends now *my* friends."

"Nope. Don't even think that's possible."

She laughed. "Oh, I think it is. Just wait until I get back to work, you start returning tattered books again, and I have to ride your ass about it."

She was taking a month off. And even better, Rick had left. Yep, that was right. He'd made the decision to leave Cradle Mountain. She wasn't sure of all the details of what went on between him and Olivia, but she knew that the woman had used him. Filled his head with negative gossip about Fiona, probably while sleeping with him. And when Rick had learned the truth, it had just been too much—and too embarrassing—for him to deal with.

"I told you, I'm going to look after my library books from now on. I have to, living with a librarian."

She scoffed. "I'll believe that when I see it." She'd seen one too many folded pages and stained covers.

Callum lowered his head, his breath brushing her lips as he spoke. "I'll prove it to you. Every. Damn. Day."

Then he kissed her, a long, deep kiss that made her feel loved. Safe. And protected.

CHAPTER 34

*L*iam couldn't help smiling at the sight of Callum and Fiona's embrace. He was happy for his friend. Hell, he was happy for all his friends. Seven business partners. Seven men he'd been through the hell of Project Arma with. And seven guys he considered brothers. They'd all found women they wanted to spend their lives with. Women who'd proven they could go through hellish experiences of their own and come out stronger.

He wasn't sure if he'd ever find what they had. He'd never even come close. Short relationships? Sure. Dates and flings? Yep. But he'd never felt the connection he saw between his brothers and their women.

He stepped back as a few waitstaff moved past. The engagement party was in a function hall, and the setup was in full swing. The room wasn't too large, and he knew from seeing the invite list that the space would be packed.

A hand clamped his shoulder, and he turned to find Jason smirking at him. "You watching them because you want some of that?"

Liam lifted a shoulder. "If the right woman came along, I'd be open to it. Not actively looking, though." He was happy with his life.

"Well, Courtney *did* mention she could set you up with—"

"Nope. Not gonna be set up with anyone the women know."

Jason's lips twitched. "There's nothing wrong with her friends."

"Her friends are the women in this room. I don't want to be paired with some woman who walks into her coffee shop that Courtney thinks is cute and would make a good match for me."

Jason chuckled. "Fair enough. Could be missing out, though."

He'd take that chance. The last couple dates hadn't gone too well.

"Your sister and the Marble Falls team get in okay?" Liam asked, keen to change the subject.

The team from Texas should have arrived already. All the men were friends with their team. Plus, Jason's sister, Sage, dated one of the Marble Falls crew.

"They sure did. I think they took up half the plane."

Liam chuckled. "Safest damn plane trip around. It'll be good to see them again."

They hadn't all been together since Luca and Evie's wedding. His skin still went cold at the memory of that day. It had been the wedding from hell, and they easily could have *not* made it out as free men.

"It really will. And I always love time with Sage." On cue, Jason's phone rang, and Sage's name popped up. "How's that for timing?"

Jason gave his shoulder another squeeze before stepping away and answering. Liam was about to find Cassie and ask what his next job should be when someone bumped into his back. He turned in time to see a waitress falling, a serving tray already tipping from her hands.

The tray full of glasses shattered, and he grabbed her arm moments before she landed on top of the sharp shards.

The woman gasped, her ice blue eyes hitting his. "I'm so sorry! I was walking behind you and tripped."

"Are you okay?"

"Yeah. I'm fine," she said quickly. "I mean, my pride's a little hurt, and I'm sure I'll get a firm talking to in the kitchen, but yes, physically, I'm okay."

He took a moment to run his gaze over her pink cheeks. The thick auburn hair that was pulled up into a tight ponytail. And those lips, so plump and red.

Fucking gorgeous.

"Let me help you clean up," he said, voice rougher than he meant it to be.

He bent down and carefully helped her shift the biggest shards of glass onto the tray. "I'm Liam, by the way."

"Nylah."

Damn, she even had a sexy name. "You working the party tonight?"

"I am. I'm new in town and was a last-minute hire. Thank God, because I really need the money." She smiled and a dimple cut into her cheek. "Are you a friend of the engaged couple?"

He lifted another shard. "I am. We run Blue Halo Security together. All the guys in the room are in the business."

"No wonder you look like a bunch of soldiers."

He lifted a shard just as Nylah went to grab it, and her finger slid against the sharp edge. She gasped, and before she could lift her hand, Liam wrapped his fingers around her wrist.

Immediately, something spidered up his arm. Something intense and hot. Like a zap of electricity. Connection.

His gaze flew up to see her lips part, her eyes locked on his.

Holy shit, who *was* this woman?

Forcing his attention away from her face, he grabbed a fallen napkin and wrapped it around the cut on her finger. "We need to get you a Band-Aid."

She swallowed, and it was damn hard not to stare at her delicate neck. To not run his eyes over those lips again. He wanted to shift forward, lean in, see if her lips were as soft as her hand. See if she tasted as sweet as she looked.

"I can get one from the kitchen." Her words were almost a whisper. Because she felt it too?

He kept his hand on her wrist, and with his other, he grabbed the tray of broken glass as they stood. "You sure you're okay?"

"Yes. But thank you for your help." She slid the tray from his hand and stepped back. Immediately, he hated the distance. Which was crazy because he didn't even know this woman. She smiled hesitantly. "I'll, um, see you later."

"Looking forward to it." And he really was.

As she walked away, his gaze never left her. She shot a final glance over her shoulder before stepping into the kitchen.

And *damn*, but he was suddenly excited for the party.

When he finally looked away, he noticed men in the corner of the room. Four of them, all working on something behind the small stage. But one of them, a tall guy with dark features, was watching him closely. Liam's eyes narrowed and the guy's gaze quickly flicked away.

He shook his head and turned away. He was just tense because of the effect Nylah had had on him. Jesus, he needed to get a damn life. All this love in the air had clearly gone to his head.

Still…he shot one final look at the guy to find him working, before shifting his attention back to the kitchen doors, just waiting for another glimpse.

Order LIAM today!

ALSO BY NYSSA KATHRYN

Declan

Cole

Ryker

BEAUTIFUL PIECES

(series ongoing)

Erik's Salvation

Erik's Redemption

Erik's Refuge

JOIN my newsletter and be the first to find out about sales and new releases!

~https://www.nyssakathryn.com/vip-newsletter~

ABOUT THE AUTHOR

Nyssa Kathryn is a romantic suspense author. She lives in South Australia with her daughter and hubby and takes every chance she can to be plotting and writing. Always an avid reader of romance novels, she considers alpha males and happily-ever-afters to be her jam.

Don't forget to follow Nyssa and never miss another release.

Facebook | Instagram | Amazon | Goodreads

Made in United States
Orlando, FL
19 September 2023

37094528R00168